A Thirst to *Die* For

A Thirst to *Die* For

A POLITICAL MYSTERY

IAN WADDELL

NEWEST PRESS

National Library of Canada Cataloguing in Publication Data
Waddell, Ian G
A thirst to die for

ISBN 1-896300-55-3

I. Title.
PS8595.A335T44 2002   C813'.6   C2002-910992-2
PR9199.4.W32T44 2002

Editor for the press: Don Kerr
Cover image: Mike Reichert Steinhauer
Cover design: Ruth Linka
Interior design: Erin Creasey

The Canada Council   Le Conseil des Arts
FOR THE ARTS   DU CANADA
SINCE 1957   DEPUIS 1957

Canadian   Patrimoine
Heritage   canadien

The author wishes to thank his editors, Stephen Reid, Audrey McLellan and
Don Kerr, and all his former staff, and all those who served as role models for
the characters in this book.

NeWest Press acknowledges the support of the Canada Council for the Arts
and The Alberta Foundation for the Arts for our publishing program. We
also acknowledge the financial support of the Government of Canada
through the Book Publishing Industry Development Program (BPIDP) for
our publishing activities.

NeWest Press
201-8540-109 Street
Edmonton, Alberta
T6G 1E6
t: (780) 432-9427
f: (780) 433-3179
www.newestpress.com

1 2 3 4 5 06 05 04 03 02
PRINTED AND BOUND IN CANADA

To all my friends.
Thank you for putting up with me over the years.

PROLOGUE **1961**

CORPORAL PETER GREENE LOOKED OUT THE WINDOW of the small aircraft. The Twin Otter bearing the markings of the Royal Canadian Mounted Police hung over the Mackenzie River, which snaked through a delta of myriad small lakes and tributaries on its way to the Beaufort Sea in the Canadian Arctic. Peter was leaving Aklavik, a village in the delta, and would cross the Richardson Mountains to the west before flying down a flat unglaciated area known as the Crow Flats to the most northerly village in Canada's Yukon Territory—Old Crow.

As he watched, Peter saw part of a migrating Porcupine Caribou herd. There were hundreds of animals on the tundra below, flowing over the land and splashing across the river. From the plane it looked like a gathering of brown shadows, but Peter could imagine the shaking of the earth and the noise that must accompany the herd's movement. For a moment he was taken back to his school days in Regina, reading about buffalo herds that used to cross the prairies. But all too soon his mind focused again on the present.

He had only recently graduated from the RCMP Academy in his Native Regina, and this was his first real posting other than traffic duty in Saskatchewan. He was used to the cold prairie winters, but how would he react to the long dark Arctic nights? Would he find friends in Old Crow or would he be The Policeman—someone to be avoided and mistrusted, forced to spend his time alone, reading, or writing home? What would he do if he wasn't accepted?

Two hours after leaving Aklavik and the caribou far behind, Peter was shaking hands with Don King, the Mountie he was replacing in Old Crow. Don, a confident little Calgarian, was clearly glad to see Peter. He quickly loaded Peter's gear into the grimy blue police truck, the only vehicle in town, then pulled away from the dirt strip used as an airport and headed down the quarter-mile, bumpy grass road into the Gwitch'in village.

"This is the only road into or out of this town, if you can believe it," King said. His right hand grasped the steering wheel and his left elbow hung down outside, brushing the gold RCMP decal on the truck door. "These people get around by boat or dog team or foot. They don't even know the twentieth century is here yet. Anyways, I'm out of here in a few days after I get you settled. Thank God."

Peter Greene was quiet, only half listening, his gaze fixed out the other side window on the old log houses built in long rows on the banks of the fast-flowing Porcupine River. A few little boys who were fishing off the grassy bank of the river looked up as the truck crawled past them. They stared at Greene with those curious looks that all small children seem to share. Peter smiled back at them.

King spent the next three days showing Peter around and teaching him the daily routine. Most of the time seemed to be taken up with filling out paper reports, all in triplicate, to be put in the weekly mail pouch. On Thursday, Peter drove King the same quarter mile back out to the little airstrip and watched him fly out. Then Peter opened the truck door, paused to look up at the sky, took a long breath of cool air, and felt the wind on his face.

The next morning, coffee cup in hand, Peter responded

to a knock at the office door and was greeted by Jim Sichinly. King had told Greene about Sichinly. Part Anglican minister, part hunter, part trapper, elder, raconteur, Jim was said to be one of the most outgoing fellows in town.

"We wanted to see who was the new fellow in town and whether he would bite us or not," Sichinly laughed.

"I'll try not to."

"Well, let's get right down to it. Do you hunt? Because if you do, you're invited over to my place on Sunday after church to eat some of that caribou that my son got yesterday. Will you come?"

Peter smiled. "My father hunted in Northern Ontario. Yes, I'll come. Thank you."

⬥

On Sunday, Peter saw the grey smoke coming from the chimney of the Sichinly cabin. It was one of the bigger cabins in the village with a large, enclosed side porch near the entrance and a nice view of the river. Once in the porch he took off his large brown leather boots and, like everyone else, left them just inside the entrance. Joining four or five other of Jim's friends in the big main room of the log house, he could smell a stew of caribou meat simmering on the stove in the open kitchen area at the back of the room. The conversation that afternoon was caribou—five hours of stories about caribou. No sports, no gossip, just caribou. Hunting, chasing, sneaking up on them, getting them into a fence, skinning them, tanning their hides, cooking them dozens of ways.

"What's the best way to hunt caribou?" Peter asked somewhat naively.

Three people tried to answer him at once. Peter laughed first and they all laughed together.

"Please Jim, tell me more about the great fences."

Sichinly put down his pipe and looked up at Peter. "They were one of the wonders of our ancient Indian world, Peter. Stones were piled up across the land in a large funnel shape, wide at the opening and then narrowing at the end. Our elders tell us that it was a great way to herd in those animals. Damn hard work though."

They all laughed. And the afternoon went on—lots of coffee and lots of caribou.

After they had eaten together, Peter got up to leave and looked for his boots. Five or six little children were playing in the house. One of them had put one of Peter's big leather Mountie boots in a bucket of water. At first there was silence from his hosts, but when Peter began to laugh at the situation, all the adults in the house erupted in laughter with him.

A couple of the men gave Peter their shoulders to lean on as he hopped on one foot over the mud out to the RCMP truck. One of Jim's nieces carried the wet boot to the truck. She had barely spoken a word all afternoon, but now she said, "I'm sorry my brother did this. I think he thought he was helping to clean your boot. I hope it is not ruined."

"No, no," Peter reassured her, smiling into her solemn brown eyes. "It's fine." And if my boot is ruined to make me a part of this community, it's worth it, he thought. The shared laughter made him feel like he had been accepted by Jim, and his family and his friends.

Most days after that Jim Sichinly would come to visit Peter at his office and talk philosophy and caribou, and hunting and caribou.

"You know, Jim, I thought I liked the outdoors, especially when I was a kid, but you and your friends really love this land—the birds and the animals and the plants, all of it. You really do. It's amazing."

Jim looked at him, shook his head and laughed as loudly as Peter had ever heard him.

"You know, Peter, I do believe that you're beginning to understand us. Just beginning."

He smiled, and Peter poured him another cup of coffee.

Jim made sure Peter got out to meet the people in the town. One day Jim invited Peter to have coffee over at the fur co-operative where some of the village women sewed muskrat furs, taken from the hunting grounds in the Crow Flats north of Old Crow, into beautiful fur coats. Among them, sitting very quietly, was Jim's niece, Georgina. Peter noticed right away her large brown eyes, the dark hair combed out long. This was the young woman who had brought him his wet boot; he recalled that very soft smile.

A few weeks later, when the ice had finally broken up after a long, long winter, Jim asked Peter to go along with him to visit his fish camp up the Porcupine River. Georgina came with them in the small boat with the "kicker" or outboard motor at the back. After a few hours on the river, during which few words were spoken and Jim constantly smoked his pipe, they arrived at the site of the fish camp. It consisted of a couple of old log buildings: one of them with a large drying rack and the other a small cabin for shelter. Both buildings were built on the grass just beyond the sandy bank. Together they cleaned up some pieces of wooden debris from the area and pulled some nets out of one of the log huts. Then they strung the nets across part of the river. Jim took Peter over a hill above the river and pointed out caribou in the distance. With Jim as guide, both men crept up close to the animals. Peter slowly raised his rifle, fired and shot his first caribou. Georgina joined them and helped to skin and cut the animal. Then they packed the meat and fur into the boat. Nothing was wasted.

When they returned to Old Crow, they distributed some of the meat to a number of families and kept the rest for themselves. At the end of the day, Peter felt very happy and at home, perhaps for the first time since coming to the North. He had enjoyed being on the land and he had enjoyed the company of Georgina.

In the days that followed he saw Georgina around the village. She always managed to give him a quick smile, then seemed to disappear into one house or another. A month later, Jim arranged for them to return to the fish camp to unload some nets, but that morning when Peter arrived at the boat, Jim wasn't there. Georgina was waiting and they waited together in silence. Soon a small boy Jim had sent came running to them. The boy had come to tell them that Jim had the flu. Would Peter mind going to get the fish, and could Georgina go along to help Peter?

"He's almost never sick," said Georgina. "I'm not sure I can go."

Before Peter could stop himself, the words seemed to pour out of his mouth unbidden: "I would really appreciate your help. I can't get the nets in myself."

Georgina hesitated, but when the boy repeated Jim's request that she help Peter, she agreed to go.

The weather had turned very quickly and was now warm. The sun only set for a few hours each night and would soon be a full midnight sun. The journey up the river was very pleasant. They did not speak to each other but felt comfortable in the silence. Peter kept a firm hand on the handle of the "kicker" at the back of the aluminum boat. He felt the soft wind flowing over the bow past Georgina and heard the flap of the wake behind him.

Once they arrived at the fish camp, Georgina and Peter worked hard pulling in the nets and cleaning the fish. The nets had been set just over a week ago by some of Jim's friends. They were now heavy with fish. After three hours, and with a little over a hundred fish in the bottom of the boat, they looked up and smiled at each other. They sprinkled some handfuls of salt over the mound of fish and covered them with a brown tarpaulin. Then together they prepared a fire and Peter began to butter a frying pan to cook some fresh fish. Georgina began to laugh.

"Why are you laughing?" Peter asked.

"I'm surprised you are cooking for us, but I am glad of that. I'm also laughing at how much of the fish we cleaned is all over your hands and shirt."

Surprising himself, Peter looked up and said, "Well, you're right, but we can fix that. We can have a little dip before dinner."

"Are you kidding? In the Porcupine River? I know my ancestors came here thirty thousand years ago from Asia, so we are tough—but not that tough."

"I have a surprise for you, Georgina. Come with me over the bank and through the bush for a little way. Something I saw from the airplane."

Not too far from the river bank was a small shallow lake; the delta was full of them.

As he took his clothes off, so did she and they both jumped into the water. It was cool, but after the work and the warm sun, they both needed it. They splashed and laughed together. Suddenly, the formality was gone. He couldn't help noticing her firm small breasts and how her nipples stood out from her brown skin. As Peter saw the sun's rays glance off the water droplets on her legs, she noticed his face begin to turn crimson. When she looked down at him and laughed he turned away with some embarrassment. When they came out of the water they lay down together on the grass above the bank. Peter put a blanket over them because of the bugs. This made them laugh again. But the laughing stopped when he put his arm around her. At first tentatively, and then passionately, they made love.

Later, as Peter cooked the fish, he knew his life had changed. He didn't feel guilty, he didn't feel awkward, he didn't feel sorry. He felt happy. And he felt at home. Afterwards, when they returned to Old Crow, they found Jim outside his house.

"I thought you were sick, Uncle," Georgina called to him.

Seeing them, he smiled. "I was but I seem to have gotten better fairly fast."

Peter and Georgina looked at each other and giggled.

They saw each other every day after that, often just to walk on the land together in silence. Peter went to Jim and then to Georgina's parents, Victor and Bertha, to tell them he wished to marry their daughter. He was pleased with their acceptance and the warmth of their congratulations. After the wedding, he left his room in the detachment office. They found a small cabin to live in and Georgina told him she was pregnant.

As the time of the baby's birth approached, Peter realized that there was no doctor in Old Crow, only a nurse who was getting old. Recently, some babies had died at birth. He decided, against Jim's advice, to send Georgina to Edmonton for the birth. His parents were living there now and they could help her. It was a sad day for him when Georgina left on the monthly plane to Edmonton. But the birth went well. On the radiophone, Peter could hear her voice. It was clear and strong.

"Why don't we name him Clayton, after your dad?"

"What about your Uncle Jim?" Peter replied. "He really brought us together."

They agreed to name their son Clayton James Greene.

Georgina had to remain in Edmonton for three weeks before she could come home on the regular monthly charter that went to Whitehorse, then up to Old Crow. As he waited for her on the day of the flight, Peter was playing cards with Jim and some of his friends in Jim's house. It was warm inside and the aroma of the caribou stew on the stove filled the cabin. But outside, the weather had turned bad. It was the tail end of an Arctic winter. The wind was blowing gusts of new snow between the log cabins. He heard the howl of the neighbour's dogs and the curses of the neighbour as he huddled in the blizzard to tie them down. Peter had brought his portable radiophone with him from the detachment office. The DC3 had apparently left Edmonton on time, where the weather was fine, and had refueled in Whitehorse, where it was overcast and gloomy, but flyable. On board the DC3 were two pilots, a lot of cargo, two students coming back to Old Crow for the summer, an elderly couple who worked at the general store, Georgina, and baby Clayton.

The card game seemed to go on forever. The plane was already late and the weather was not getting any better. Peter knew the airplane had not turned back to Whitehorse, and there was little to do but wait. They waited and waited. They played hand after hand. Peter tried to eat but couldn't. He learned that the last radio contact with the airplane came from Dawson City, but after that there was nothing.

Finally Peter slept. When he awoke there was still no word from the plane. Many times in the past he knew airplanes had put down, even on the tundra, to wait out a storm. If that happened they could be out of radio contact, he thought. The only thing they could do was to continue waiting.

After another full day of waiting, the village met at the co-op.

"I'll take out one of the skidoos with extra gas in a sled behind and I'll go to . . ." Before Peter could finish, Jim's arm slipped around his shoulders.

"We all know how much you love her, but we know this land. Let us find them the traditional way. You operate the radio and tie in with the Twin Otter that is leaving Norman Wells and the other DC3 that'll be leaving Whitehorse. I will take our dog teams out of here in an hour."

Reluctantly, Peter waited. And waited. He began to lose hope. Finally, after five days, the village was awakened around midnight by the yelping sounds of the returning dog teams. Peter was half asleep at the RCMP station when he heard the commotion. He went out into the snow and saw the sleds packed with what looked like bodies wrapped in furs.

Jim Sichinly came up to him. "I'm sorry, Peter. She did not suffer; it happened quickly. I saw the crash site. The baby survived the impact and so did the two old people. They were injured but tried to look after him. There were tins of condensed milk which they fed him. First the old man died. Then the old woman. They left a saucer of condensed milk for Clayton. We arrived about three days later."

Just then, a woman came from behind Jim and handed Peter a bundle. It was a baby boy. And he was crying.

⟶

One night, a long six months later, Peter was with Jim and Victor and baby Clayton. He was just beginning to get over his grief. The baby was now crying less as he got constantly passed from relative to relative so he was never out of someone's loving arms.

"Jim, I couldn't really ask you until now. How did the baby survive?"

Instead of answering directly, Jim told a story: "Many years ago the family of an old chief was out on the land, in the Crow Flats in the spring, hunting muskrat. It was a clear day so they decided to go out farther without their tents, towards a lake they had heard about. This lake was so far away that no people had been there; it was near the mountains to the north and west, near the great bear country. A huge blizzard blew up and the family huddled together to wait it out in some small trees. But this storm, unlike others in our springtime, didn't quickly blow itself out. They soon ran out of food and in the cold the parents and the older child died. We found them together, and the baby survived somehow."

"How, Jim?"

Jim looked up at Peter and said solemnly: "We also found bear tracks."

"Are you saying the bear suckled the baby?"

"The baby grew up to be one of our greatest chiefs. You see, we believe nature and the land will look after our children."

"Are you saying a magic bear saved my child?"

Jim laughed. "Maybe little Clayton here was just lucky."

Some time later, Peter Greene requested RCMP headquarters in eastern Canada for a reassignment; the memories at Old Crow were just too painful. He decided to take young Clay with him. Saying good-bye to the inhabitants of Old Crow was hard. When he told Jim about his plans, he could see the hurt in his eyes. But Jim never openly expressed his feelings, except to remind Peter of the importance in life of the land, and the spirits associated with it.

"Don't forget us, Peter. Don't let young Clay forget us either." Nothing more was said.

CHAPTER I

CHIEF JUSTICE MACKINNON MOVED FROM SIDE TO SIDE on his red leather chair. Finally comfortable, he took a fountain pen out of the pocket of the vest inside his crimson robes, took the top off the pen and opened up a large writing book. He then turned his head slightly to his right and looked up to the clock hanging high above him.

The old clock looked out of place. It was of the schoolroom variety, round and plain, white with a black rim. It peered down into a courtroom with soft yellow oak panelling and bright red carpets.

That old clock showed 11:30 AM.

The court clerk, below the judge, stood up. He looked around the courtroom for an instant, cleared his throat and, like a minor stage player whose moment in the play had come, proclaimed: "In the Supreme Court of British Columbia at Vancouver, Thursday April 20th, Greenpeace Society Inc., Lyle Stewart et al, versus the Attorney General of Canada."

"My Lord," said the lawyer on the judge's right, "my name is Tom Scott and I appear for the plaintiffs, the Greenpeace Foundation and Lyle Stewart, its president. Ms. Patricia A. Nelson is with me."

Scott was about sixty-five, known to be thorough and determined and well-respected as a lawyer for progressive causes. He had made his reputation when he brought the first Native rights case to court in the early seventies. They had laughed at him then, but he had doggedly plugged away until Aboriginal rights, as they came to be known, were made part of the new Canadian Constitution in the early eighties. A host of other law cases and land claims negotiations like the Nisga'a settlement followed.

"May it please your lordship, G.A. Starrup appearing for the Attorney General of Canada. With me is R.G. Marbutt from our departmental office in Ottawa."

The chief justice nodded to the lawyers with perhaps a bit of an extra nod to Mr. Marbutt who, being from Ottawa, was welcomed almost as a foreigner.

The older lawyer, Starrup, wore the silk gown of a Queen's Counsel, and as he rose again he tugged it down and said, "My Lord, counsel has prepared a written outline of fact and argument for this case which will assist the court and I will hand my copy to your lordship."

At this moment, a young woman who had been observing the proceedings from the back of the courtroom began to scribble a note. She tore the page out of her notepad, folded it, took it down the side aisle to the gold bar that separated the spectators from the lawyers and quietly handed it across to Patricia Nelson, the lawyer who was "junioring" Tom Scott. She then left the courtroom.

The lawyer quietly opened the note, smiled and whispered to Scott. He turned to the government lawyers.

"I wonder if my learned friend, who is so organized in these matters, has an extra copy of his written argument for my junior counsel?"

Starrup was a bit taken aback, but in the courtly manner of a QC he looked at the chief justice, who was already thumbing through the documents and was oblivious to the request, and then he turned to Scott and smiled. "Yes, I think I can provide my friend with an extra copy."

He handed a copy to Scott, who let it sit on the desk beside him. At the back, outside the courtroom, the woman who had written the note paced nervously.

The chief justice looked up. "I take it Queen's Counsel will not be calling witnesses but will be relying on this written material and, of course, argument. Now let me see if I have all the material and that I have it in the proper order."

As the judge continued to thumb through the material before him, Nelson picked up the copy, put it into a file folder and quietly got up from the counsel table with some other files under her arm, crossed the bar, walked down the centre aisle and out the open door at the entrance to the courtroom.

"Really, Janet, you asked a lot there. You're lucky Tom's a cool guy, unlike some of the other counsel around here." Nelson took a copy of the government's thick brief out of one of the file folders and handed it to the other woman.

Janet Wong was not yet thirty and she sparkled with energy. She flipped back the long black hair hanging over her face with one hand, and with the other she took the brief.

"You know I wouldn't ask if it weren't really important. The boss says his intuition tells him there's a big story here. And usually his intuition is right on. Thanks for this, Pat. I think this is going to be huge. I'll try to keep in touch, really. I owe you one."

The lawyer smiled and quietly returned to the courtroom as Scott said, "My Lord, this case is an action to set aside an order of the Government of Canada, the first of its kind we believe, to allow the export of a large quantity of water from the Canadian western provinces to the United States of America."

Janet had no time to listen to more. She hurried down

the hall outside Courtroom 30, slipping past other litigants waiting for their cases, and headed for the Barristers Lounge where she could find a table and a phone.

The Barristers Lounge looked a bit like a tennis club locker room. Inside, there was a door leading to lockers and washrooms where the lawyers could change into their gowns before going out to the court battles, and where later they came back to wash off the grime of their daily work. The lounge itself was one big room containing wooden tables, battered leather furniture salvaged from the old courthouse, now an art gallery, and old fashioned phone booths up against the wall.

Janet could use the lounge because she was herself a member of the bar. The daughter of a corner grocer on Commercial Drive in East Vancouver, she had fought her way through Templeton high school, and on to UBC Law School where she had finished at the top of her class. From there she spent a year articling for a labour law firm in Vancouver. But at the end of that year she was not yet ready to follow her colleagues into the boredom of a big law firm. A job had opened up in the office of Clayton Greene, the Member of Parliament for Vancouver Centre. She wanted the experience of a year or so in Ottawa, and at about $35,000 a year it paid better than a first-year lawyer could get—there being a surplus of lawyers these days. Besides, it was an opportunity to work outside of Vancouver for a while. But only for a while because Janet loved Vancouver deeply. She thought of Vancouver as her town, and she knew it better than most. After all, her ancestors had come to the *Gum San*, the Golden Mountain, three generations ago.

She also knew that something had clicked between herself and Clay Greene from the beginning. She remembered the interview and her nervousness, which made her even more talkative than usual. She remembered how informal he was, so youthful and open for someone in government. She especially remembered how he focused on her in spite of his telephone constantly ringing, and in spite of all the people outside waiting to see him. As she expressed her interest in the environment and talked about poverty issues, she especially noticed his eyes, which became more intense and even more focused on her. She just knew she could work well with this man—and they did, perfectly and effortlessly. It was a good fit.

God, she thought, this brief is too long. Typical of Crown Counsel, wordy and not much to the point.

Finally, under Tab Five, she found it. Reaching for the phone, she dialed nine for an outside line and then a local Vancouver number, 666-5511.

"Government of Canada, gouvernement du Canada," the operator answered, the first phrase a little more carefully pronounced than the second.

"My code is 3477435, and I want to call Ottawa, 996-8036." Janet looked at her watch. It was ten minutes to twelve, which would mean ten to three Ottawa time.

"I'm sorry, the line is busy. Please try again, will you?"

Frustrated, Janet closed her eyes and began counting to ten, first in English, then in French and finally in Cantonese. She tried again.

She could hear the ring on the other end. "House of Commons, Chambre de communes, Opposition Lobby, Antichambre de l'opposition."

She thought she recognized the voice as a young page, one of the student messengers in the House, the boy from rural Alberta who could actually pronounce the French.

"Could you get me Clayton Greene please. I believe he's in the House."

A minute passed and Janet thought she had been lost on hold. She hated that feeling and considered dialling yet again.

"Clay Greene here."

"Clay, it's Janet. I have the information. Have you got a pen?"

As he listened in Ottawa, Greene, like the three political assistants lounging on chairs nearby, watched Question Period as it was broadcast on the TV monitor hanging on the wall opposite.

"Yes, that's what I need Janet. Read it again."

After he hung up the phone, he pondered the information for a moment, gazing absently at the portraits of J.S. Woodsworth, Tommy Douglas and other departed political leaders, now called statesmen, who watched from their position of honour on the wall of the Opposition Lobby.

Greene scribbled some further notes and ran up four large steps to a glass and wooden door which opened onto a small passageway behind thick green curtains. On the other side of those curtains was the Canadian House of Commons where 301 members, or, more correctly, the 150 that attended the daily Question Period, were supposedly governing the country.

As happened every time he entered, he was struck by the atmosphere of the place. It was like entering a large arena, but instead of ice and floorboards there were green-leather-topped desks, each one seating two MPs, in five raised rows facing five other rows of similar desks opposite. Two members would sit in green-covered chairs like school kids sharing the one dark brown wooden desk. High above this political arena were the visitor's galleries where the fans sat, and above the galleries, wonderful stained-glass windows that let in some real light.

Greene looked to his right, down to the second row of the official opposition seats where a member was on his feet.

"I want to ask the Minister again, why for heaven's sake is this government backtracking and once again letting the Spanish come in and overfish off Canada, and thus continue to destroy the livelihood of more Newfoundland fishermen?"

"Let me tell the member from Gander-Twillingate, as I have in the past until I am almost blue in the face, that this government, unlike the previous Liberal government to which the member subscribed, has no intention of signing phony deals or selling Canadian fishermen out, and is at this very moment negotiating a firmer and better deal with the Europeans over these disputed waters."

This caused the predictable jeering and cheering, and in the midst of it Greene spotted his party's whip, who was responsible for the order of their allotted number of questions in Question Period. The whip was a short, red-headed, balding man, a bit puffed up with his importance as a minor power broker in this particular House.

"I need to get a question, Rod. It's serious."

"Well, we only have one question left, if that. I would have to ask one of our members to take a dive until tomorrow. They might be more willing to do that if their Minister wasn't in the House today. I'll see."

But the whip was clearly in no hurry. Greene was. He scribbled a note to the Speaker—"John, I need a question. Clay."—and signaled for one of the pages to deliver it. He spotted his favourite page, the young man from Red Deer with the big smile and the bright wit, and handed it to him.

Question Period was supposed to run for forty-five minutes and end, under the strict rules of the House, at 3 PM sharp. Clay had about two minutes.

Lately, Question Period had become a shouting match, dominated by those MPs who could, and would, say the most outrageous things in the hope of getting on the evening TV news with a much sought-after twenty-second or, more accurately, ten-second clip. Sometimes however, Question Period could be a stirring experience, the best example of a parliamentary democracy. After a tragedy like a lost oil rig, or an air crash, or a mine disaster, a Minister would be asked for, and he would provide, the latest information on the tragedy, to a silent and attentive House. At other times, when, for example, contaminated shellfish was released to the public, or job creation funds were funneled to government MPs' ridings, a Minister would be grilled during Question Period and made to be held responsible. If the Minister faltered, he or she was a goner.

In any case, with this televised House, Question Period attracted a wide audience and could make or break a minister's or a member's reputation. Somedays it could be riveting; other days, simply boring.

"Order, order," barked Mr. Speaker John Lentil, as he rose from his imposing green chair at the far end of the House.

This Speaker had been a member of the House for almost twenty years, and he usually got order since he in turn seemed to understand the frustrations of the backbenchers who elected him and who made up the majority of the House.

"The Question Period is almost over. I will permit just one question from the Honourable Member from Vancouver Centre without the usual supplemental question." As Clay Greene rose, he could see the Prime Minister and the Deputy Prime Minister just across from him. Tradition has it that the government and the opposition in the British parliamentary system sit only the distance of two sword lengths apart. In the Canadian House the separation is a bit wider, but not much. Greene's third-row seat was just behind his party leader, Jack Hepburn, so he could see the PM clearly. Cool and organized as usual, the Prime Minister was packing his briefing notes and smiling to a government MP who had yelled something at him.

"My question is addressed to the Prime Minister. What involvement does the Prime Minister have with Western Energy Incorporated, and why was it necessary for his government to pass a secret order-in-council to allow the export of as yet undisclosed amounts of water from Canada to the US?"

"Oh, there they go again. What's the NDP got against the Americans?"

Greene could hear the laughter and catcalls from the government backbenches.

"Order," said the Speaker. "Prime Minister."

John Alexander MacKenzie, or "Sandy" as his friends called him, was a shrewd Scot from Cape Breton. His quiet way, in marked contrast to some of his predecessors as Prime Minister, belied a razor-sharp mind.

But after Greene's question, for an instant or less, a strange frown appeared on the face of Sandy MacKenzie. Still, he was quickly on his feet.

"Mr. Speaker, I welcome the Honourable Member's question, but I am unaware of any secret Orders-in-Council." MacKenzie emphasized the word secret. "Unlike other governments in the past, this government has always operated openly and above board."

"Hear, hear! You tell them Sandy!" Clay Greene could hear the heckles from the government members. So, too, could the Speaker.

"Order. Orders of the Day. Presenting reports of the standing committees."

With that, Question Period was over. The Prime Minister picked up his papers and left the House, not pausing to talk to his back bench MPs as he usually did.

CHAPTER **2**

CLAYTON GREENE RETURNED TO THE OPPOSITION lobby, where the leader of his party, Jack Hepburn, was discussing the Atlantic fisheries situation with his press secretary and his chief of staff in preparation for press questions outside the lobby. The discussion centred on what they could do to prevent the opposition Liberals from monopolizing media coverage on the issue. Perhaps this time the NDP would call for Canadian Navy ships to challenge the Europeans in the disputed waters.

Greene, having decided he should stay in the lobby until Hepburn had faced the media, went into a small phone booth in the opposition lobby to get a little privacy and called his office. In the West Block, the building just next to the main Parliament Buildings, Ann, his secretary, answered.

"What was that question all about, Clay?"

"I'll tell you shortly. What's up there?"

"Lots. You have to go to a meeting of the Environment Committee this afternoon to plan the future global warming hearings. And the whip just called and asked you to fill in on the Justice Committee tonight, says you owe him one. And if you can believe this," Ann continued, "we have constituents in town—the Beckett family. He says he contributed to your last campaign and wants an invite to lunch in the Parliamentary dining room. Says he heard on TV that it has sumptuous food and is cheap to boot. Oh, and Janet wants you to call her at a number at the law courts in Vancouver. And you've got lots of mail, so come back to the office as soon as you can."

Hanging up the phone, Greene paused in the privacy of the little booth and closed his eyes for a moment. Sandy MacKenzie's momentary hesitation puzzled him. The PM was usually unflappable, in complete control of himself and the House. At age sixty-one, this bachelor politician had been thirty years in politics and seemed to have spent most of that time learning all there was to know about every department and every ministry. A little more than two years ago, his long experience had allowed him to pull off a minor miracle.

The Liberal government of the time had been flying high in the polls and had enjoyed a long honeymoon with the voters. But the Liberals had become overconfident and internal dissention, coupled with an unexpected recession spurned on by a severe downturn in the US economy, hurt them further. When they cut the health care budget, and when Canada suffered a withdrawal of foreign investors, the Liberals' love affair with the Canadian voters was abruptly over. It was all so sudden and unexpected, and this wily man, who took over the leadership of the Conservative Party after two leaders had come and gone, had pulled through the election with the largest number of seats, thanks to the Maritimes and Ontario, provinces which once again did a flip-flop and abandoned the Liberals for the Tories.

However, MacKenzie was forced to form a coalition government with the Western rump of the old Reform Party now called the Alliance Party, leaving a dispirited Liberal Party in official opposition, a rejuvenated NDP just behind them, and an assortment of Bloc Québécois members who had chosen to continue in the federal Parliament after the referendum. Indeed this was a remarkable House of Commons; it was almost evenly divided among the parties.

The joining with the Alliance was not easy, and like the good sailor he was the Prime Minister tacked through his government's legislation, appealing sometimes to the left and sometimes to the right, sometimes to the Liberal and NDP opposition, sometimes to his Alliance allies, and sometimes, when the wind was almost out of his sails, to the handful of Independents and the Bloc. He often looked uneasy in his dealings with his Alliance ministers, including his Deputy PM, but he had managed to keep this coalition afloat. MacKenzie was known as a pragmatist, as well as an honourable man, and Clay couldn't imagine that he'd get himself involved in secret dealings. But if he had, he wouldn't be the first PM to do so.

It was time to head for the office and see what Janet had dug up. Clay came out of the phone booth, walked a few paces out one lobby door into a hall between the Opposition and Government Lobbies, and out another door to the grand foyer in front of the House. He found himself in a large open expanse of marble floor, the marble broken in places with tall, grey stone pillars. He knew this was the playing field for the game of political rugby that Canadians watched each night on the television news. This was where the politicians would be surrounded by the "scrum" of reporters, cameras, and mikes. On the floor in the midst of this noisy activity, Clay could look up at a beautiful collection of Inuit tapestries on the walls between the offices on the floor above.

About twenty reporters, along with three TV cameras, some radio reporters with long micophones, and the print media with their notebooks and small tape recorders were "scrumming" Hepburn on the Atlantic fishery issue.

Various backbench MPs stood around the foyer trolling for press interest, but most were coming up empty-handed.

Greene thought he was different. He believed he had a certain credibility with the press. They knew he was always well-informed and that he picked his issues carefully, even if they had other doubts about him. It didn't hurt, either, that he had—much to his amusement—been chosen best-looking male MP earlier this year. So after his leader had been thoroughly grilled, about one third of the press pack descended on Greene.

"What secret Order-in-Council?" asked the CBC national radio reporter, a short guy with a big voice.

"You should check out a court case being argued in Vancouver today, Greenpeace Foundation v. A.G. Canada. Check Tab Five of the Crown's argument where they admit for the first time that Orders-in-Council were passed to sanction water exports."

"Are you saying the PM benefitted, that he's up to some hanky-panky?"

"No, I'm not saying that."

"Well, what's the big deal?" barked the CTV reporter.

Just at that moment there was movement in front of the Prime Minister's office on the floor above. The reporters looked up, turned around and raced for the stairs at the other end of the foyer. They wanted to nail the PM with their questions on the Atlantic fishery.

"Well, Mr. Greene, there goes the pack, eh?"

It was Marianne Tremblay, a fairly new reporter for the Canadian Press—the press pool that is Canada's national wire service.

Greene thought Tremblay had an independent, no-

nonsense air about her. She wore her blond hair a bit short and she carried her tall thin frame with confidence. Clay Greene liked that. Unlike a lot of young reporters lately, she didn't appear to take herself too seriously. Yeah, she sure is attractive, worth some follow up, he thought.

"I don't know what you're on to, but I thought the old man looked a bit taken aback when you asked him that question. And that is unusual for him."

"It is," said Greene. He noticed her white blouse and the way it clung to her body. His eyes caught the faint outline of nipples under it and above them the small gold chain and locket that hung from her neck.

"And from where I was sitting, from the press gallery above the Speaker's chair, I get to see most of the cabinet. They didn't pay much attention to your question except for the Deputy PM."

"Sorry—"

She could see that Greene seemed distracted. "I said, they didn't pay much attention except the Deputy PM."

"Well, I wasn't paying much attention to him," replied Greene.

She began to feel uncomfortable about the way that Greene was looking at her; he was what the boys in school would have called "checking her out."

"He took notes and sure looked interested. It was the only thing in Question Period that he paid any real attention to. And, of course, the Minister of Fisheries was ready to kiss you. He thought you were going to ask another fisheries question. So, what have you got?"

He thought how serious she was, and how that was an attractive quality about her.

"Marianne, I think I've got wind of some "fishy" things happening on the Pacific Coast. Greenpeace has long claimed that the federal government wants to sell our water to the Yanks. For the first time the government has admitted this— in court documents filed today. I have other leads that I'm following up too."

She looked interested, he thought.

"We'll file the story on the court case, although I doubt if the others, except for CBC radio, will do much. My bureau has been thinking about doing a piece on water exports as part of a longer story on the environment. Perhaps we could co-operate?"

"Well, that could be worthwhile. Who knows what might happen."

She was just about to tell him she didn't need another arrogant MP when a guard reached over Clay's shoulder with a small piece of paper. "Mr. Greene, your office called again."

"Okay, I'm going." Greene turned back briefly and looked intently at Marianne. "This issue of water exports is going to be huge, I'm sure of it. I'll talk to you soon, Marianne, and stay tuned."

As Greene descended the marble stairs from the foyer, to the Member's Entrance door, Marianne wrote down a few notes, flipped her notepad closed, then turned and quickly walked away. She thought: How can a guy like him be an arrogant prick one moment and charming the next?

Out of the corner of her eye Marianne saw the CBC radio reporter coming away from the PM's scrum and down the far stairs towards her. She knew this guy, Michael Leslie, who was maybe short in stature, but big in experience on the national and international parliamentary scene. He also had the sharpest tongue in the Press Gallery and an engaging smile to go with it.

"So, did you get anything more out of Mr. Narcissus MP?"

"Pardon me?"

"Oh, it's just that Mr. Handsome MP thinks he knows it all. Arrogant plus. Lots of promise, but not much there I fear, my dear. He's the 'love 'em and leave 'em type,' they say."

While fiddling with the buttons on his tape recorder Leslie went on to tell Marianne about the time he invited Greene to his first Parliamentary Press Gallery dinner. The dinner is held once a year and traditionally a journalist invites an MP as his date for the party that can go on all night. It's a chance to find out a lot about the MP. It seemed to Leslie that Greene's life before politics consisted of booze, frat parties, and trying to get laid. Greene spent the evening flirting with just about everything in a skirt. He ended the evening getting really pissed and talking to himself. Finally at the press club's so-called breakfast, he barfed all over some PM staffer.

"It wasn't a pleasant sight, I can assure you."

Marianne had a puzzled look on her face. She said, "Oh, come on Mike. You tell everyone you're gay. Maybe it was you who struck out."

"Touché, ma chérie, but not so. The Gallery dinner is a working night for me, well maybe the odd joint, but that's all. I'll say this though. He's got a good hunting instinct for some issues. Take water, it's a great issue, but can he deliver? Or will he get sidetracked, if you know what I mean?"

With that the diminutive reporter put one arm around

Marianne's waist and winked at her with his left eye. Then he ambled down the corridor still adjusting his recorder. She heard him say over his shoulder.

"Don't say I didn't warn you."

As he finally put his tape recorder into a black shoulder bag, she didn't hear him mutter under his breath, "handsome boy chick meets new beautiful nerd reporter, a new definition of mission impossible."

One floor down, near the Members Entrance, Clayton Greene had picked up one of the guard's phones, dialed through to Vancouver and was listening to the voice of Janet Wong.

"Clay, I got another lead and, by the way, that was a great question. Finish your committee work tonight and get the 9:50 AM Air Canada flight tomorrow morning to Vancouver. I'll pick you up at the airport and we'll visit my source. This one is fabulous!"

Greene smiled to himself, hung up, thanked the guard and went out the door to a small green bus that waited to shuttle MPs and their staff between the House in the Centre Block and their offices in the West Block, the Confederation Building and the old Justice Building. As he waited to board, he watched a large black Cadillac limousine move off from beneath the Peace Tower, followed by an escort of two RCMP Buicks, red lights on their roofs. As the limo passed he caught a glimpse of the Prime Minister, head deep in briefing papers. For a fleeting moment, the PM looked up and their eyes met.

CHAPTER 3

THE AIR CANADA 737 WAITED ON THE TARMAC IN front of the Ottawa Airport. Clay Greene was in the Air Canada Maple Leaf Lounge. Like all MPs, he had a complimentary pass to these lounges at airports all over the country, and they were a godsend to him. He could use the phones, get a coffee, read the country's main newspapers, wash up, even "buy" someone a drink. Of course, it was all free, which made it even better. Since he was first elected, he had got to know the Air Canada and Canadian hostesses at Ottawa, Toronto, and Vancouver so well that they had become like family to him. Unlike some MPs, he actually talked to them and listened to what they had to say.

As the morning sun shone over his shoulder, Greene sat down at a small desk in the lounge and dialled his Parliamentary office: "I'm about to get my flight. Call Janet in a couple of hours, so you don't wake her up in Vancouver, and tell her to pick up my old Volvo and meet me at the airport. We arrive at 12:50 Vancouver time. She tells me she's got a great lead on this water export case."

"What am I to do with the folks from Vancouver, your constituents, the Becketts?" protested Ann.

"Check with Joan in the community office in Vancouver later this morning. She knows who really helped in the campaign and who didn't. Whether they helped or not, give them my apologies, your best smile and tickets to the Member's Gallery for Question Period. And let them use our phone to call their friends or neighbours at home. That should do it."

"It's okay for you to say. I'm the one who has to deal with them."

"But you always do it so well, and . . . "

The Air Canada stewardess came over and touched him gently on the shoulder. "Excuse me, Mr. Greene, first boarding call for your flight."

"Thanks." After a quick nod to the hostess he continued on the phone. "And Ann, tell Joan to arrange some constituency appointments tomorrow morning in the Vancouver office, those pending immigration cases, and get me a return flight tomorrow at 2 PM, the one that stops briefly in Calgary. I'll get an electronic ticket at the airport. I have to get back to the House."

Clay hung up and went back to sit at the small bar. He began to gulp his coffee. While jotting down in his diary the arrangements he had just made, he was aware of a woman sitting at the end of the bar. It was Marianne Tremblay.

"What are you doing here?" The words came out a little too fast.

She seemed surprised to see him. "I, I have a sister in Vancouver and I'm on my way to visit her." Tremblay slowly finished her glass of orange juice. "You know, I looked up some of my files on water exports, or at least the past debate and coverage on them. It was pretty extensive."

Greene smiled. "I told you, Ms. Tremblay, you ain't seen nothing yet!"

"Oh, you don't have to convince me about the issue and I know your track record on some of the issues you've pressed."

As soon as the words came out of her mouth she

thought of yesterday's conversation with the CBC's Mike Leslie. She wished she had chosen them a bit more carefully.

"So, what do you know about my 'track record,' as you call it?

She hesitated and finally replied, "Well it's my job, and I do remember that you stood up in the House a few years ago. In one of those sixty-second statements before Question Period, you warned about Khalistani agitators in Vancouver, predicted violence, and even said an Indo-Canadian lawyer friend of yours, a moderate, had been beaten up. We didn't cover your statement. A few months later an Air India jetliner was bombed."

"So you think I may have something to say?"

Tremblay smiled ever so slightly. "We'll see, won't we? Anyway, I believe the real stories happen outside of Ottawa. It's just too easy covering Question Period, period, as most of the Ottawa media do."

"With thoughts like that, good luck to success in the press gallery, Marianne."

Before she could reply, the hostess reminded them that the final boarding call had been made.

"Where are you sitting, Ms. Tremblay?"

"I'm using my points and I'm not sure exactly which row, but . . . "

"Actually we can help you, Ms. Tremblay," interrupted the stewardess. "We've oversold the flight in economy, so I can put you up with the big shots in executive class, across from Mr. Greene."

Tremblay looked a little taken aback. Greene grabbed his briefcase and smiled.

"Fancy that. If we're going to spend five and a half hours

together, you'd better call me Clay."

"You can call me Marianne."

Clay Greene generally tried to work on airplanes. He had found in his many trips to the constituency, averaging one every two weeks, that flying could give him the illusion he was working without any actual work being accomplished. So he turned down the offered copy of the *Globe and Mail*, opened his briefcase, and pored over the six immigration cases he would deal with tomorrow.

Looking across the aisle he saw that Marianne had dozed off. He knew he had to be careful with a reporter there, even a pretty one. When he first came to Ottawa, he had gone drinking with an old experienced reporter from the Global TV network who told him the three cardinal press rules for new MPs. One, nothing is really off the record. Two, don't piss on skunks, meaning don't waste your time criticizing the media for the stories they write about you. And three, don't get into bed with them. Actually, Greene liked the media, finding them more interesting people by far than the average MP—and it showed in his easygoing manner with them. He wasn't sure however, if the interest was mutual. And, he knew instinctively that there had to be that distance, however little. Too bad, he thought, and he returned to the immigration cases.

As lunch was about to be served somewhere over the Manitoba-Saskatchewan border, Clay heard a soft voice say, "Tell them to get to the Immigration Appeal Board."

"Hey, you're not supposed to be looking over my shoulder. How do you know anything about immigration?"

"Remember, I used to write local stories and we often featured the heart-rending story of some poor family getting thrown out, or about to be thrown out of the country back to Honduras."

"If they would just stay away from those immigration consultants, sharks that they are, it might be easier in the long run for them to get landed in the country. Why don't you do a story about those consultants?"

"Another of your House Statements. See Hansard page 60357."

"You know a fair bit about me, don't you?"

"Well, I confess, I have to write a feature about a few typical MPs—and you're to be one of them—but all I know about you is what I've read in Hansard and what I've seen in the newspapers or on TV."

"You sound like one of my constituents, except they don't read Hansard."

Just then, the luncheon tray arrived. Greene quickly put away his immigration cases and relaxed back into his seat. He still had to remember not to break any of the rules.

"I also know that you were elected nine years ago, at age thirty-two, in a surprise by-election victory, and that you have been re-elected twice by big margins since then. Your constituents apparently love you. What I don't know is how you got to Vancouver, since you were born in Edmonton, right?"

A slight scowl crossed Greene's face and he looked down at his books.

"Actually, I spent my early years in the North. When I was five my father, a widower, moved to Montreal where I went to school."

"That explains why you can speak French so well. Tell me how you got settled in Vancouver?"

The smile returned to Greene's face.

"When I was eighteen, I left home and took a train to Vancouver. I walked around Stanley Park on a beautiful June day and read a book. I can even remember the title, *Zen and the Art of Motorcycle Maintenance*. After each chapter I would sprawl on the grass and sleep awhile. It took me all day to walk around the park. But what a day. I fell in love with the place. In what other city in Canada could you lie in a T-shirt on green grass and look up at mountains with snow on them? I lived for a while at Long Beach, on the west coast of Vancouver Island between Tofino and Ucuelet, and I even tried to stay for a few weeks on Wreck Beach, the nude beach near UBC.

"I'll bet you were a knockout at eighteen at Wreck Beach."

At that comment the smile got bigger and Greene's eyebrows noticeably lifted.

"Let's just say I did all right. Life seemed so easy then."

"Did you work?"

"For some reason, I became interested in philosophy and anthropology, and I enrolled at UBC. I was pretty quiet and introspective then, a bit dreamy, and had lots of long hair. I worked part-time at Orestes, a Greek restaurant on West Broadway. Do you know it?"

Marianne noticed he didn't mention the frat parties; she did notice his glancing at the stewardess who was bending down and pouring a cup of coffee at a neighbouring seat.

"MacLean's" magazine once called Orestes a real 'in' place. I remember going there when I lived in Vancouver for a

year—it was quite a Yuppie hangout and the two guys who ran it, Aristides and Blaine, were pretty amazing. But it's closed now, isn't it?"

"Well, I was anything but a Yuppie in those days. I had an old Volkswagen, my only possession, and I lived in two rooms on Kitsilano Point. Oh, I did have an old dog, a Labrador that for some reason I called 'The Judge,' and I took him everywhere with me. The Judge and I were a pair. I considered myself a radical, most likely a Marxist, but sometimes I was attracted to Oriental philosophy. I suppose it could be said that I was, happily, all over the park."

"What about relationships? You know, women, men, what have you?"

"Oh," Clay Greene paused, and seemed to draw into himself.

Marianne Tremblay continued. "Around the gallery there are lots of rumours. After all, you're still a bachelor."

Clay smiled. "I don't know about the rumours, but I was pretty wild in those early days in Vancouver. I loved the experience of falling in love. My problem was that I didn't stay in love long. And I did the seducing, except occasionally when I found I could be seduced intellectually. But really I was never very serious about anything."

Marianne wondered what he meant by "seduced intellectually," but decided not to pursue it. He sure can skip over things, she thought.

He continued, "I liked my life—my old car, my dog, my frat. Life was easy until . . . "

"Until what?"

"I got thrown in jail during a demonstration against logging in the old growth forest. Those were the days of confrontation—us, the people as we liked to call ourselves, against MacBlo and the other big forestry companies. At one demonstration the police really got out of hand. They charged us with billyclubs, and tear gas, and many of us who had been there peacefully were arrested. I was released without charge a day later, but I was a little bitter. I also experienced a real cell in a real jail. I was shocked at all the poor, Native people in there." At the reference to Native people he paused slightly and turned away from her for an instant.

"Let's just say I didn't like the way the cops treated them—like dirt."

"Did you go to law school after that?"

"Yes, one of my friends was applying, so I did too. I don't think anyone in my family had ever gone to university, much less to a professional school. I hated the first year but it became easier and easier after that. I articled for John Hurley, one of the best criminal lawyers in town—but an incredible drunk."

"Did you practice law?"

"The word practice is too nice. I lived it. I took a small office in the Ford Building at the corner of Main and Hastings in the eastside of Vancouver. They called it 'the corner' because it was the centre of the heroin trade, even though the police station was across the street. Junkies, whores, dope dealers, shoplifters, impaired drivers, petty B and E artists, you name it, they all came into my office. It really toughened me up. And I never had trouble getting a table in a Vancouver restaurant because I usually had defended one of the waiters on a marijuana charge." Greene tossed his head back and laughed to himself as the stewardess took away their trays and left the coffee.

"Why did you go into politics?"

"Oh, I suppose I felt strongly about all the individual day-to-day wrongs that I saw as a criminal lawyer and I thought I could change them."

"Do you still feel that?"

"No, but I have got a sense now of the larger problems— sort of Canada's problems—and with a bit of effort and luck I can have some influence there."

Marianne kept thinking that this guy just throws off the words so easily, but at least he does so in a charming way. Maybe Michael Leslie was wrong; maybe he is capable of more.

Greene paused slightly, stared ahead and then Marianne saw the sparkle return to his eyes. "You know, in many ways Canada is still young, a work-in-progress. I feel lucky to be here in this place, in this moment. Look out that window to the prairies down there. This country is so big, but it is also so fragile, strung along the American border, struggling to be independent and to be civilized. Sometimes I feel like we take a couple of steps forward, and then at least one back at the same time."

"Is that why you're interested in this Greenpeace lawsuit?"

"Sure. Look at that big river over there. Canada has water in abundance and the Americans, and indeed other parts of the world, would like to get their hands on it. So the nature of the suit interests me. Also, I hate secret government and I don't like the way these Orders-in-Council were passed. I'm a bit of a stickler for laws and detail. It's the Scots side of me. And there is another reason."

"What's that?"

"There's a mystery here. My nose tells me that the Prime Minister is connected to this. That's a real mystery. Like most people, I guess, I'm intrigued by mysteries."

Greene reached down to the tray for his coffee cup, hesitated for a moment and then turned to face Marianne. She could see the change in expression, that worried look, the guard going up, a door closing. She had seen it come before in people she had interviewed, but perhaps not as suddenly as this.

"You know this is getting to be a bit of a cross examination, Marianne. It's my turn to ask a few questions. How about you? How did you get into journalism?"

She just smiled, "It ran in the family, I guess. My father worked for *Le Devoir* and for awhile Mum even did some editing for the *Gazette* in Montreal."

"Wow, that must have made for good dinner conversation," Greene chuckled and continued: "Anyway, tell me why you got into political journalism and why you know about the water export issue?"

"The answer to the first question is simple. My editor sent me to Parliament Hill. As to the second, I . . . I guess I'm interested, like you, in creating a country, although we may differ in the details."

Greene's smile was a bit tentative.

Marianne continued, "Besides, this will grow as an issue and I want to be in at the beginning. That's being a good journalist, I think."

"So you think you're a good journalist?"

"I try to be."

Greene looked down, began to yawn, tried to catch

himself, and then smiled again softly. He knew the conversation was over.

"Excuse me, Marianne, I'm a bit tired."

As Greene closed his eyes Marianne turned away and opened her notepad. She wrote a few lines and paused. She wondered why she hadn't told him the truth. Her dad was not just a writer for *Le Devoir*, he was editor. As such he had been, until his retirement, one of the leading intellectual voices for Quebec sovereignty, for the separation of Quebec from this Canada in which Clayton Greene saw so much promise. She loved her dad and had, they said, inherited his brains. But she had also inherited her mother's caution, and yes, a bit of shyness. She would never forget the look in her father's eyes when she told him that she doubted his views on the future of Quebec—that she wanted to be a citizen of the world and didn't like narrow nationalism. He had exploded. Was this his girl talking, his pride and joy who had been as a child at all the rallies, at all the Levesque speeches, at all the concerts? When she started living with an anglo stockbroker in Montreal he had cut her off. It almost broke her heart. So, why hadn't she told this to Clay? Maybe he would have asked her why she wasn't with the anglo boy now. She didn't want to get into that. Yes, she could have been more forthcoming. After all, he was pretty open with her. Or was he? Tired, she too closed her eyes.

When Clay woke, the 737 jet was descending to land.

"Do you need a ride into town?" he asked Marianne. "Janet Wong, my executive assistant from Ottawa, is meeting me at the airport. She's temporarily back in the riding to help me with the water exports investigation. Janet found out about the water export Orders-in-Council and she's apparently dug up another lead. If you're interested in this water export story, you might want to talk to her about it."

Marianne replied, "I would be interested. I don't know if any newspapers will be, though. I filed the story about the lawsuit, and about your question, and made sure the *Vancouver Sun* got a special copy on the wire. I emphasized you are a Vancouver MP, no kidding, so expect a short blurb there, if nowhere else."

"Thank you."

CHAPTER 4

JANET WONG DIDN'T DISAPPOINT. AS CLAYTON AND MARI-
anne emerged with their luggage through the door on the
arrivals level, Janet was arguing with one of the security
guards whose job was to move the traffic in front of the airport. When the security guard saw Greene, his whole
expression changed.

"Sorry, sir, didn't know it was your Volvo."

"That's what I told the stupid jerk, if he would only listen. Anyway, how are you, boss? Boy, we're moving on this
thing. Your question was great!"

Greene smiled broadly at Janet and said, "Janet this is
Marianne Tremblay of CP. Janet Wong, my able and
demanding assistant."

Janet barely paused to nod in the direction of Marianne.

"We didn't actually get much interest," said Clayton as
he did up his seat belt and looked at Marianne in the back
seat.

"Article in today's *Sun*, page A15, not bad for a starter,"
barked Janet from behind the wheel.

"A starter?"

"Yeah, I got a real lead, but maybe I'll tell you later."

"Marianne wrote that *Sun* article, Janet. You can be
open with her. She's going to help us with this thing. As a
matter of fact, she's the only journalist who's shown any
interest at all."

Janet looked a little incredulous, but without missing a
beat continued: "Okay, we're going to the Bayshore Inn near
Stanley Park."

"But we've already had lunch," Greene and Tremblay said almost in unison.

"This is not lunch, this is a boat trip! We're going around Stanley Park to English Bay, to a freighter, to meet its captain. My uncle, Tommy Gow, is the President of the Seaman's Union. He got a tip and he'll meet us on the freighter."

Marianne Tremblay looked at Janet Wong. "I've seen that name in a *New York Times* article I read recently."

"I'm not surprised. My Uncle Tommy is famous in world shipping circles. He's the man foreign crews call when they're treated like slaves—overworked and not given paycheques. Tommy and his members will throw a picket line up around a visiting freighter in dock. No back pay, no leaving Vancouver. It usually works. Tommy's won the confidence of seamen all over the world."

———

The newly renovated Bayshore Inn, a Vancouver landmark where Howard Hughes and scores of other famous people and legions of tourists had stayed, sparkled like a jewel in the afternoon sun. Its side door faced the entrance to Stanley Park; its back faced the snow-capped north shore mountains topped by twin snowcapped peaks called the Lions. Just past the parking lot a gleaming white cabin cruiser waited for them at a new wooden dock. Marianne could smell the fresh cedar.

"Ms. Wong, is it?" said Captain Don Fenwick.

"Yes, thanks for the fast service."

"Not at all, your uncle's a good friend of mine. Jump in and we'll be off."

Just as they were about to board the boat Marianne Tremblay interrupted: "Can you give me a moment to call my sister and tell her I'll be delayed? I'll go into the Bayshore lobby and call from there."

Janet Wong reached into her black leather shoulder bag and pulled out a small cell phone.

Marianne at first hesitated and then walked quickly to the side door of the hotel lobby. Over her shoulder she muttered, "There's a washroom there too."

The Captain laughed, "Didn't she know we do have heads in these modern boats?"

Janet Wong scowled, "I don't know about her, Clay."

Clayton Greene just laughed. In a few minutes Marianne Tremblay returned from the hotel lobby and politely thanked the group for waiting.

"Would you mind holding on for a few more minutes? My office is sending a fax to the hotel. It's important to me."

Janet Wong was about to speak when Captain Fenwick invited them on to the boat to have some freshly brewed coffee while they waited for Marianne.

Janet Wong threw up her arms.

Greene was first to hop on board. "Come on, gang, it's gorgeous. It certainly beats Ottawa. We can enjoy the day for a few minutes. I'll use your cell, Janet."

Marianne went quickly back to the hotel lobby. Fifteen minutes later she returned, apologetic. Janet Wong didn't look at her.

Clayton felt the cool ocean breeze and smelled the salt in the air as the launch pulled out of the dock area. They watched the joggers going around Stanley Park.

The launch turned left after passing under the Lion's

Gate Bridge and sped into English Bay toward one of the seven freighters waiting for port berths in Vancouver's inner harbour. As they approached the freighter, Marianne Tremblay noted its name and homeport in her notepad, *Akuru Maru, Yokahama*. Clayton could see the short burly figure of Tommy Gow on the deck. As they climbed up the rope ladder to the freighter's deck, Tommy reached out his right hand.

"Hello, Clayton, good to see you. I've just arrived myself."

"Tommy, this is Marianne Tremblay."

"What's happening here, Tommy?" Marianne asked.

Tommy smiled briefly and then frowned. "The captain is a Korean. His name is Kim and he was supposed to be on the bridge to meet me."

Another man, probably Korean, came up to them and motioned for them to follow him. Clayton, Marianne and Janet followed Tommy past the bridge to a side door and a small ladder that led to a lower deck. As they stepped inside the captain's cabin, scattered papers lifted off the floor and swirled around them in the draft from the door. A small man dressed in black pants and a white shirt with gold stripes on each shoulder was sprawled across the desk, a pool of blood soaking into the papers around his head on the desktop. Marianne gasped as Tommy rolled the man's head slightly and they all saw the bullet hole in his temple. Even as Tommy reached to feel his pulse, it was clear he was dead.

The doors of the desk were all opened and papers scattered on the floor.

There was a sudden roar as a motorboat started on the other side of the ship. Greene scrambled back up on deck and arrived at the rail just in time to see a small boat pull away from the freighter with two men on board.

"Tommy, check things out here," he called down the hatch. "Call the harbour police. I'll meet you at the Sylvia Hotel lounge in a couple of hours." Then he was over the side and dropping down the rope ladder to the launch.

"Do you think you can catch that boat?" he asked. "I think the men in it just killed the captain."

"I'll give it a try."

The other boat had a good headstart, but Fenwick's launch was bigger and faster and began to close the distance.

The first boat was heading for False Creek, past the highrises of Vancouver's West End. As they approached the Burrard Street Bridge, Greene began to notice small, irregular splashes in the water around their boat.

"They're shooting at us!"

Fenwick slowed down his launch for just a moment, but it was enough to let the first boat slip into a marina off Granville Island. Fenwick steered the bigger boat after it, but in the maze of sailboats and motorboats moored and moving, backing out and docking, the first boat seemed to have disappeared. There was nothing they could do. Fenwick slowly turned the launch around and headed back to Coal Harbour.

———

Two hours later, Greene entered the lounge of the Sylvia Hotel, small and ivy-covered and right across the street from English Bay. Tommy, Marianne, and Janet were already there, sipping beers and hashing over the day's events.

"Sorry to abandon you like that . . ." Greene began. "I

thought there was a chance to catch that boat, or at least identify it, but when we got close, they started shooting at us. Oh, this is my friend Jerry Howie, Professor Jerome Howie to be exact, of UBC. He's an old friend of mine and we can trust him."

Marianne and Janet saw a good-looking man around sixty whose hair had turned from blonde to grey—a shorter man than Greene—but better dressed and with a quiet solid air about him. Before either one could say anything, Tommy Gow responded.

"It's amazing and it happened so damn fast. Those guys are no amateurs. That was a professional job on the poor captain."

Janet Wong nodded her agreement

"The cops are there, on the freighter now, and I told them all I know—well, almost all," said Tommy.

Janet and Marianne piped up at almost exactly the same time, "Well, tell us all, Tommy."

"Captain Kim was to take the first load of water from up the BC coast to southern California. Apparently only last month the federal government gave permission for it. Not many people seemed to know about it. Kim was going to take on supplies and further crew in Vancouver. Apparently the *Akuru Maru* is specially outfitted. I got backpay for Kim years ago. He never forgot, poor bugger. Rumour on the waterfront is that big money is involved and this could be the beginning of a lot more. Leasing papers and other correspondence, which Kim was going to show us, have disappeared. People say that a company called Western Energy is involved. Don't know who they are. I did find this matchbox, sort of before the police arrived."

He handed the matches to Greene.

"Thanks, Tommy," said Greene. He glanced briefly at the matches and put them in the right pocket of his jacket and quickly downed his glass of beer. Marianne noticed that Jerry, Clay's older friend, poured some of his remaining beer in Greene's empty glass. Jerome Howie called the waiter to bring another round for the table and paid the tab.

Greene took a sip of the new beer and said: "Janet, can you do a companies search tomorrow and meet me at our community office at 12:30? And have another look at those court papers. I'm leaving for Ottawa on the 2 PM Air Canada flight. I've got some more questions for in the House. What about you, Marianne?"

"Well, considering I'm trying to come to terms with almost witnessing a murder, I'm going to file a story and then go to my sister's."

Greene looked to Marianne. "I didn't even get to say welcome to Vancouver!"

CHAPTER 5

A FEW STEPS EAST OF THE GRANVILLE ISLAND MARKET, about a kilometre from the Sylvia Hotel, in a dimly lit boat shed hidden behind a boat-building shop of corrugated iron, were two men wearing dark windbreakers and jeans. They reached up and took down two grey business suits off of hangers, changed into them, and put on black street shoes. One of the men transferred some papers to a slim leather attaché case; the other bundled the casual clothes into a canvas bag. The taller of the two felt into his suit jacket for a pack of Benson and Hedges, took one out and fumbled through his pockets for a match.

"Have you got a match?" he asked the other.

"Sorry, Pierre, I don't smoke."

"Never mind, we have those matches from the boat."

Pierre reached into the canvas bag and began to search the pockets of the jeans but couldn't come up with anything.

"Mon dieu, I've lost my matches."

"Probably they fell out of the boat," said the other, with a look that showed his growing impatience. "We'd better go. We have to get these papers to his house—and fast."

The men retrieved two small revolvers from under the floorboards of the boat. They slipped the guns into holsters inside their suit jackets as they left the boat shed by a side door. A long black Chrysler New Yorker waited beside the door. Pierre got into the driver's seat and reached into the glove compartment for a cigarette lighter. The cheap Bic he found wouldn't light at first and he cursed at it until a small orange flame finally appeared and he lit his cigarette. Then he started the car and floored it out of the alleyway beside the boat shed. As it turned left onto one of Granville Island's narrow roads, it almost struck a lone bicyclist who was forced to pull sharply to the side to avoid the car. The cyclist landed in a large puddle of inky rainwater at the side of the road.

"Shit, who do those guys think they are?" groaned the cyclist as he shook his fist at the departing car.

———

Clayton Greene came out of the small workroom at the back of his community office on Davie Street.

"If I have to listen to another immigration case this morning, I'm going to die."

"You should complain, I have to do this every day while you star in Question Period—and go to all these diplomatic receptions," responded Joan.

"You know I hate diplomatic receptions and, perhaps you've noticed, I haven't been exactly a star in Question Period since the MacKenzie government signed that draft ozone treaty with the Yanks."

"My, we're in a bad mood this morning." Joan smiled and handed Clay a cup of coffee as she opened out the front page of the *Vancouver Sun*.

"Perhaps this will pick up your spirits."

MURDER IN ENGLISH BAY, screamed a headline at the top of the page. There was even a by-line: "Marianne Tremblay."

"Kim Joe Lee, 48, captain of the Japanese registered ship the *Akuru Maru*, was killed late yesterday afternoon in the cabin of the ship he captained. Two men suspected of the murder escaped by boat." The story described the scene, with quotes from Tommy Gow and some crew members. There was mention of a pursuit into the network of marinas around Granville Island, but the pursuers' names were not mentioned. "The incident is seen by some sources to be related to the issue of water exports to the US and to the question on this subject recently raised by Vancouver Centre Member of Parliament, Clayton Greene, in the House of Commons."

Greene smiled.

"Why do politicians always get off on the fact that their name is in the paper—a double climax if it's on the front page?" grunted Joan Sanford as she picked up some of the immigration files.

"I wasn't getting off on it, as you so crudely put it."

Greene was smiling at the discretion Marianne Tremblay displayed in her reporting. Maybe here was one journalist that he could trust.

"You've got a pile of calls to return, messages that I took while you were seeing your constituents who, as you know, always come first. Ottawa office, your dentist, Ottawa office. Whip's office—they want to know if you'll be at the next Environmental Committee meeting—if not, you'll have to find a substitute—you are the critic after all. Then there's the provincial party secretary about another fund-raiser, Louie Raymond of the Arts Club, again your Ottawa office and . . ."

"Why was Louie calling me?"

"Maybe they want another grant—you've helped them in the past."

"Could you get him on the line for me, and could you get the phone number of the Vancouver Coroner's Office please?"

In a couple of seconds Louie Raymond, stage manager of the Arts Club Theatre, was on the telephone.

"What's up, Louie, got some good tickets for me?"

"You know, Mr. Greene, you've always got two comps waiting for you at the Arts Club or the Stanley Theatre. We appreciate all the help. But I was calling you about that story in today's *Sun*."

"What about it, Louie?" said Clay, turning serious.

"This may be off the wall, but late yesterday afternoon I was riding my bike to the theatre to set up for last night's performance, and a big-mother-of-a-black-car shot out from around those marinas—you know, near the boat-building sheds behind our theatre. They just about wiped me out so I tried to get their licence number. It was ARB, but I couldn't see the rest."

"Thanks, Louie."

"The plate was an Alberta one, which made me even madder. As I said, this may be off the wall, but I thought I should call you since the *Sun*'s story said you were looking into something."

"Thanks again, Louie. I'll pick up those comps some time soon. Bye."

"Here's the coroner's number," said Joan as she passed a piece of paper through the office door.

Clayton Greene dialed the number and when the switchboard answered he asked for extension thirty-one.

"Dr. Christopher Blake here."

"Hi, it's Clay Greene here, Chris. You remember when I used to cross examine you?"

"Oh yes, that was before you were a big shot. What can I do for you?"

"Off the record, and just between you and me, have you done an autopsy on Captain Kim? And what does it look like?"

"You know Clay, I always liked you because you always treated me with respect in cross-examinations, unlike some of those other young liars, or lawyers as they call themselves. I even voted for you, although my Conservative father would turn in his grave, God bless him!"

"Well?"

"Fairly professional. They didn't waste any bullets. Probably wanted to learn something first."

"Why do you say that?"

"There were some cigarette burns on the body."

"Thanks. One of these days, I'll stop by for lunch just like old times."

"Do that. And keep up the good work in that House of Conmen, or Commons."

With that the coroner hung up. Clay searched his jacket pocket and pulled out the matches that Tommy Gow had retrieved from the Captain's cabin. The cover said "Tony's Restaurant." A phone number, 685-7221, had been scrawled inside. About half the matches had been used.

He picked up the phone and dialed the number; after a few rings, an operator's voice came on the line.

"We're sorry, this number is not in service."

Another call came in as he hung up. Joan was on the other line, listening to a caller who seemed, from what Clay could hear, to be complaining about his income tax. Greene pressed the second line button to pick up the new call.

"Clayton Greene's office."

"That's unique, a big shot who answers his own phone,"

said Marianne Tremblay in a confident voice.

"You're the second person who's called me a big shot today. I suppose I should feel good, but I don't. I feel frustrated about this murder."

"You know, Clay, I share your frustration, but I figure we need to have more background on the water export issue before we can start looking for the killers."

"So, Marianne, what do you propose we do?"

"I don't know about you, Clay, but I'm going to that big library you have here in Vancouver to look at their files and to check out the net. I've also got some sources in Toronto to check out by phone."

"Well, imagine that. A journalist who actually does her own research!" Greene laughed.

"Now, don't be nasty."

"As a matter of fact, I'm not nasty. Things may be looking up after all. I've got a bit of my own research to do. How would you like to go to dinner tonight, an early one because I'll be catching the midnight flight afterwards to Ottawa."

Marianne smiled—it was amazing what one little mention in an article would do to hook a politician. "Now you're talking. I really did want to sample some of Vancouver's great Chinese restaurants."

"Actually, I was thinking Italian, in fact the place where those matches on the freighter might have came from. Meet me at Tony's Restaurant, 1400 block Seymour, at a quarter to eight."

"Italian, Tony's? Okay, if you insist. See you then," said Marianne.

"Joan," Clay called to the outer office, "will you make a

reservation for 7:45 at Tony's Restaurant and change my afternoon flight to the midnight one."

"Fine, but you know how cranky you get when you take the red-eye flight. And tell Mr. Tony that I didn't see a 'Vote Greene' sign near his restaurant in the last election campaign. Will the reservation be for two?"

Janet Wong caught that last remark as she came into Greene's Office. "Morning, boss. I don't know if you want me to join you at Tony's, but if you don't mind I'll take a pass. I've already got dinner plans."

"Too bad. It might not have been a bad idea to have you along. I'm going to see Marianne Tremblay about water exports." He didn't sound very convincing.

Janet frowned. "Look, Clay, she seems nice and all that, and we could certainly use her research help, not to mention her contacts, but—"

"But what, Janet?"

"Well, she was on the same plane flight as you, and you told me she sat beside you, and then she made that call from the Bayshore, the one to her sister. Then the fax. It was like she was trying to delay us. And you know those guys beat us to the freighter. And Captain Kim was killed. If we'd been there sooner, it might not have happened."

"Oh, come on Janet, let's be serious!"

"I am being serious, boss."

"Look, get to know her. Go for a beer together. Talk. She's a reporter, not a spy. Anyway, I'm off to Fairhaven Seniors home for my weekly tea. I'll pop back later if you want me to see some more constituents. Then I'm going for a game of tennis at the Jericho Club with Howie Jerome, and a good dinner after. See you both later."

Clayton knew Tony from ten years earlier, when Tony had been a co-owner of a restaurant in Gastown with another guy, Luigi. After a hard day in his law office, Greene used to go down and share a bottle of wine in the kitchen with the two restaurant partners who had just worked a full day. But Luigi insisted on drinking his limited success away. Tony, younger and more ambitious, went on to open his own restaurant. He was now the most successful Italian restauranteur in Vancouver and had even been featured in the "Gastronomique" section of Air Canada's inflight magazine.

"For old times, please have this bottle of wine on me," said Tony as he poured some Okanagan cabernet into Marianne Tremblay's glass, "and bring this lovely woman to my newest restaurant, which has just opened at Whistler Mountain."

When Tony had left their table, Clay raised his glass. "A toast to a mystery and to where it takes us to solve it."

After the glasses clinked they spent a few moments discussing the menu, but after the waiter had taken their order, Clayton Greene wasted no time.

"Well, what have you found out, Marianne?"

"I thought I would try to get a handle on water exports. I phoned a few specialist journalists in Toronto and some of the environmental lobby groups in Ottawa. Then I sat down at the library."

"And?"

Tremblay opened up her note pad.

"Ben Franklin actually said it all, 'When the well's dry, we know the worth of water.' Trouble is, Canadians think

Canada is awash with fresh water. They're right, too. Canada possesses about 25 per cent of the earth's fresh water, and we have less than 1 per cent of the world's population. Our rivers have a combined flow of sixty-eight thousand cubic metres per second, enough to fill all the country's bathtubs every ten seconds, as a journalist would put it. Our Great Lakes alone contain 18 per cent of the planet's surface fresh water."

"Lucky us," said Clay as he refilled Marianne's wineglass and ordered a plate of antipasto.

"Problem is that other countries, especially our great friend and neighbour to the south, as the expression goes, are facing a water shortage. A group called the Council on Foreign Relations, a Canadian-US group of highly credible academics, has said that fresh water will be *the* major long-range resource issue on the continent. Water is the most precious of all continental resources. This issue is going to make the controversy over acid rain seem like child's play." Greene was listening and trying to digest the details.

"Have there been any studies on this?"

"One of your local academics, Professor Peter Pearse, perhaps one of your constituents, did a study a few years ago on federal water policy. Turns out, shortfalls in the west, southwest and western Great Lakes regions of the US will reach crisis proportions in a few years. There have been some megaprojects proposed. Ever heard of NAWAPA?"

"Yeah, wasn't it some big dam in the Rockies?"

"It stands for the North American Water and Power Alliance, an idea conceived by an engineer named Ralph Parsons. In 1964 he proposed that an 800-kilometre length of the Rocky Mountain Trench in BC be flooded and two canals be built: one 190 metres wide by 11 metres deep to flow to the southern US, another 23 metres wide by 9 metres deep across the Canadian prairies to link to the St. Lawrence system."

"No kidding. How much would it cost?"

"About $300 billion, excluding the social and environment costs, of course. A volume of 250 million acre-feet per year, roughly equivalent to the average total discharge of the St. Lawrence, is envisaged. North America, as seen from outer space, would resemble Schiaparelli's depictions of the canals on Mars."

"Impossible."

"Look, if you can have a continental oil and gas policy, why not a water policy? Reagan and Mulroney have now left the political scene but water is included in the fine print of their free trade deal. Besides, there's more."

"More!"

"Ever hear about the GRAND Canal, or more correctly, the Great Recycling and Northern Development Canal? Tom Kierans proposed that James Bay be turned into an immense freshwater reservoir by building a dike across the Bay where it meets Hudson's Bay. The water from this reserve would be pumped and diverted south through a series of canals and the Ottawa River to the Great Lakes, from which water would be transferred to the USA through a waterway called the Chicago Diversion and other possible diversions."

"How much?"

"About $100 billion over eight years."

"What about environmental costs?"

"Well, a canal between Canada and the US could provide

a route for undesirable plants and animals. In the early years of the twentieth century, lampreys invaded the upper Great Lakes following the opening of the Welland Canal and decimated the commercial fisheries. People say the changing drainage patterns around the Garrison Dam will have similar undesired side effects in Manitoba."

A large caesar salad for two had appeared, and Greene was wasting no time in tackling it. After a few mouthfuls he looked across to Marianne. "Didn't one former Canadian Environment Minister, I think it was Charles Caccia, a good Italian Canadian, say that water is not for export, period?"

"So have a few provinces, including British Columbia. But this new Canadian government has no firm policy. I've heard that there's a struggle in cabinet. And there have been some powerful voices calling for exports. You know who supported water exports and the GRAND Canal? None other than Simon Reisman and Robert Bourassa. Reisman spoke about Canada trading access to its water in return for better access to US markets."

"I suppose, as one of my old Marxist professors used to say with a sigh, the basis for the Canadian economy has always been exports of renewable and non-renewable natural resources—grain, timber, minerals, oil and gas. Why not also water? Once a colony, always a colony."

Tremblay put down her cup and looked momentarily at the steaming plate of fettuccine in front of her. "There will be one helluva fight with environmental and Native groups, not to mention the provinces who probably own the water. Maybe on this issue, Canadians might just say, 'Wait, stop!'"

"I thought for a moment you were going to use the word gutless, as in 'gutless politicians.'"

Marianne looked intently at Greene.

"If the shoe fits, wear it."

"Oh, maybe I'll just let that one pass. Instead, tell me if you found anything about the more limited idea of exports by tanker?"

Marianne didn't lose a breath.

"The plan is to ship to the southern US and to Mexico. There are already moorage facilities in Hotham Sound, north of Vancouver." Marianne turned a page of her notebook. "The water would come from Freil Lake, which is about ninety kilometres up the Sunshine Coast from Vancouver. Freil Lake empties into the ocean through a waterfall. Maybe this was where poor Captain Kim was going."

Clay Greene looked at Marianne Tremblay with a new appreciation. "That's not bad research. And it shows what a huge political issue this is. With tanker exports, you can at least turn off the tap. With the others, it wouldn't be so easy. We really would be joined, wouldn't we?"

"And there's big money, bigger than any Canadian megaproject so far. This is even bigger than hydro, telephone, or oil and gas exports combined."

At this point, the waiter came and asked if either of them would like another glass of water.

As they both laughed together, Tony came to their table with two glasses of sambuca.

"These are only part of the dessert. You have to try our tiramisù. It's the best in the country."

"We'll do that, Tony, if you can answer me a question," Greene smiled.

He took the box of matches from his pocket and showed it to Tony, including the phone number inside. Tony didn't recognize the number and said he gave out thousands of boxes of matches. Greene glanced at Marianne and turned back to Tony. "Joan Sanford, my constituency assistant here in Vancouver, said to say hello, and in her usual direct way, wondered about election signs in the last campaign."

"I'm sorry, Clay. Your people never asked me. We had a Conservative sign up because Senator Murphy, who eats here a lot, asked me and you know I can't turn a good customer down. But you and I go way back, Clay. I appreciate those early days. You know I voted for you, Clay."

With that, Tony was gone to attend to some minor crisis in the kitchen.

"Do they all vote for you?" asked Marianne as she sampled the tiramisù and looked at the sambuca.

"They all tend to say that—luckily for them it's a secret ballot."

"Pierre Trudeau once said MPs were nobodies off Parliament Hill, but you seem to do all right. Do you like being an MP?"

"Sometimes, but not tonight. When I have to take that overnight flight, no. But when I accomplish something, yes, I like it."

"If you were in another party, you could more easily become a cabinet minister, couldn't you?"

"Maybe, but what's so great about being a cabinet minister anyway? People like Tommy Douglas with medicare, and Stanley Knowles with his persistent work over the years for better pensions, or Grace MacInnis on the early women's issues, have accomplished more than most cabinet ministers."

"There are some exceptions," interrupted Marianne.

"I suppose so, like Ron Basford's work on getting federal

government money to re-create Granville Island here in Vancouver. But most cabinet ministers work like hell and accomplish very little when all is said and done."

"How about the top job? Prime Minister?"

"I've never thought about that. I suppose you could move this country if you were strong and you had a vision for it, but there's no chance for me to be a cabinet minister— wrong party. So I decided I wanted to be a good MP and I picked an area like the environment on which I could concentrate."

Greene realized he was opening up a lot more than he intended. Remember, he thought, you could read this word for word in some magazine article or worse. For a second he thought of Janet Wong's warning. He ordered coffee and decided to switch the topic.

"What about you? Do you want to be a big shot columnist like the late Marjorie Nichols, or an Alan Fotheringham, a Michael Valpy, or, God forbid, Geoffrey Simpson?"

"I don't know if I could take the social life that seems to go with it."

"Oh, come on, look at the money and the power people like Peter Mansbridge or Pamela Wallin have."

"TV's not my medium. I'm an old-fashioned print researcher."

Clay looked at the top of her blouse. "I think that you could do TV."

"Thanks, but I really feel that today's journalists are short on detail and real analysis. You see this in politicians too, with some exceptions. Name me the contemporary Canadian politician who can handle a science matter or a complicated health issue like AIDS—stories that don't fit easily into the twenty-second clip. The politician of the future, says David Suzuki, probably another constituent of yours, will be the one who handles these kinds of issues. I agree with him. It's the same in journalism. Day-to-day rumours, polls, the Question Period, they're easy to cover. But there has to be more to journalism than that."

Greene laughed. "Boy, I thought *I* was idealistic."

"I think I'm realistic and, I also think I'm good at what I do."

"You certainly are determined, and that was a good quick piece of research on water exports, almost enough for an article."

Marianne Tremblay didn't respond and for a long moment neither of them spoke.

Greene folded his napkin and leaned over the table slightly towards her. He caught a small whiff of very light Armani perfume and he liked it.

"I suppose I could postpone my flight tonight and we could go for a nightcap."

Marianne didn't even hesitate, or smile.

"You're a free man, go ahead, but I'm going down to Chinatown to have a beer and a talk with Janet Wong. I still have some things to take care of."

CHAPTER **6**

THE AIR CANADA 767 LEFT VANCOUVER RIGHT ON TIME, fifteen minutes before midnight. Clayton Greene stretched back in his Executive Class seat and thought of the airline's ad with the line "Arrive refreshed for a day's business in Toronto."

"Shall I wake you for breakfast, Mr. Greene?" purred the stewardess.

"Please don't."

Greene knew he would need all the sleep he could get, even if it was only three and a half hours. Tomorrow, or today now, would be a long and important one. Normally he tried to avoid the "red-eye" or the "cardiac express," as the overnight flight from the West Coast was sometimes called. But he had needed to stay in Vancouver that afternoon for the phone calls. Or was it really the dinner with Marianne? Was he being too open with her? It was unlike him; he was normally a cautious person. She *was* a superb researcher. But didn't he already have staff for that? It was good to have a media perspective on the issue. Anyway, she turned him down at the end of the dinner. It wasn't the first time a chick turned him down, he thought, although it hadn't happened often. He must be getting too serious, too into this job. Enough, go to sleep, forget her. He tried to meditate. He stilled his mind. He watched it wander from one thought to another. And he stilled it again.

He had just shut his eyes, drifted off, and tossed and turned a bit, when he heard the announcement to fasten seatbelts for landing in Toronto. It was just after 7 AM

Toronto time, 4 AM Vancouver time, and he thought, no wonder it's difficult for a homegrown BC politician to achieve supreme power in Ottawa. He wondered whether life wouldn't be a lot better and a lot simpler if he returned to his Vancouver law practice and got to sleep in his own bed.

After changing planes to the 8:15 shuttle flight from Toronto to Ottawa, he looked around him and saw row upon row of freshly-shaven and showered blue business suits with the occasional woman here and there in the plane. The smell of after-shave lotion was a bit overpowering. Most of the people, he knew, were going to Ottawa for a day of lobbying one government department or another, or just to "consult." He realized that an MP, especially one in opposition, knows only a small part of government. He wished that he had taken some more time to find his way around all the government departments. But he did know the Hill and the House procedures and perhaps that was enough for the time being.

Boy, are you jet-lagged, he thought. Tired, and feeling a little grubby, he accepted the breakfast tray and some coffee from the ever-smiling stewardess. The passenger next to him, who had been reading the *Globe*, put the paper down to eat.

"Do you come often to Ottawa?" his seatmate asked Greene, between bites of a muffin.

"Yes, I work here."

"You don't sound too keen about that."

"I'm a bit tired, just came from Vancouver."

"What do you do in Ottawa?"

"I'm an MP."

"Oh, what's your name?"

"Clayton Greene, and yours?"

"John Graham."

They shook hands over their breakfast trays as the stewardess refilled their coffee cups.

"Say, I just read about you in the morning paper. Water exports, a murder . . . strong stuff."

Greene looked at Graham a little more closely. He seemed about fifty-five, his hair sprinkled with grey, his white shirt crisp and freshly laundered, his tie conservative and carefully chosen to match his suit. "What do you work at—can I call you John?"

"Yes, certainly. I'm with the Bank of Nova Scotia, Scotiabank, but I guess you NDPers don't like bankers."

"Well, I think banks should pay their fair share of taxes and so on, but I've never had anything against bankers as people. After all, you're Canadians too."

They both laughed. Greene had learned through many aircraft flights not to provoke arguments with the passenger next to him. However, he had nothing against a good intellectual discussion. He found business people often very naive about public affairs, and in many respects they were prisoners of the narrow perspective they received from business columnists in the *National Post* or the *Globe and Mail* or *Vancouver Sun*. Greene was a tolerant debater when he was in the mood for it and had a talent for shifting the other person's point of view—often planting a small seed of doubt that he knew would grow if the person thought about it. He was also a good listener.

Graham asked more questions about political life, especially about the honesty and commitment of present MPs. Greene said that he really thought most members on all sides, in all parties, were there out of a sense of public service. They certainly weren't in it for the money.

When he mentioned money, Greene noticed a strange look pass fleetingly across John Graham's face. Graham sipped the rest of his coffee. "I want to ask you . . ."

At that moment the stewardess stopped at their row to pick up the trays. Graham became silent. The jet began its descent into Ottawa.

As the plane arrived at the terminal he turned towards Greene and quietly said, "I'll give you my card. Perhaps we'll meet again."

After disembarking, Greene breezed through the terminal and caught a cab to Parliament Hill. As the cab passed Carleton University and turned onto Colonel By Drive leading down the canal, he reached into his pocket and brought out the banker's card. It read "John R. Graham, Vice President, Caribbean Region, Bank of Nova Scotia."

———

Ten minutes later, precisely at 9:30 AM, the cab stopped at the Members' Entrance of the House of Commons. Greene paid and tipped the driver and took the marble steps two at a time, past the guards, to the entrance of the House. He turned right and continued down the corridor to the Commonwealth Room, a small room with a beautiful fireplace and grand mirror, used for receptions and meetings. About twenty of his colleagues were there, seated around a large green table. They were discussing the line-up for the day's Question Period.

To an outsider, Question Period looks spontaneous, with the Speaker recognizing standing members randomly for questions. In reality, the line-up is predetermined by the parties' executives, who meet in the morning. The Speaker is slipped a typed list just before the questions start. In the old days Question Period was indeed spontaneous, and it was up to the Speaker to choose who got to pose the questions, which usually went to the more senior members.

Usually the party leader got the lead-off question, or more accurately, a question and not one but two supplementals. This day the party research director suggested the leader go with a question based on rumours of yet another renewal agreement with the Americans to continue cruise missile testing in Canada's North. Other members had submitted questions which were listed by the party whip, and that member or the research assistant could make a pitch to get the question. As on most days, there were about fifteen questions submitted for six spots. The final selection was determined by the caucus executive, a group of five members including the House leader.

When his turn came, Clay outlined the Greenpeace court case and the subsequent murder in Vancouver. Bob, the whip, commented that the question Greene wanted today was a little vague, as indeed it was. Besides, he said, he thought Greene's previous question had not really gone anywhere.

Just as it was beginning to look like Greene wouldn't get a spot that day, the party research director mentioned that the morning's *Globe and Mail* had an article on the subject on page A4 and that the writer had speculated there would be further questions in the House today. Attitudes seemed to change.

Greene sent a silent thank-you to Marianne and smiled.

He left the executive meeting after he made his final pitch for a question and returned to his office in the West Block to drop off his briefcase and check in with Ann. Then he went further down the Hill to the Confederation Building to use the members' gym on the eighth floor. After a workout and a shower, he felt like a new person. When he arrived back in his office, Ann greeted him with a smile.

"The whip's office just called. You have fifth question. Lucky you!"

———

A Member of the Canadian Parliament gets a global budget of approximately $200,000 to hire staff and pay all office expenses. Most MPs keep three staff members in Ottawa and one in the constituency, with a little money left in the budget for some special research contracts and for a contingency. Greene sometimes hired a temporary worker to input lists of names on his office computer so he could send letters and reports to his constituents, or to special groups of constituents on particular issues. Already copies of his question to the PM on water exports were being mailed to those constituents who had shown an interest in environmental matters.

The constituency or riding, or district as the Americans call it, usually with a population of about 100,000 people, was the number one priority of each MP. Even the PM had to watch his constituency because, unlike the American chief executive, he had to be re-elected personally in the riding at each election. A good MP respected his constituents, who in turn gave him the legitimate political strength to be equal to any other MP in Parliament.

The budget didn't allow for huge salaries for Greene's

four employees, but this suited him fine because it meant he got bright young people as researchers. They were usually bilingual, even those from the Canadian West. The researchers stayed for a couple of years and then moved on to other professions. Greene believed this meant less bureaucratic thinking, and he hated bureaucracy with a passion. The two secretaries, or chiefs-of-staff as they jokingly called themselves, in Ottawa and Vancouver, had been with Greene since his first election, and there was a bond of loyalty and trust between the three of them. The better MPs tried to cultivate this bond because their secretaries virtually ran their lives.

Rob Faulkner, a tall blond young man from Kingston, Ontario, was Greene's research assistant. He was holding up the Ottawa end of Greene's office while the other assistant, Janet Wong, was still in Vancouver. People liked Rob for his easygoing ways, but behind the smile was a keen political mind. For some reason, which Greene claimed not to understand, Faulkner wanted to be a political party organizer even after Greene had warned him that it could be the most thankless job in the world.

Over a coffee in his office, Greene brought Rob up-to-date on the past days' events. He showed him the matchbox from Tony's Restaurant and the phone number inside.

"Call for you, Clay," yelled Ann from the outside office.

"Hold my calls, will you? Rob and I are going to work on my question."

"This is from Janet—I can feel the vibes even from five thousand kilometres."

Greene picked up his phone and he too could feel the energy.

"I think I've struck something, boss. I just pulled the company's records in Victoria and I know who the directors of Western Energy are."

"I'm waiting with bated breath."

"George Smithers, Gene Pantalone, René Mercier, and Mrs. René Mercier."

"So what?"

"Gene Pantalone is a big Conservative organizer on the coast, chief bagman we think, although he wasn't a MacKenzie supporter in the last Tory leadership convention. I called David Strauss, remember him? He used to have my job with you, now a stockbroker, a lefty stockbroker if you can believe it. Anyway, he's amazing. He got me the name of the major shareholder of Western Energy. Turns out it's British Properties Investments."

"So what?" Greene teased.

"Well, back to the people in Victoria's Companies' Branch and guess what? The owner of Britprop, the correct name, is none other than Senator George R. Murphy."

Clayton Greene looked out of his office window at the silhouette of the Gatineau Hills in the distance and sighed. "What did Mao say? 'A journey of a thousand miles begins with the first step.'"

"What's the next step, Clay?"

"Why don't you call Marianne at CP in Vancouver and tell her to watch Question Period. Call me later this afternoon, and . . ."

"Yeah?"

"Great work! Ciao!"

While Greene was on the phone, Faulkner had stepped out of the office. Now he returned, holding the matchbox.

"Call this number again, Clay."

Greene dialed 1, then 604, the British Columbia area code, and 685-7221. Again, a voice told him that the number was not in service.

"Try this." Faulkner switched on the speaker phone, dialed 8 for local calls, then the same number. As the phone rang, he put his finger to his lips.

"Senate of Canada, Senate du Canada. Office of Senator Murphy, bureau du Senator Murphy."

Clay clicked off the line and his face lit up. "Looks like we have just taken the second step, Rob."

"Pardon?"

"Nothing, just something I said to Janet. Tell me all you know about the honourable senator."

"You recall, Clay, when the Conservatives had their last leadership convention, Senator Murphy managed James Roberts' campaign for leader. The convention couldn't stomach that guy's extreme right wing views. So they chose MacKenzie as a compromise. As you know Roberts is now the Deputy Prime Minister."

Greene interrupted. "MacKenzie turned out to be a good choice. A Maritimer and someone who would offend no one, or so they thought."

Rob continued. "In the election, Sandy MacKenzie's campaign manager was sidelined by a heart attack and so he turned to the old pro, Senator Murphy, to take over the campaign. Old pro—our organizers think he's an old sleazebag. The campaign became a lot dirtier from there."

Clay lifted his head and sighed as he recalled the thirty-eight days of the campaign.

"When the Libs collapsed in Ontario, MacKenzie's

Tories squeaked ahead of the Alliance and again stopped an anticipated eastern breakthrough. After the election he brought some Alliance members into his minority government, including Stan Knight as the Defence Minister. The NDP, which had made surprising gains, and the Liberals, now a bit dispirited, were both reluctant to defeat him. Brilliant!"

"But what of Murphy, Rob?"

"Senator Murphy and his friends, including the Deputy PM I suspect, were not happy with the direction of the government. My feeling is that Senator Murphy has been frozen out, abandoned by a very smart MacKenzie. Oddly, the Alliance MPs are still on board, but it isn't a very happy alliance. I bet Murphy wishes the Deputy PM were the actual Prime Minister."

Clay Greene listened intently as he gazed out his office window at the Centre Block and the Peace Tower.

"Okay, Rob, let's get going and draft my question."

———

Five thousand kilometres away, a petite woman in a white apron brought a silver tray of pastries and croissants outdoors. She placed them next to a coffee urn on a white iron garden table. The table sat under a fully blooming Japanese cherry tree, behind which stood a huge, wood-beamed house. It was part of the British Properties, an exclusive area on the flanks of the north shore mountains above Burrard Inlet, with a gorgeous view of the city of Vancouver below, including a panoramic view of English Bay and the freighters at anchor there.

The group of seven men who were gathered in the garden

began to help themselves to the goodies. Another servant pulled a TV set outside between the white table and the pool. Senator George Murphy, in slacks and silk shirt, was in the process of pouring himself another cup of coffee from the urn. A huge gold chain hung from his thick, hairy wrist.

"What time is it, Pete?"

"It's already 11:30," answered a blond, muscular man in his mid-thirties.

Senator Murphy barked, "Turn on the TV. We'll catch the Question Period and see if the opposition follows up that *Globe* article. Those assholes never think for themselves, so they just might."

When both opposition leaders opened with questions on the cruise missile testing, the group began to talk about other matters and refilled their plates.

Question Period was almost over. Senator Murphy, in the garden in the British Properties, was reaching over to turn off the TV.

"The Honourable Member from Vancouver Centre," announced the Speaker.

Murphy hesitated.

Clayton Greene rose. "My question is directed to the Deputy Prime Minister in the absence of the Prime Minister. Is the government aware that by approving, allegedly secretly, various Orders-in-Council, they have made it possible for a company, Western Energy Incorporated, to make a fortune selling water to the US?"

The Deputy PM, James Roberts, rose in his place and adjusted his glasses. A short, slender man with a twist to his mouth that made him look like he had just sucked a lemon, Roberts was not popular in the House. "I don't accept for a minute the Honourable Member's premise that secret government orders were passed. As to that old canard about certain companies making money, isn't that typical of the Honourable Member and his party? They don't want a Canadian company to make an honest dollar."

"Hear, hear," came from the government backbenchers.

Clayton Greene held himself back. He had learned the hard way that too often a quick quip sidetracks the issue or, worse still, brings the Speaker to his feet to interrupt and tell the questioner to get to the point. He'd blown questions in the past because of an unfocused supplemental, or as a young MP called Bob Rae had once termed it, "the irresistible smart remark."

"Supplemental question. Is the government aware that the major shareholder who will gain from the water exports is Senator George R. Murphy, the former chair of the last Conservative election campaign?"

All hell broke loose in the House. Cries of "Shame!" "Get out of the slime!" "Sleazy!" came from various government backbenchers. The Speaker rose to shout, "Order, order!"

Greene looked to the Press Gallery, above the Speaker's chair and just below one of the public galleries. The journalists were picking up their pens.

The Deputy Prime Minister rose again, this time a little less cocky. "The government is not aware of the shareholders of Western Energy, the company in question, nor whether the Honourable Senator is involved in the company. He is obviously not here to respond to the Honourable Member's innuendoes and insinuations. Again, may I remind the Member that it is no crime to invest or even to make a reasonable profit, at least not yet, in this country, unless in the unlikely event that the Honourable Member's party ever achieved power."

More cries of "Shame!" along with "Answer the question!" "More Tories at the trough!" and others came this time from the opposition benches.

"Order! Order!" cried the Speaker, as he moved on to another question.

This time in the scrum outside the House, Clayton Greene was surrounded. He called for the government to come clean about what it knew about Western Energy and the water exports.

In West Vancouver, Senator Murphy angrily clicked off the TV and grunted and turned around. "We've got to stop that guy Greene. He's dangerous. This thing has been going well." He paused for a moment and then looked straight at the younger man across from him.

"Pete, find a way to shut him up."

At that moment the housekeeper came back out into the garden. "Senator, a gentleman from Broadcast News is on the phone. He says he'd like to interview you."

⎯⎯⎯

When Clayton Greene arrived back in his office, Rob Faulkner was there to greet him.

"I liked it, Clay. You stuck to the facts. You've received a number of press calls already."

"Let's ignore the calls for now, Rob. Let's get over to the Finance Committee and see if we can't get the water exports on the agenda."

"Funny thing, I took the precaution of calling the whip's office and getting you put on that Committee today. We have two members on the Committee, you're only an alternate. But you're on for today.

Greene was finding out by experience that what topics Committees consider, and how controversial they get, depends on the chair of the particular committee and on the ability of the members to work together.

The Tory member from Saskatoon Centre, Don Harris, was a gritty former business college teacher, part-time farmer, part-time businessman. He obviously figured he wasn't destined for the cabinet, so he was determined to be an active and independent chair.

Clayton Greene had once told a group of college students visiting the House that, in his opinion, Canadian parliamentary committees were much too tame, too afraid of embarrassing the government, and that they should become, within limits, more like the American Senate and Congressional committees. Under Harris, the Finance Committee was the exception. Although right of centre in his politics, a sort of populist Conservative, Don Harris presided over the committee like a genial uncle. He was proud of the work and the independence of his committee. And he wasn't afraid of his own government.

"Now tell me why a finance committee should hold hearings on water exports?" asked Harris with a broad grin on his face.

"Because future water shortages will be an important issue, especially if our farmers experience shortages as a result, something an MP from Saskatchewan should be especially concerned about," replied Clayton Greene.

"Close, tempting, but no cigar."

Greene lowered his voice and leaned closer to the bulky chairman. "I'm telling you, Don, there's a lot more here than meets the eye. Trust me."

"Well, here's what we'll do, my friend. Today we have to wrap up the last of the witnesses on international banking centres. You can propose at the beginning that we hold hearings on the water exports, financial implications on Canada's future balance of payments, and so on, and I'll allow that to sit on the table for consideration by our steering committee. Okay?"

"If that's the best I can get for now, I'll take it."

With that, both men entered Room 208 in the West Block, where the committee was meeting.

An hour later, Greene returned to his office. He left his colleague from Nova Scotia to do the questioning on the banking centres. As a new member, she was keen on the topic.

"Jack Hepburn called," Ann told him as he came in." He asked you to drop by his office when you had a moment."

Hepburn, the NDP leader, was a former trade unionist who had come up through a steelworkers' local in northern Ontario. He was tough, straightforward, and honest—as well as being a workaholic. He prided himself on knowing every area of government and spent long hours in his office working when he wasn't travelling on party business. Greene sometimes wished he would relax more. There were rumours in the press of heart trouble, which Hepburn emphatically denied. Today he looked pale, his skin patchy, and he had deep bags under his narrow eyes.

"How much have you really got on this, Clay?" asked Hepburn.

Greene was hesitant. MPs are always afraid another MP will "seagull" or steal their issue. But Greene always co-operated with his leader.

"I'm still accumulating facts. To be honest, I don't know the next step, but we do know Senator Murphy is up to his ears in the exporting company, and we expect a court decision shortly on the legality of the government's approving order."

"I was just wondering whether I should go on it in Question Period tomorrow. If Jourdain or another Liberal goes on it, I may have to join in. We'll play it by ear. Keep in touch, Clay, and we can discuss it at caucus executive tomorrow."

As Greene was returning to his office, he paused in the now empty hallway, put his head gently up against the wall and silently asked himself: just what was the next step?

CHAPTER 7

THE GOVERNOR GENERAL OF CANADA DIDN'T OFTEN hold parties for members of Parliament. But when a new session started, she invited members to Rideau Hall, the Governor General's mansion in Rockcliffe Park, for dinner, drinks, and dancing. It was an opportunity to meet the new members and to gossip. Her Excellency had delayed the party because of the uncertain situation in the new Parliament and then because she had been ill. Now she had recovered and the minority Parliament, which no one had expected to last, looked like it might even go a full term. So it was time for the Governor General's party, and Clayton Greene, like most of the others, wouldn't miss it.

Early in the evening, Greene worked out in the members' gym. He was doing sit-ups during the CTV six o'clock news, and glanced up to catch a shot of his question. A radio beside him was tuned to CBC Radio's "World at Six," Greene's favourite news broadcast because of the quality of the reporters and because it gave more extensive coverage of each item. The CBC news nicely made the connection between the Senator and former Conservative campaign manager and water exports. Greene made a mental note to phone the people at Oasis, Parliament's in-house TV system with multiple channels, and ask them to record the six o'clock BCTV news from Vancouver. It would appear at 9 PM Ottawa time, when he would be at the Governor General's.

Greene put on his tuxedo in his office and went into Ann's office, where she was waiting for him in an elegant light green evening dress.

"Wow, it's a dark Robert Redford! You look great, Clay. I'm glad my boyfriend won't be seeing you. He'd give me a hard time for being your date."

"You're looking fabulous yourself, Ann."

In fact, Ann was the perfect date for a Governor General's dinner. She was attractive and could mingle with the guests with little effort. She knew all of them and none of them knew her, and it was amazing what MPs would tell a good-looking woman after a few glasses of champagne. Once or twice in the past she'd had to politely excuse herself from the Governor General's arboretum when conversations got a bit too close.

As Greene's Honda Civic, his Ottawa car, entered the stately portals of the Rideau Hall grounds, almost directly across from 24 Sussex Drive, the Prime Minister's residence, Ann commented that they sure were arriving in style—Greene's style. They wound their way up the long driveway, passing numerous RCMP cruisers discreetly parked at the edge of the road under the border of maple trees.

"Leave your weed behind this time, Ann."

"Clay, be nice. I think this is going to be a good night."

She was glad to see him relaxed tonight. It was not always so. She loved working for him, but was only too well aware of his dark periods, sometimes days of introspection, gloom and brooding. He seemed to retreat into himself, searching for something—she couldn't figure out what. It frustrated her, all that potential. This guy could really make a difference in Ottawa. Was it some sort of deep shyness? Could be, some politicians are surprisingly shy in private. He tried to break out of this, she thought, by flirting and what looked to her like old-fashioned womanizing. Such old-style politics were unbecoming to him. Then, the next day, some-times the next hour, he would focus on the topic at hand and she could see the potential, the passion that absorbed him. She was close to him in a professional way and didn't think her job was to criticize him. Indeed, as with all good secre-taries on Parliament Hill, he couldn't have survived without her. Yet there were some subjects, like his dad and his fami-ly, that were off limits. Maybe someday he would open up, but that was his business. Anyway, she guessed that his mind was working over the puzzle of the water export case. She knew that he had a lot of unanswered questions. Perhaps tonight they would get a few answers.

They parked behind Rideau Hall, an old rambling mansion that would fit better in a movie about the American South than among the Canadian pine and maple trees. They looked at each other, laughed, and then pulled themselves up as straight and formal as they could and walked through the large doors. Once inside on the crim-son carpet, Clay veered to the men's coat check, to the right, and Ann to the women's, on the left. They met again at the bottom of the stairs, grabbed hands, and walked together up a bright red carpet to the top where they were greeted by the Governor General's aide-de-camp, a young man in a braided military uniform. He directed them ever so gra-ciously into a line-up, where they waited outside the main ballroom.

"Look at those MPs constantly adjusting their bow ties and cummerbunds," Ann whispered to Greene. "They look like nervous penguins."

Greene stood, Ann noticed, a little off to the side of the line-up and smiled, a bit detached.

After five minutes they had advanced to where the Governor General and her husband stood together, formally shaking each guest's hand after an introduction by another aide. Greene remarked how well the GG looked, and she smiled and leaned towards Greene's right ear for the briefest of moments. A photographer took pictures and then they were squeezed through the receiving line and into the main ballroom where the RCMP band was playing the opening strains of a Strauss waltz.

"What was that all about?" smiled Ann.

"Search me. She wants to meet me in the arboretum around eleven."

"What did her husband have to say about that?" teased Ann.

"Oh yeah, sure, Ann. We're even now. May I have the first dance?"

"Of course."

After enjoying a few dances, they strolled from room to room, looking at the collection of Canadian art that adorned the walls and the Inuit sculptures that sat on turn-of-the-century Québécois tables. At the buffet they ran into the chair of the Finance Committee, who had a woman on each arm and was gazing at a huge plate of sweet desserts in front of him.

"How's your diet coming, Don?" Greene asked gently.

"I'm stuffing myself," beamed the portly MP as he looked to his left and then slowly to his right, "and enjoying every minute of it. Say, don't give up on your hearing request. This thing gets more interesting daily."

"You can bet on that, or should I say, invest in that," Greene shot back.

"Young man, you'll learn that there are real investors who make this country grow, damn it, and shysters who give the whole thing a bad name."

"That's why we should catch them . . . the shysters, I mean," said Greene as he moved with Ann to find a seat at one of the tables. The large room where the tables were set up was decorated like a big orange-and-white tent. They finally found two empty seats.

"Mind if we join you?" asked Greene.

"Not at all," came a voice with a decidedly Québécois accent. It was the Honourable René Jourdain, leader of the Liberal Party. Given the electoral jolt that party had received in the last federal election, Greene was surprised at how relaxed he looked.

"Very debonair, monsieur. You and your madam make a very attractive couple." Jourdain took Ann's hand, bent over, and kissed it somewhat theatrically.

"You don't look bad in that tux yourself," replied Greene.

"Thank you. It took me a long time to put the jacket on tonight. You would have problems too if you had as many knives in your back as I have these days," said Jourdain.

The table collectively laughed. Greene liked the man— at least he could continue to joke.

As eleven neared, Ann grabbed Greene's hand under the table and said, "Will you get me some more of that cheese-cake?" As she spoke, Ann pinched Greene's arm lightly. "It's only eleven o'clock. We'll be staying a little longer, won't we, Clay?"

Greene nodded, took the two dessert plates, and excused himself. He put the plates down at the end of the desert buffet table and noticed people were coming back for seconds, or was it thirds? He then made his way down a long corridor lined with old military prints. At the back of the mansion he opened a glass door and stepped into a forest of greenery the length of a football field. The fragrance of beautiful flowers and the damp, warm air enveloped him. The glassed-in arboretum was a unique and beautiful spot built on the end of the old house. A few couples were talking more intimately here; the atmosphere inspired it. At the end of this indoor garden, he stopped near a fountain and waited. After a few minutes he was aware of a woman moving up beside him. It was the Governor General.

"Your Excellency, may I say again how well you look and tell you truthfully that you looked terrible the last time we met."

"Thank you again. I really have recovered. It was touch-and-go there for awhile."

There was a pause, which Greene was determined not to fill with small talk.

"I know this is unusual, but there have been some strange things happening that I can't tell you about. You know the Crown or the Crown's representative never gets involved in partisan politics. I of course intend to respect that, but I think we have a special relationship with MPs of all parties. According to my dear old friend the late Senator Forsey, and some other constitutional people including my husband, if there is a government crisis I apparently have a sort of reserve power to . . . how should I put it? . . . with which to sort it out."

Greene liked the GG's direct way and sharp mind, and could understand why the Canadian people had a lot of respect for her. He also believed there was a tough woman underneath that gentle smile.

"One of my predecessors, Edward Schreyer I think it was, kept Prime Minister Joe Clark waiting all morning before he agreed to dissolve the House and permit a winter election, and of course there have been other cases in Canadian history.

"In any case, that is not the situation at present. However, there are other issues, which I am not free to discuss, that worry me about this water export matter. You have, if I may be permitted to say this, raised it well in the House."

The Governor General paused for a moment, looked around, and then looked directly at Greene. "You know that I'm commander-in-chief of the Armed Forces. Keep pressing the matter, young man, but do it responsibly."

She smiled and touched his wrist. "Now I must go to dance. The fast stuff is coming up."

A few minutes later, Greene returned to the table with two plates of blueberry cheesecake. Ann had two Liberal MPs and one New Democrat in rapt conversation. "No, Ottawa is only the second-coldest capital city in the world. The coldest is Ulan Bator in Mongolia," Ann exclaimed as the dessert was laid in front of her.

After they ate and finished their coffee, Ann declared that she wanted to catch some of the music the orchestra was now playing.

"I'm even more interested in hearing what happened," yelled Ann, as they rocked to a surprisingly fast tune played by the RCMP band.

He bent over and yelled into her ear, "Encouragement. I'll tell you later in the car."

Just after midnight the Honda scooted out of the Governor General's estate and onto Sussex Drive. Ann lived in the Sandy Hill area of little shops and Victorian buildings near the University of Ottawa, and Greene headed in that direction to drop her off before heading to his own apartment in the Glebe, just south of the Queensway freeway.

"She's worried about things she can't tell me about," Greene explained to Ann, "and she encouraged me to keep on the water export case and do it properly, or rather 'responsibly,' whatever that means. And she reminded me she is commander-in-chief of the forces. All told, a strange conversation and very, very unusual."

As Greene was saying this, he glanced up at the rearview mirror and noticed that a black car, which had left Rideau Hall behind them, seemed still to be following them, much as a policeman follows a suspected impaired driver before the cruiser lights go on. Greene had only had one glass of white wine, so he wasn't worried about being pulled over, but there was something about the car that didn't seem right. Something told him it wasn't a police car.

He pulled a quick right off Dalhousie Street into the Byward Market area. The Honda was much more maneuverable than the larger car, and he had turned so quickly that he caught its driver unaware. As Greene went down St. Patrick Street, crossing Sussex again, he saw in his rearview mirror that the large car had managed to find him and was speeding to catch up. He proceeded to cross two intersections near the National Gallery of Canada. An Ottawa police car didn't quite make the second light and stopped for it, which meant that the large car had to stop too.

Thanks for that, thought Greene as he followed the

speed limit on Alexander Street glancing at the American Embassy down to his left. He sped up when he turned the corner past the Rideau Mall and made a quick left past the Westin Hotel, then a quick right, a left on Laurier, and into Sandy Hill. There was no sign of the black car.

"Had you forgotten where I lived?" Ann asked lightly, though he could sense concern in her voice.

"I think we were being followed. When I pulled into Byward Market, the car behind made an obvious effort to get back on our tail and catch up. I think we're okay now."

"Well, it was a good evening, Clay. Thank you."

"Well, thank you, Ann, for a lot of work. I must say I enjoyed the evening too, but it was rather strange." He gave Ann a soft kiss on each cheek, smiled tiredly, and let her out of the car

On the way home he flashed back to his law school days at UBC. Maybe it was something about tonight's car chase that did it. He recalled that awful rainy winter night in Vancouver. It was Friday night, after a long evening at the fraternity house, and stupidly he had driven his girlfriend home—or at least, tried to. She lived somewhere in the Vancouver suburb of Richmond just near the Fraser River. He should have known better, especially when he had fumbled initially with the car keys, but he hadn't wanted to disappoint. He thought he was invincible in those days; in fact, he had been right out of control.

It all came suddenly back—the road on the dyke, the rain, the ditch, the dirty water, and, above all, the horrible realization that she had hit her head on the windshield. He remembered the police, the flashing lights of their car, the sound of the ambulance siren. He recalled feeling dazed as he sat with the policeman in the cruiser. Then there was the phone call he was allowed from the Richmond police station. He hadn't called his Dad, who was in the Maritimes. Uncle Jim was too far away in Old Crow. For some reason, he had called his law professor. When he first met Jerome Howie the older man had taken a liking to him and had given him his card. That card was in his wallet that night. He couldn't believe it when Jerry came down to the police station and took charge. Jerry took him home. Jerry cleaned him up. Jerry assured him his career, his life, was not over, that everything would be okay. Jerry had saved him.

As the Ottawa snow began to fall gently, Greene again looked in his rear view mirror. No car; he was safe. He turned the corner towards his apartment.

Before going to sleep he rolled the night's events around in his mind. Keep on the water case, the Governor General had said, act discreetly, but act. Commander in Chief. It was getting pretty weird.

And yes, he was scared. He thought of Marianne in Vancouver. He hesitated.

Then he picked up the bedroom phone and called Jerome Howie, as he often did, to talk over his current problems with his old friend. He always felt better afterwards, as if the call made his day complete.

CHAPTER **8**

"**N**EVER LET IT BE SAID THAT I DON'T HAVE SOME style," Greene said as he came into the office, late as usual. "Here, this is for your hangover, Ann." He pulled a latte in a tall paper cup from the brown paper bag he carried.

She looked up at him and frowned. Greene went into his own large office and handed another of the coffees to Rob, who was arranging for a playback of the previous night's BCTV newscast, then settled onto the black leather couch to read the morning's *Globe and Mail*.

A story at the top of page two, datelined Vancouver and with Marianne Tremblay's byline, delved into the corporate connections of Senator George Murphy.

> Business circles are abuzz with talk of water exports. Officially, Canada's 1987 water policy bans large scale water exports but allows small ones, in bottles or possibly tankers, though tanker exports are less assured. The provincial government of British Columbia, for one, has legislated a moratorium on large-scale water export.
>
> The federal government may be on a different tack. Documents released this week in a lawsuit in the Supreme Court of British Columbia reveal that the federal government quietly approved a study by a BC company, worth $4.5 million over two years, and some trial exports of water as part of the study. Western Energy

Incorporated was the lucky recipient of the study grant.

It appears that the converted tanker *Akuru Maru*, whose captain was recently found murdered, was used on such a trial run. Although federal permission was granted, it appears that any shipment of water would violate the BC government moratorium. Some corporation lawyers in Vancouver question whether the province has the power to ban such exports under the terms of the North America Free Trade Agreement.

Western Energy Incorporated is controlled by Britprop Inc., whose chairman, Senator George Murphy, has close links with the MacKenzie government. Murphy was the national campaign manager for the prime minister in the last election campaign. MP Clayton Greene (NDP Vancouver Centre) has pursued these links with questions in the House of Commons about the new Orders-in-Council which appear to reflect a change in government policy.

Britprop Inc. itself is linked to Houston Energy Corporation through a member of its Board of Directors. That member is Jeffrey Conway who headed the American water import consortium before he was elected vice-president of the United States. Conway, a strong religious fundamentalist, was an activist for the Christian Right and a leading businessman in the energy sector before he joined the presidential ticket in the recent American elections. Houston Energy has recently moved out of oil and gas pipelines in a slumping market and into the potentially lucrative southern California water market.

Arlon Russell, an American energy economist, recently estimated a typical tanker shipment of water, bound for drought-plagued California, is worth approximately $800,000. Jeffrey Conway, in a speech last year to the Oregon Chamber of Commerce, was quoted as saying that filling Los Angeles' water gap alone would require 1,600 tanker trips per year.

Greene noted that the article closed with a terse "no comment" on the water issue from the good Canadian senator.

The image on the TV screen continued to say, "Stand by for your request." Then the tape started to roll, and BCTV's news anchor, appeared. He briefly recapped the murder of Captain Kim to introduce a story on the link to Western Energy through Greene's question in the House. Some stock footage of waterfalls and lakes accompanied the reporter's comments on Canada's plentiful water supply, "the envy of the world," and the Greenpeace lawsuit. Then some charts tracing the corporate connections flashed on the screen before footage of the last political campaign showed Senator Murphy's role in assuring MacKenzie's victory on election night.

Clayton Greene drew closer to the TV set when the scene shifted to an enormous home in the British Properties, which was obviously staked out by the news team. As Senator Murphy emerged from the front door to walk to his car, a rotund BCTV reporter followed Murphy down the sidewalk and, almost out of breath, fired questions at him.

"Of course we knew nothing about that unfortunate crime, Harvey. We just chartered the boat." Then a pause. "Surely a businessman is entitled to pursue foreign trade, which is good for the country. The connection to the government means nothing; nothing illegal has been done here. I dare anyone to say otherwise, and I'll be making a statement tomorrow in the Senate on a matter of privilege."

With that the Senator slipped into his car and drove away, followed by another car.

Greene took a sip of his coffee, thought for a moment, then motioned to Faulkner. "Rob, tell them to run it again, twice."

When the story was repeated, Greene watched intently and waited. "Did you see that, Rob?"

"See what? I just saw one uncomfortable senator."

"Look quickly at the licence plate on the car that followed the senator."

As the story was repeated for the third time, Faulkner watched as the TV camera followed the departing senator and the second car before it returned to the reporter to wrap up the piece. He could see an Alberta plate with the first initials ABB.

Rob left for the morning caucus meeting, and a few minutes later Ann came in with the mail. "You have some telephone calls, too," she said. "Not very important, but perhaps you should check this one." Ann, after all these years, had the amazing knack of choosing the letters or the phone calls that Greene would want. He took the slip from her. "John Graham" and a Toronto number. "He called about fifteen minutes ago, but you were busy with the news clip. I told him you'd get right back to him." With that, Ann began to leave the room.

"I thought you quit smoking, Ann."

"How did you know I started again?" She frowned at him.

"Old tracking skills."

She laughed and left the room while he dialed Toronto.

"Mr. Greene, Clayton, I must tell you this is a call I hesitated to make, but I read the *Globe* story this morning. I also remember your saying to me on the plane that bankers are Canadians too. That's not often said by politicians. I like your work on the environment. Also, I have some personal reasons for talking to you. I can't say much now—please meet me early this evening for a drink and maybe a quick bite at the restaurant in the Windsor Arms Hotel near Bloor, just west of Bay here in Toronto. Know where it is?"

"I can find it, but first tell me . . . "

"See you there around six. Please make sure no one sees you going there if you can." With that, Graham hung up.

Clayton Greene had just begun to tackle his ever growing "riding correspondence" file when another call flashed on his phone.

"Clayton, how are you?"

It was the unmistakable voice of Marianne Tremblay.

"I wanted to tell you that I'm continuing to research the

source of some offshore funds. I couldn't put that in the article because it's not fully nailed down yet."

"OK, Marianne, actually I'm going to Toronto to meet a possible source of that kind of information, a banker of all people. I'm seeing him at the Windsor Arms Hotel near Queen's Park."

As soon as the words were out of his mouth, Greene regretted them. He promised John Graham that he would keep things confidential.

"Oh, well, keep me informed, Clay. I'll get back to you."

Marianne was quickly off the line just as Rob Faulkner came into Greene's office.

"The leader is going to go on the Murphy issue. They're going to try to tie it in with the scandals of the previous government. Do you want to follow up his lead question?"

"I don't think so. Besides, I've got to go to Toronto."

"Toronto!"

"Yeah, I have to see my banker."

That afternoon, Question Period degenerated into general name-calling. Both opposition party leaders probed the government connection with Senator Murphy and the work of the energy export company, and constantly alluded to the scandals of a previous Conservative government.

In response, Prime Minister MacKenzie insisted he ran a clean ship and challenged the opposition to disprove it. Besides, he argued, his government was aiding in yet another revival of the western Canadian energy industry. Surely the opposition leaders weren't against western development, or were they?

Greene sat silently throughout the show. He could see the Press Gallery waiting for him to rise, but he had long since determined not to ask a question unless he really had some new material. That strategy had paid off in the past because the media knew he didn't ask a question unless he was serious.

As he was returning to his office to leave for his flight to Toronto, he stopped by the TV monitor in the Opposition Lobby. The government House Leader had just risen on a point of privilege after Question Period. He said that the Honourable Member for Vancouver Centre had breached privilege by raising false insinuations yesterday in the House of Commons, insinuations that one of the Honourable Members who sat in "the other place"—the formal Parliamentary term for the Senate—had profited by some sort of undue influence in the sale of Canadian water by a company in which he had an interest. There was no proof of this at all. The Honourable Senator could not reply to such spurious and, if said outside the absolute protection of the floor of the House, libelous statements.

Greene strode back into the House of Commons, almost knocking down a page who was bringing a glass of water to a member. He rose in his place and was recognized by the Speaker. "Mr. Speaker, I do not admit that I have breached the privileges of the Honourable Senator, but in the interests of fairness I am prepared to allow you to rule that there has been a prima facie breach of privilege and, by our rules, the matter would then be referred to a House committee to conduct inquiries, with witnesses."

The Speaker of the House of Commons rose, smiling. "I thank both Honourable Members for their assistance. I note the Honourable Member from Vancouver Centre is prepared to, as he put it, allow me to refer this matter to a committee. If I may say so, that is very clever of him, although may I remind him that the rules and precedents, not he, allow me to rule on a breach of privilege. Here the rules are clear. A member of this House must be affected, his or her privileges affected. Not so here. The senator is, of course, not a member of this House, so there can be no prima facie breach of privilege. Orders of the Day, please."

Greene looked across at the government House Leader. They had made their point. The government was going to get tough on Greene.

———

The Air Ontario Dash-8 landed at Toronto Island airport which was only a five-minute shuttle bus ride to the Royal York Hotel in downtown Toronto.

Clay Greene left the Royal York and took the TTC subway up to College Street. He came out of the subway station and walked north to Queen's Park, the building that housed the Ontario Legislature. Once inside, he went to the office of the former, provincial Minister of the Environment—Ruth Jones, who was a small woman, full of energy, with a ready smile. Greene had travelled to her East Toronto constituency during the last provincial election and knocked on doors for her. He had been struck that at every second household, it seemed that someone said Ruth had helped them with a personal problem. It reinforced for him the importance of being a good constituency politician.

He also liked to talk with his provincial counterparts in the environment field, and he was proud that his party was united in both the east and the west on environment and energy policies. That was no mean feat these days, and it was largely his doing because he kept in touch constantly.

"Clay Greene, what are you doing here?"

"I came to see my banker."

"What?" She spoke with just the slightest Scottish accent and seemed to purr out her words.

"Oh, I'm only half joking. I'm here for a meeting and I'm sort of undercover."

"Well, you're here at a convenient time. The environment committee of the Ontario NDP, the activists anyway, are meeting in my office tonight. We'll be discussing nuclear power, the Great Lakes pollution, and probably your water thing."

"Great. I'll try to drop by later, probably just after eight. Don't tell any press I'm here, please."

It was ten to six. Greene excused himself, slipped out the side door of the Legislature and crossed Queen's Park, the park to the north of the Legislative Building, towards Victoria College, part of the University of Toronto campus. As he passed the main college building, he looked up at the carvings above the great doors and read the inscription: "The Truth Shall Make You Free." If only I could find it, he thought, and continued through a gate past the grey stone buildings of Burwash Hall, a student residence that had housed young Lester Pearson. Greene pictured the earnest young students of those days, discussing the possibility of Canada achieving independence in foreign affairs, and he smiled to himself.

As he left Victoria College, walking east for a block, he passed St. Michael's College before turning north towards

Bloor. The Windsor Hotel was on his left, and behind it was a small restaurant.

John Graham was at a corner table, nervously fiddling with a glass of scotch. Graham rose when he saw Greene. "I'm pleased you came, Clay, on such short notice."

"Not at all."

"Can we order now, since I have to get back to work? Bankers don't really keep bank hours, you know. May I suggest their house special."

Greene nodded and looked closely at Graham. Tall, well-dressed, neat, very sincere. United Church background, he thought.

"You must understand—confidentiality is everything in my business. Well, almost everything. There are other principles, too."

"Like what?"

"Like honesty. You know, I've had very little to do with politics, although I once worked for Mike Pearson when I was a student because I thought he was great for Canada on the international scene. And I liked your Tommy Douglas. He was honest and straightforward. They don't make them like that anymore. My experience, my job, is in international banking, currently in the Caribbean where our bank has many branches. As such, I look after the transfer of money from Canada to these Caribbean accounts, mainly to the Bahamas."

At this point, the waiter put two plates of chicken parmigiana, the house specialty, before them. Greene suddenly felt hungry.

"This is a very good restaurant. I think you'll like this main course."

"I'm more used to eating at a Greek restaurant on the Danforth, but I believe you." Greene picked up his knife and fork. "But please, continue."

"There has recently been a large amount of money transferred to our Scotiabank branch in Nassau in the name of people in very high places in the Canadian government. Normally I turn down deposits from Third World dictators or suspected drug dealers because we're a clean bank, but I can't question Canadian government officials."

"How much?"

"I really can't say."

"A million bucks?"

"More."

"Five million?"

"More."

"Double that?"

"You're close. That's all I can really say."

"In high places—how high?"

"Very high. That's all I can say, too."

"Why did the *Globe* article prompt you to call me?"

"Well, the money came in with other deposits. One was from Britprop Corporation, which was mentioned in the story on Senator Murphy. Coincidentally, I had your card handy."

"Where did the money come from?"

"I don't really know. I tried to check with our Montreal office through which it came. A Mr. Jardin or maybe Jardine was involved, I think, but my information is really hazy here."

Over the rest of the meal, Greene pumped the banker about the workings of international accounts. He learned that these Bahamian accounts were a bit like Swiss ones, closed, and secret. As he savoured the last bite of chicken, Greene thanked Graham for the information.

"I believe in this country, you know, although I may not be of your political persuasion. I've lived and worked in some tin-pot dictatorships and some corrupt so-called democracies. That's not my vision of Canada. If I can get more information to you, I will. Please don't quote me or call me at the bank."

Graham gave Clay his home phone number, and the dinner and the conversation were over.

Greene retraced his route to the Ontario Legislature. As he was crossing Queen's Park, he was dimly aware that the darkness had cleared the park of people and that he was alone. At least he thought he was, but as he passed a statue of an obscure general on his horse, somewhere in the middle of the park, he sensed someone was near him and turned around in time to see two men almost on top of him.

As a fist came towards his face, Greene shot up his right hand to block it. Then he grabbed the arm, spun himself around, and lifted the burly man over, throwing him onto the ground. As he did so, the other man, also bigger than Greene, came at him. Greene shot out a fist and hit the man in the stomach. All that work in the Tai Chi classes on those long Ottawa nights had paid off, at least for a moment.

Greene was agile, but he couldn't hope in the end to match his two brutal assailants. He used his surprise resistance to his advantage and took off across the park towards the lights of the Legislative Building. It took seconds for the attackers to follow, which gave Greene enough of a start to arrive at the red stone buildings ahead of them.

As Greene passed the guard at the side door of the Legislature, he glanced back and saw his pursuers falter as they entered the circle of light outside the door. They quickly disappeared in the darkness.

Sweating, he showed his MP's card. The guard indicated that Ruth Jones was expecting him and he was to go right up to her office.

Greene entered the meeting room, where a small group of party activists were sitting around a table. One woman looked up. "Mr. Greene, tell us about this water export deal, will you?

"I wish I knew the answers," he said as he slouched down in a chair to join the group's discussion.

CHAPTER 9

BEING IN THE CANADIAN SENATE IS LIKE BEING IN A time warp. It reeks of the nineteenth century. That's not all bad—as the rich red carpets, the tapestries and murals, and the normally sedate nature of the debates suggest a gentler, more innocent time. But in the modern world only Canadians would tolerate such an institution, filled mostly with hacks and flacks appointed for life, or to age seventy-five, by the prime minister of their day. It's been said that an appointment to the Senate is like going to heaven without the necessity of dying. The Senate is full of party bagmen, failed politicians, backroom movers-and-shakers of past eras, and even the friends of former Prime Ministers' wives. Only a handful of senators do any work, though their efforts almost make up for the indolence of their colleagues.

A few people, Senator George Murphy among them, took the institution seriously. Clayton Greene had sent his assistant, Rob Faulkner, to the public gallery of the Senate. He was one of three people in the gallery, the other two being student guests of a Senator Lapierre. Murphy rose in the Senate on a point of privilege. Rob had done some quick research and talked to his contacts in the Senate staff. Senator Murphy was apparently a bit of a loner in spite of his intense political background. He hadn't, like some Senators, been born with a silver spoon in his mouth. He came from a family of small merchants in the hardware business in Winnipeg. He himself had made some money in the pork futures market. In politics he had a reputation of being thorough, very calculating and smart, although a little thin skinned to criticism. This was no Huey Long, the flamboyant old Louisiana Senator. This was a guy who liked the backrooms, at least until now. Faulkner was surprised to see him on his feet, arms gesticulating and face reddening. Senator Murphy blasted that young member of the House of Commons, "that other Chamber," who had implied scurrilous things from the fact that some Senators, including himself, engaged in running a business.

"These Senators," he proclaimed, "actually work in the real world, where jobs are created and where money is earned, yes earned, and reinvested, leading to economic growth in the country. This may be hard for the young member to understand, since he has no background in business. That's why he also doesn't understand that I don't personally charter the ships that might do some work for the company. This is all done by management, the trustworthy, responsible people I hire to run the company. The member knows, or should know if he understood business the slightest bit, as a Senator I am not involved in its day-to-day management. In any case, the unfortunate death of Captain Kim is not connected to the company or to the directors. The member's implication is leftist, socialist muckraking at its worst. If they get tired of criticizing our American friends, they pick on Senators."

He sat down to applause throughout the red chamber.

One Senator, Godfrey Samuels, an elderly lawyer from Montreal, did rise to put a question to his honourable colleague. Senator Samuels quietly asked how Western Energy managed to get the Canadian government to pass such "accommodating" Orders-in-Council that clearly did benefit the company.

Senator Murphy, somewhat surprised by his colleague's

interest, repeated that the day-to-day management of the company was not in his hands and he couldn't speak for the government since he wasn't in the cabinet. Besides, those Orders-in-Council were subject to a lawsuit, so he couldn't comment further, nor should the Senate now debate this issue. With that he sat down and the matter was ended, or so he thought.

———

When Greene showed up at his office at 9:15 AM, Rob Faulkner briefed him on the previous day's Senate sitting. Greene in turn relayed the story of his meeting with the banker, leaving out the events in Queen's Park.

"Close to ten million bucks in an account in the Bank of Nova Scotia in Nassau, in the names of high Canadian government officials. Why and from whom?" As Greene was wondering this aloud, Faulkner scribbled notes.

"The other clue, Rob, is a Mr. Jardin or Jardine."

"There used to be a good French restaurant in Ottawa, in the market, called Le Jardin. There's Jardine-Matheson, one of the Tai Pan companies from Hong Kong in James Clavell's novel."

"You have a wandering mind. Be serious, Rob."

"There's Alphonse Desjardins."

"A famous Quebecer."

"That's right, Clay. Desjardins was the founder of the Caisse Populaire Desjardins du Quebec, unfortunately long dead."

"That's one of Quebec's largest financial institutions, isn't it?"

"Yes."

Greene looked up at the light fixture above his office. He brought his right hand to his chin and held it there for a few seconds. Then he looked back at his assistant. "Rob, you might just be getting serious."

Greene asked Ann to get Gaston Samson on the telephone. Samson, an actuary, worked at the head office of the Caisse Populaire Desjardins in Levis, the hometown of Alphonse Desjardins, directly across the river from Quebec City. Samson had gone to school with Greene in Montreal and later moved back to his home in Levis to work for the Caisse. He was now its vice-president.

Rob Faulkner was reading out of a parliamentary guide: "Alphonse Desjardins, journalist and French-language stenographer in the House of Commons. In 1900 established a co-operative savings and loan company in Levis, Quebec."

Looking up from the book, Faulkner spoke more slowly. "I remember from my history lessons that Desjardins used European savings-and-loan companies as models for his enterprise and encouraged workers to save and plan for the future—the collective financial future of Quebec. Also, many Caisses were tied to churches and had the support of the clergy. And the Parliamentary Guide says: 'Desjardins' successors established ten regional Caisses Populaire, which today form la Federation de Quebec des Unions regionales de Caisses populaires Desjardins, with its head office in Levis.'"

Ann indicated that Samson was on the line, and Greene picked up the phone, slipping easily into French as they exchanged pleasantries and he asked Gaston if they could meet.

"Of course, I would love to see you, Clay. Why don't you join my son and me at a hockey game tomorrow night?

The Hull Olympics are playing our Quebec team. This is junior hockey, but it's the way hockey should be played, rough and tumble. I have an extra ticket."

Greene accepted with relish. He had a fondness and respect for Samson. Greene had been invited to his friend's wedding ten years earlier—probably the only Anglo in attendance. He remembered his surprise when he left the tourists of the old town of Quebec City and crossed the St. Lawrence by ferry to find a small Quebec town. The other guests at the wedding, most of them from Levis and nearby small towns, made Clay feel at home. He remembered thinking that if only neighbourhoods in different parts of Canada, both English and French, could spend a warm summer evening together, the country's future might be much brighter and smoother. He learned a lot that night at the wedding in Levis.

No sooner had he put the phone down than Janet Wong was on the line from Vancouver.

"The Chief Justice has just handed down his decision in the Greenpeace case. Ruled against the good guys, boss, though he said that while the government may have technically acted legally, the whole procedure stinks. The judge, of course, used legal language. He said it was too secret, the orders were too broad; they could ship out all the rivers and drain all the lakes under these permits, and they were granted amazingly quickly. Sounds like you can have some more fun in Question Period."

"Thanks, Janet. That's interesting. Fax me the reasons for judgment."

"By the way, boss, over Peking duck at my Uncle Louie's restaurant last night, I was thinking about you."

"You know I like Peking duck, right?"

"No, not that. I was thinking about getting some of these questions before a committee so we can subpoena witnesses. Remember the Stats and Regs Committee, now just called Regs, I believe? Try it. Call you later."

"Rob, what do you know about the Regs Committee?"

"It's an odd one, Clay. A joint House/Senate committee, one of the few, meaning it's composed of both MPs and Senators, and its job is to oversee the thousands of government executive orders and to make sure they meet certain legal criteria. The committee writes to government departments and gets bureaucrats to change their policies on executive orders. It's a slow job. Believe me, Clay, you want to avoid sitting on this committee."

"Tell me more. I'm fascinated."

"At my arcane knowledge, or by the committee?"

"Actually, both. But tell me more."

"Well, one year the committee pointed out that the government had wrongly cut off applications for home insulation grants and it forced the government to change its timetable for ending the grants, much to the embarrassment of the Energy Minister. The success of the committee was mainly due to the dogged work of the co-chair, an old Senator near retirement."

"What's his name?"

"Are we playing Trivial Pursuit this morning?"

"I'm not kidding."

"I'm looking it up. Here it is. His name is Senator Godfrey Samuels."

"Get him on the phone, will you, please?"

Senator Samuels said he would be only too pleased to raise the matter of the water Orders-in-Council at next

Thursday's committee meeting, and yes, he would appreciate a copy of the reasons for judgment of the learned Chief Justice of BC in Greenpeace v. the Attorney General of Canada.

After he hung up, Greene went to chair a luncheon meeting of the BC Caucus of his party. They talked about how to raise more BC issues in Question Period. Off and on, they had discussed this same subject since he had been elected to Parliament.

In Question Period, the big story of the day, and hence the subject of the lead questions by both opposition party leaders, was the Canadian Wheat Board's payment to grain farmers. The farmers were outraged because the payment was much less than expected. The opposition leaders' questions stressed broken promises, fiscal mismanagement, farm bankruptcies, and suicide rates of farmers. The government responded, citing the glut of grain in the world market and the amount of previous payments by this government compared to past governments as the reasons for the reduced payment.

Greene was far down the list with fourth question for his party. "My question is for the Prime Minister," he began. "Just over a week ago I asked the Prime Minister about the Orders-in-Council passed by his government to facilitate Western Energy Incorporated in the export of Canadian water, and he replied that there was nothing secret about those orders. In view of the fact that the Chief Justice of BC has expressed the view that these orders were granted too hastily and too secretly, has the Prime Minister had occasion to change his mind about them?"

"Oh, oh!" came taunts from Greene's side of the house.

The Speaker rose. "Prime Minister."

"Thank you, Mr. Speaker. The answer is no. The Honourable Member should tell the House that in the case of Greenpeace v. the Attorney General, to which I think he is referring, the learned Chief Justice held the orders in question to be legal."

The Prime Minister smiled across at Greene and sat down.

"Supplementary question. The Honourable Member from Vancouver Centre."

Greene was sorely tempted to point out that the judge had actually said that, although legal, the method of passing the orders was questionable. He could see the members of the press gallery had begun to pick up their pencils. It was all he could to restrain himself. He swallowed hard and continued.

"Would the Prime Minister have any objection to a committee of this House examining all aspects of the orders in question?"

The pencils were rather quickly dropped, and Greene felt the disappointed sighs from some of his colleagues.

"Prime Minister."

The PM certainly was expecting a different sort of question, and he paused slightly before responding to the Speaker.

"Thank you, Mr. Speaker. I don't know about the phrase 'all aspects,' but I have no general objection. The agenda of the committees are, of course, determined by the committees themselves, and this is especially so given the open, unsecretive ways this government has dealt with committees."

There was scattered applause from the government backbenchers, and the Deputy Prime Minister actually showed the slightest hint of a smile.

It wasn't a spectacular question, thought Greene, especially from the point of view of the press gallery, but it would make it difficult for the Conservative and Alliance members on the Regs Committee to object to consideration of the Orders-in-Council. Patience, he thought, a little bit of progress at a time, the hardest thing for a politician to learn.

Besides, Greene had noted from the corner of his eye that the Honourable Member from Saskatoon Centre, the Chair of the Finance Committee, had been listening particularly intently to the PM's answer.

Back in his West Block office, Greene checked in with Ann. "Did Marianne Tremblay call, by any chance?"

"No, she didn't." Ann lifted up her head with a glimmer of a smile. "Something wrong?"

"No, everything's fine."

"Thinking about going back to the riding for some unfinished business, are you?"

"Cut it out, Ann. You have to admit, Marianne's been very helpful, and she is, well, nice."

"Clayton, I've worked on the Hill a long time, and the best advice my old boss used to give to new members was: 'Remember young fellow, the press are not your friends.' Be careful."

"Ann, don't worry. Besides, I'm going in the opposite direction, to Quebec City. Do I have enough special trips?"

An MP is allowed trips back and forth to his or her riding each year, and a number of special trips to other destinations in Canada. Greene liked to travel Canada and meet people face to face on party speaking engagements or on environmental issues.

"You should be okay. What do you need?"

"Can you get me a flight to Quebec City for tomorrow? And a return Saturday afternoon."

"Big speech?"

"No, a meeting and a hockey game, actually."

"Very Canadian."

Greene was putting some papers into his leather shoulder bag when he looked down at the phone. Should he call Marianne? An odd thought struck him. I did tell her about Queen's Park and they attacked me there. Was that coincidence? He knew he wanted to talk to her again.

"It's you, Clayton." Marianne's voice was clearly excited. "I am glad you called."

"I haven't a lot to tell you. Just wanted to talk, I guess."

"Don't apologize. I was about to call you as a matter of fact."

Then, as if he couldn't help himself he blurted out: "Marianne, I'm going to Quebec City."

"Why?"

"I've got an old friend I went to school with, a guy I trust. He might open up for me a Quebec connection here."

"Be careful, Clay."

CHAPTER 10

GREENE SAT BETWEEN GASTON SAMSON AND HIS TEN-year-old son, Pierre, near centre ice in the Colisée arena. The rink was completely packed. The crowd exploded at each end-to-end rush. Hands came up as fans rose in waves around the sides of the arena.

Greene sat on the edge of his seat, holding a white plastic cup of beer. He had enjoyed watching his beloved Canucks in Vancouver, but it was never like this. This wasn't the NHL. The fans were right into the game. Cheaper tickets meant lots of kids with their fathers or mothers.

The enthusiasm made it hard to hear Gaston talk. Samson was a small, energetic man with a slight mustache, much too athletic for an actuary. Greene remembered how he had always lost to him at racquetball. He had tried without success to get Samson to run for Parliament. The previous member from Levis had been ineffective, and Greene liked Samson's poise. He also felt there was some real idealism under all those numbers.

"Is the Caisse investing in the Caribbean now, Gaston?" Greene yelled above the crowd.

Samson leaned towards Greene's ear. "You know, Clay, when the Caisse opened on 23 January 1901, twelve people paid a total of $26.40 as first payment on their shares. The first savings deposit was only five cents."

"I know you are proud of the Caisse, but that wasn't my question, Gaston."

"Today we have over four hundred branches and assets in excess of $20 billion. We have investments everywhere."

"Including the Caribbean?" Greene tried again between bites of a hot dog. "Less PR, Gaston, just a simple answer."

"Well, it's a good question. I've never heard of any. But if you stay over tomorrow, I can go into the office and make some discreet inquiries." Samson winked at him. "Besides, Hélène wants you to taste another one of her lemon pies."

Deliriously happy Quebec fans, parents and kids, whose team had just won three to two with a last-minute rush, poured out of the Colisée arena. This was what a hockey night used to be like in Canada, thought Greene.

A small ferry in the Lower Town, just below the bulk of the magnificent Chateau, waited to take cars and passengers across the fast-flowing St. Lawrence, which grew wider and wider as it flowed farther out into the gulf and on to the Atlantic Ocean. The ferry ride took only about twelve minutes, but halfway across the swirling water Pierre, who had fallen asleep, woke up and asked Gaston to take him to the washroom.

Clayton Greene got out of the car and walked a few feet on the silvery ferry deck, past a van, to the port side of the old boat. He leaned over the wooden railing and gazed back towards the Lower Town and to the magnificent Chateau above. A dark spot to the left of the Chateau he knew was the Plains of Abraham. He could imagine the events and the history of this place. Coming from the Canadian North as a boy, he pictured in his mind's eye another era here, when it was like a small village in today's North, with Native canoes on the shoreline and the garrisoned village of Quebec, New France, above. He thought of another village, Old Crow. Look at it today and you can see the past exactly, Greene thought. He closed his eyes and imagined the fires and torches that would have lit the old town of Quebec, and he opened his eyes again to marvel at the receding twinkle of lights of the modern city full of tourists.

He didn't notice the back doors of the black van behind him quietly open. But he did feel a heavy object come down on his head. The lights, both ancient and modern, quickly went out.

Greene woke in a darkened room, which seemed to move under him. It smelled of oil. His hands were chained to the floor and his mouth was very dry. He realized he was on a ship, and it was cold and very damp. He wondered how long he had been here.

A heavy iron door opened and two men entered. They left the door, a hatch door, open slightly, and Greene could see what looked like open sea outside and an early morning light. He could also make out what seemed to be part of the deck of what he presumed was a freighter.

The men were Asian sailors. One was middle-aged and the other younger. The older one put a ladle of water up to Greene's mouth and Clay eagerly sipped from it. Before it was empty, the sailor flicked the remainder of the water over Greene's face and laughed. A mean son-of-a-bitch, thought Greene. The younger sailor stood behind the other and looked a bit scared.

Greene could feel his head throb and he spoke. "Please, tell me where I am."

The older sailor just snarled at him, turned, and directed the younger man to go outside, which he did. The older sailor, closed the door behind him with a clang.

Greene fell asleep again. When he awoke, he didn't know how much later, he felt a pang in his stomach and his tongue circled around his mouth, trying to find just a bit of saliva. Visions of lemon meringue pie kept going through his mind. His head hurt. He shook it a bit and looked down at his wrists. He realized why they were paining him when he saw the tight chains.

Greene was in agony for what seemed an hour, and he was about to lose consciousness again when the hatch door opened. The light outside seemed brighter, and the younger man was there alone. He had a bowl of water with him. Greene wiggled his wrists and grimaced to show that they were too tightly bound. The young sailor ignored this and slowly lifted the bowl to Greene's lips. Clay slurped up the water as fast as he could. He muttered "Thank you" to the boy. The sailor said nothing and turned to the door to leave. As he was about to leave, Greene said, "Kamsa Hamnida." It was Korean for "Thank you," and Greene had learned it from a Korean parliamentary delegation that had come to Vancouver. It was the only Korean phrase he knew.

The young sailor paused, turned around, and with a very slight smile, reached down and loosened Greene's chains so his wrists could move slightly. When they heard some voices in the distance, the sailor quickly left.

Greene looked down at his wrists. He was thankful the pressure was off them. For the first time in his life, he wished he had smaller wrists and arms. He began to wiggle his hands. After a while he found that he could raise them slightly, and he began to beat the chains down to the iron floor. The door was closed and apparently the sound didn't carry outside. Greene didn't care anyway. He could only guess what his fate would be in the near future if he didn't get off this ship. His guess was not optimistic.

In the corner of the room he saw a rusty oil can. He reached over with one of his legs and hooked his foot around the can, then carefully pulled the can towards him until he was able to reach down and, with his head, squeeze the can. His contortions would have done his yoga teacher proud. Some oil spilled out of the can and he rolled one of his wrists in the black goo. Bringing his left arm over and holding his right wrist, with a lot of effort he managed to slip his right hand through the loosened chains. Then he was able to pry the chain off his left wrist. He was free. Or was he?

Greene opened the door slightly and saw the deck of a freighter and the black shape of land far off. He had no way of knowing how far the boat had come down the St. Lawrence, but he assumed it was a substantial distance.

He slowly opened the hatch door fully and crept out on the deck. He thought he saw figures on the bridge of the boat. The ship looked like it had once carried a load of cars, perhaps it had been a Hyundai transport ship, but it was empty now and moving pretty fast. There was a large, flat, rust-coloured deck in front of him.

Just at that moment, someone came out of the main cabin on the bridge. Greene recognized the middle-aged sailor—the cruel one—just as the man looked his way, paused, and went back to the bridge. A minute later he came out again, moving towards Greene with a long semi-automatic rifle in his hand and looking like he had every intention of firing it.

Greene glanced back at the small cabin where he had been chained, but then asked himself what was the point of going back to be trapped in there. He knew the first thing a hunted animal did to avoid the hunter was to move without any hesitation. Immediately he stood up and began to run, zigzagging across the flat steel deck to the side of the boat, and dove.

He could feel the coldness of the water. He also could hear small splashes near him. Realizing that they were caused by bullets, he took a deep breath and went under the water.

As a small boy he had experienced the coldness of the Arctic lakes—even in summer when they dared swim in them they were cold. Now he thought of those days and decided that if it came down to a bullet or the coldness of the water, the choice was obvious. He kept swimming downward. When it was impossible to hold his breath one second more, he switched direction and slowly hit the surface, gulping for air. As he had calculated, the current had carried him some distance from the freighter, which was travelling a lot faster than the current. He felt exhilarated.

That was until he realized he was in the middle of the St. Lawrence and it would soon be dark. He began to swim towards the dark grey landmass on the horizon. His stroke took him a good distance and warmed him up. Thanks to his years as a scuba diver, Clay was used to swimming, but he knew he couldn't swim to shore. He began to float on his back and to think like a scuba diver in difficulty—don't panic. He decided he would swim for short periods and then float for longer periods. He was lucky that the waves were small and gentle.

After a few hours in the water he began to feel for the first time that he wouldn't survive. He could sense the cold creeping into all parts of his body. He knew what hypothermia meant. He forced himself to think of what he wanted to do in his life, what he had yet to accomplish. Strangely, he saw the face of Marianne, sitting next to him in a restaurant and she was opening and closing her little notebook and telling him about the new facts she had found. He began to think; he had told her about his trip to Quebec. Had she tipped them off? Whose side was she on? Was she working with these people? Was he losing his mind? Then he saw a candle burning. And it was just about out.

He heard a growl, like a bear's. It woke him from his dream. He swam a bit more, then floated again on his back. He began to slip back into sleep. He fought it. Again sleep. And again a growling sound and a strange musky smell that floated over the waves. He decided to swim to get away from the smell, but the odour followed him. The swim made him more alert and ever so slightly warmer. But he was getting very tired.

Another growling sound made him look up. As he lifted his head out of the water he saw a small boat was coming in his direction. He began to kick his feet and splash as much as he could.

The boat came closer. He could now see the large letters "Les Ballaines" on its side—it was a whale-watching charter. He thought he could make out the name Tadusac, a small town about two hundred kilometres down the St. Lawrence from Quebec City. Then he heard the frantic and surprised shouts.

After they pulled him into the boat, one of the passengers told him they had been looking for whales all day without any luck, and they were on their way back to port when they spotted him. Greene almost told the passenger he had wasted his money—the white Beluga whales were being killed off by the pollution. Then he realized the whale-watcher had saved his life, so he smiled a grateful thank you and asked for something to eat.

When the boat docked at Tadusac, Greene immediately phoned Gaston Samson in Levis.

"Where have you been, Clay? A guy on the boat told me you walked off with the foot passengers. For some odd reason, my car wouldn't restart. By the time I got it going, I figured I missed you somehow. Hélène said not to worry, bachelors do weird things, especially on weekends."

"Yes, I went whale-watching."

"Eh?"

"Not really. It's a long story, Gaston. Did you get a chance to get that information?"

"Well, I went into the office. I'm only telling you because you are a member of Parliament and we are to trust our members of Parliament. Right? Five million dollars was transferred to an account in Nassau very recently. It's a secret account, but I'll try to find out how the money came into it. Be careful, Clay."

"Thank you, Gaston. Tell Hélène I must go back to Ottawa now, but I did think of her lemon pie—it kept me going. Tell her to save me a piece."

Greene dialed the government operator again, gave his code, and placed a call through to Ann's home in Ottawa.

"Where have you been, Clay?"

"Well, right now I'm on my way back to Ottawa after I get something to eat. I'm famished and I'm wet. I've lost my ticket. What time is my flight from Quebec City?"

"Clay, are you all right? You missed your flight. Today is Sunday. And by the way, you should see the *Toronto Sunday Star* right away. There's a story quoting the Liberal leader Jourdain, who says that $10 million has been put into a Bahamian account for a high-ranking cabinet minister. Jourdain hasn't ruled out the PM, he says."

"Damn it, that son-of-a-bitch. Don't trust bankers."

"Why should I start now, Clay? Look, are you okay?"

"I'm fine. Just angry, that's all. I'm going to take a bus to Quebec City and check in at the Chateau Frontenac. You can reach me there in a few hours under the name of . . . try Mr. Wolfe."

Greene ate a burger on the bus, and when he had checked into the Chateau he had room service bring him a steak. He then placed a call to Toronto. John Graham answered.

"Why did you give the Liberals the story? You knew they would go straight to the *Toronto Star*. It's almost their house organ."

"Clay, I didn't! Honestly, I swear!"

"Who leaked it then?"

"It's known, was known, to very few people, I assure you."

"Someone in your bank must have leaked it. Good-bye, see you again some time."

Before he could hang up he heard the voice of the banker again. "Clay, I'm almost sure I was the only one in the bank who knew. The bank didn't leak it. And Clay, the Prime Minister's cheque to us came from a Western Canadian branch, I believe."

Greene hung up the phone and returned to his steak. Who would leak it? he wondered. The *Star* reporters would never reveal their sources. So what now?

As Clay pondered this, suddenly the words registered: "the prime minister's cheque."

The ring of the phone in his hotel room broke his concentration.

"You really are registered under 'Wolfe,' aren't you?" said Ann. "Well, I just got another call at home. I couldn't believe it."

"Believe what?"

"It's not every day that the Prime Minister calls me."

CHAPTER 11

QUESTION PERIOD STARTS IN THE HOUSE OF COMMONS at 2:15 on Mondays, right after the House hears fifteen minutes of short statements by backbench members. The member from Thunder Bay was on his feet and demanding federal money to widen the Trans-Canada highway in Northern Ontario when the Speaker arose and cut him off. "Oral questions. The leader of the opposition."

Greene could feel a difference in the atmosphere of the House. In a minority Parliament, tension was part of the day-to-day atmosphere, especially with the House split five ways and the three main parties having almost equal representation. Today, however, there was an added edge as MPs waited for new revelations that could alternately harm or energize their parties. He himself was sweating a bit, and more than a little angry that Jourdain had seagulled his story.

"My question is to the Prime Minister," Jourdain began. "We all know the scandals of a previous Conservative government, but we had hoped that this one would be clean. We should have known better."

Already MPs were heckling Jourdain, and the Speaker was forced to rise. "Would the Honourable Member please put his question."

Greene wished he could have asked the first question. He would go right to the heart of the matter. Sandy MacKenzie was smart, and he would seize on any aside or irrelevancy in the question and deal with it instead of the substance of the question. As a student, Greene had learned this technique while watching the former prime minister,

Pierre Trudeau, on TV. Trudeau was a master of avoiding answering questions directly.

"Given yesterday's article in the *Toronto Star*, a very impeccable source, would the Prime Minister tell the House what he knows about the $10 million deposited to a foreign account for a member of his government?"

There were cries across the House about sleaze and about the government coming clean.

Sandy MacKenzie stood up. He looked to Greene to be remarkably calm. "This government has been free of scandal or any hint thereof, Mr. Speaker, and we are proud of that." There was quiet applause from the Prime Minister's backbench, but it was muted, a nervous sort of applause. "I personally am not aware of any money deposited in a foreign account, or any account for that matter, for a member or members of my government, but I will look into the allegations."

Smart, thought Greene. He is taking it seriously, no panic there, but yielding nothing.

"As to that impeccable source, the *Toronto Star*, I've heard it tends to be a Liberal paper." There was now laughter from the PM's backbench. "When it comes to my party and the *Star*, the *Star* is about as unbiased as *Pravda*—that is, Mr. Speaker, *Pravda* before Gorbachev, Yeltsin and Putin." The Prime Minister smiled and sat down. His backbench was laughing with him.

Jourdain continued questioning in French, for the French TV news clip, but it was clear to Greene that he had no more information than the *Star* story, and he essentially repeated his previous question.

Jack Hepburn followed for the NDP, and even though

his questions were a little more precise, the Prime Minister still avoided giving a straight answer.

A page came to the side of Greene's desk. "Mr. Greene, a Ms. Tremblay is on the phone in the lobby. She wants to talk to you, says it's urgent."

Greene hesitated for a moment. Should he take the call? He got up and hurried out of the House to the lobby phone.

"Marianne, I've got second question for my party. I'm up soon."

"Okay, I'll be quick. Five million came from the Hong Kong Bank of Canada. The *Star* reporter here, who is onto that, thinks it's big Hong Kong money for a big immigration scam. I don't think so, but I'm not there yet. Use it, though, and good luck!"

As he returned to the House, he wondered again, "Is she really helping me? Is this the real deal?" He took three deep breaths and then focused his energy. He heard a Liberal question about immigration and an increase in business-class immigrants.

"The member from Vancouver Centre."

"My question is also to the Prime Minister, and I appreciate his commitment to a previous questioner to investigate these allegations. In the course of his investigations, will he look into the possibility of money coming from the Bank of Hong Kong to an account in Nassau?"

The Prime Minister rose, still looking calm but with a puzzled look on his face. "I don't know if the Honourable Member is continuing the allegations about some immigration irregularities, but I assure him that I will take into consideration what he has said in our investigation."

"Supplementary question."

"The Honourable Member from Vancouver Centre."

"The Prime Minister will note I did not mention immigration." Greene then continued in fluent French, "Will the Prime Minister also look into the transfer of money from the Caisse Populaire of Quebec to the Nassau account?"

Sandy MacKenzie seemed to sag for a minute and he coughed again. He looked older and paler than Greene had ever seen him.

At that moment, an MP yelled out, "Tell us about the other money you got from your business friend!" The heckling came from a member who had a reputation for being obnoxious, one of the most unpopular members of the House.

The PM fixed his eyes on the heckler and in formal but good French said, "They have a fertile imagination, this opposition, Mr. Speaker. Do I detect a slight jealousy that the economy, especially the Quebec economy, is going well? Well, we run a clean government and a growing economy, and we are proud of that."

His backbenchers gave him strong applause.

The Prime Minister then looked over to Greene. "I will, of course, deal with any facts the Honourable Member from Vancouver Centre provides me," he added in English.

Greene felt good. He had kept up with Jourdain in the questioning. He knew it was only a matter of time until the press found out all the details about the Nassau account. They wouldn't rest until they did. Greene told the press scrum outside the House that he was looking forward to the PM's investigation. Then he returned to his West Block office.

"Tell me about the call, Ann."

"Well, I was sort of expecting you on the phone. What other workaholic would call on a Sunday night? But it was the PM's voice, I could tell immediately. He was very polite and apologized for telephoning me at home. He said he would like you to meet him tomorrow night at L'Agaric restaurant.

"Where is L'Agaric?"

"It's in Chelsea, a little village on the Quebec side of the Ottawa River in the Gatineau Hills, about fifteen minutes from Parliament Hill. It's a beautiful little undiscovered place."

"Well, okay, I'll go. Ask Rob if he'll come with me."

"And Clay, the Greenpeace people want to see you about the water exports. They're considering an appeal of their lawsuit and they have a poll that shows Canadians are dead set against large-scale exports. We're already getting letters about your questions in the House on water."

Greene mused that it never failed—an issue would be raised in the House and usually it would take some time for it to percolate out into the country. But if it were a good issue, the public would always respond eventually. That was why it was in the government's interest to move quickly on a controversial issue, he thought, and in the opposition's interest to delay, to give the public a chance to understand it.

He realized he had almost forgotten Senator Murphy, not to mention his own escape in the St. Lawrence.

"Ann, I'm going to a steering committee of the Regulations Committee, and then to the Standing Committee on the Environment, where we'll hear some follow-up witnesses on the Ozone Depletion Treaty and maybe some more nuclear industry lobby, though I hope not. There is likely to be a vote at 5:45 on a revenue bill. After that, I'm going to the gym and then I'm going to meditate."

"Meditate?"

"Yes, it's an old yoga trick. When too much is going on, you need to still the mind."

"I prefer to play bridge."

"Different strokes for different folks."

As Greene passed Rob Faulkner's small office, he heard Rob's voice from behind a huge stack of papers, books, and Hansard transcripts.

"I've got some good news for you, Clay."

"And that is?"

"In the Regs Committee, the planning group of the steering committee has agreed to begin hearings immediately on the water export Orders-in-Council. Senator George Murphy is to be the first witness later this week. We circulated Hansard copies of your question to the PM to the Conservative members. One Tory had pointed out that the committee decided its own agenda and he was technically correct, but the rest jumped into line. There was some argument over the scope of the hearing, the whole matter of water exports versus a narrow focus on the orders in council in question. Senator Samuels said he would rule on a question-by-question basis at the time of the hearing."

"Great, Rob, well done."

The Honda Civic crossed the Interprovincial Bridge and sped along on the freeway through Hull towards Maniwaki. After five kilometres, the townhouses faded into snowy countryside. And not a moment too soon, Clay thought, as he saw the exit sign for Chelsea. Two minutes down the road to Meech Lake, at the crossroads of two rural roads, he pulled up in front of the restaurant.

L'Agaric Cafe-Restaurant was in fact a small yellow wood cottage with turquoise trim. Its own herb and fresh vegetable garden, which partly accounted for its delicious food, stretched along the side and behind to the small parking lot. Patrons sitting on the summer patio in the front could watch the cars going up to Meech Lake. In the winter, sitting cozy inside, they could watch the skiers driving up to Camp Fortune.

Rob and Clay stepped out of the car. "I'm famished," Faulkner said as he locked the passenger door.

Clay tensed as two burly men approached them from behind a nearby van. "Watch it!" he warned Rob, but then the closer of the two flashed a RCMP badge.

"You're Mr. Greene?" he asked Clay, who nodded. "Mr. MacKenzie asked that you see him alone."

Clay tossed Rob the car keys and walked into the restaurant alone. Also alone at the back of the little restaurant, and no doubt purposefully almost out of view, was the Right Honourable Sandy MacKenzie, Prime Minister of Canada. Only in Canada could this happen, thought Greene.

"Sit down, Clay, and thanks for coming. Sorry about your assistant, but I wanted to talk to you alone."

When their waiter appeared, MacKenzie indicated he did not have much time and would like to order now. As Greene looked over the menu, he noticed that the PM was smoking and coughing even more than he had noticed before. MacKenzie looked pale, except for his eyes, which were bright and alive.

"We'll have a litre of the house wine, and I'll have the house special, the lamb."

A big Scottish spender, Greene thought, as he ordered.

"I don't usually eat out. The people give me a big house, you know."

"Yes, I was hoping someday when my leader lives there, I might get invited for dinner."

"Perhaps," said MacKenzie with a slight smile on his face.

"Well, Prime Minister. You didn't summon me here alone to an out-of-the-way village restaurant for nothing."

"You are very young and determined, aren't you?"

"Well, I'm disturbed about what I've been finding out about water exports and about this latest bank account riddle."

"You may not believe this, but I share your views on water. I'm also concerned about your safety. You have a lot of courage. You didn't even report the Quebec City incident."

"You know about that?"

"CSIS, the Security Service, does actually do some things, although I know the opposition doesn't believe that. CSIS reported the incident to me, although they only found out about it after it happened."

"Were they following me in Quebec City, too?"

"Probably. Of course they lost you, as did your friend, I gather. They're investigating. We can't have people kidnapping our MPs."

The waiter brought their dinners and Greene plunged right into his meal.

"We will give you police protection if you want it. They think it's tied into the English Bay incident."

"You mean the water export Orders-in-Council? Want to tell me more about that?"

MacKenzie smiled. "You already asked me that in the House."

"And I didn't get an answer."

"So, you think that ministers are really supposed to answer the questions."

"As a matter of fact, Prime Minister, I do. At least to the best of their abilities."

"Well, you have a lot to learn, my son, but I will admit that you are one of the better questioners."

"Prime Minister, without being too dramatic, the water export issue will be one of the most important and controversial questions of the coming decade. Our own ambassador to the US, Raymond Chretien, once told the New England governors that water is bound to emerge as one of the four or five biggest issues between Canada and the US this century."

"Tell me about it. Better still, tell the President. But you don't see that part of government from the opposition benches. You see very little." MacKenzie had barely touched his food. Greene had cleaned his plate. There was a long pause, and Greene was determined not to fill it. "I would appreciate it, Clay, if you have any more information about the water exports case, that you pass it on to me in, shall we say, a less public way."

Greene began to bristle. "You're the PM. You have access to all the information. You have the full force of the civil service, not to mention the RCMP, behind you, and, as you just said, CISIS."

MacKenzie smiled and lit up another cigarette. "We used to say in Cape Breton that the boss may think he knows everything, but sometimes he doesn't. Someday, who knows, you may find out that's true."

With that, one of the plainclothes RCMP officers came into the restaurant. The PM rose and pulled from his pocket enough cash to pay the bill.

"I'll let you leave the tip, Mr. Greene. No doubt it will be ample as befits a friend of the workers. Let us know if you want additional security, and please let me know personally on the water exports. I am serious."

With that, the Prime Minister left the restaurant. Greene was left with his thoughts.

Rob Faulkner broke into his silence.

"Jesus, my big night and those guys nicely cut me out. We shared a pizza in their car. How about that? They wouldn't even let me get out of the car for a pee. Well, what did you learn? What was it all about?"

Clayton Greene folded his hands together on the wooden table and slowly looked up. "Strange. I really don't know. It's as if he really did want information from me. Maybe he doesn't know, or maybe he's even cleverer and more Machiavellian than I thought."

CHAPTER 12

MARIANNE TREMBLAY CLOSED THE STAIRWAY DOOR next to Earth Books, a small, eclectic bookstore with an aroma of jasmine on Fourth Avenue in Vancouver's Kitsilano neighbourhood. She saw the silhouette of her sister in the window of the small apartment above the bookstore and waved good-bye. As Marianne opened her umbrella to shield herself from the rain, she marvelled at how different this was from a Montreal winter night. For a moment her mind wandered back to Quebec.

A car horn honked once and then again. It woke her from her daydream.

"Here, get in. You'll get soaked." Janet Wong leaned over to open the passenger door, and Marianne jumped in.

"I like this rain, Janet. "

"You'd get over that if you lived here. I like the rain forest, but I hate the rain. In a previous life all Vancouverites must have been salmon, or perhaps ducks."

"Where are we going?

An hour ago Marianne had received a telephone call from Janet. Tired after a long day spent on the phone, in the library, and at her computer, she had wanted to relax with her sister, speak a little French, and get caught up on family talk. But Janet had been insistent and very determined. She also sensed by Janet's voice, and by her look now, that Janet was not very happy about picking her up. Marianne didn't know that Greene had called a reluctant and still suspicious Janet from Ottawa and told Janet that he needed Marianne at that night's meeting.

"We're going to the Drive."

"For a drive, where?"

"No, Marianne, to the 'Drive.' It's an area of Vancouver, a new hip area, really an old Italian area in the east end on Commercial Drive. Lots of coffee shops, Central American restaurants, etcetera. Kits, Kitsilano here, used to be the hangout for hippies and is now a bit yuppie and new age. The West End, where I live, has a lot of seniors, singles, and a large gay population. Yaletown is the new singles neighbourhood, and the Downtown Eastside is poor and druggy. But we're going to the Drive."

Marianne just smiled. Janet had lost her some time ago.

"Anyway," continued Janet without missing a beat, "I know this woman who knows this woman who works for Western Energy Inc. By day she's a secretary/receptionist and by night she's . . . well, let's say, a little different."

The Honda turned left and crossed a bridge towards downtown. Marianne could see the lights of boats below. The little car turned left again past masses of apartment towers, the white roof of BC Place, the indoor stadium. Marianne saw red neon signs in Chinese characters in the distance. After that it seemed like a long straight few kilometres to Commercial Drive, full of small cafés and fruit stores. They pulled into an alley, parked up against a community centre and started walking.

Marianne glanced at the people passing them on the sidewalk and said, "Perhaps I've overdressed a little, Janet?"

Janet just laughed. "It sure isn't Montreal, but you're OK. Anything goes here." She grabbed Marianne's arm and, narrowly missed by two women on bicycles, they crossed the Drive and entered a short squat building in need of a paint job. The sign said "Joe's Café."

Marianne looked into the café, all chrome and glass, clearly built in the 1960s. A wood-panelled cappuccino bar rose inside on the left of the entrance; some round black tables hugged the front and side windows. A couple of ancient pool tables at the back rounded out the furniture. Piles of free magazines sat on the floor near the door. Pictures of Portuguese bullfighters glared down at patrons from the walls. Two women seated near the pool tables looked up and smiled when Janet entered.

Janet introduced Marianne to Lynn, who was short and wore blue jeans and a black V-neck sweater that set off her fair complexion. She wore no make-up except for a hint of lipstick, and her hair was short with a touch of red. Her smile was instant and huge.

"Hi Janet, Marianne. This is my friend, Mary Ellen."

Mary Ellen was blonde, also with short hair, and about as diminutive as Lynn.

"You want a cup of coffee or a beer?"

"Coffee's fine," both Janet and Marianne answered at the same time.

Lynn quickly turned and barked at the bartender, "Fred, four caps." Then she laughed loudly and said, "This ain't Starbucks."

"I thought women never came to this place after the incident?" Janet said.

"What incident?" asked Marianne.

Lynn laughed again. "Joe's an old wop. See the picture of Mussolini over the bar." She swung her arm and gestured generally in the direction of the portrait. "Joe got a bit weird when he saw two women kissing there at that corner table.

He kicked them out. Big mistake. Big boycott. But I think it's finally over now. Isn't it Mary Ellen?"

"Yeah, thank God," said her friend. "The cappuccinos are great and it's easy for people to find." Both Lynn and Mary Ellen laughed loudly together.

Lynn looked at Marianne directly. "Have you figured out our geography yet, Marianne?"

"Well, we came from Kits over the Burrard Street bridge into the West End and . . . "

At that Lynn turned to Mary Ellen and asked, "What connects the fruits to the vegetables?"

Mary Ellen paused an instant, smiled, and replied "The Burrard Street bridge."

The two women laughed uproariously.

"It's an old Vancouver joke," explained Lynn. She then became serious. "Janet, Mary Ellen asked me to call you because you and your boss, Mr. Greene, helped her in the past when she lost her job unfairly."

"I've never forgotten that," said Mary Ellen. "Also, I sort of follow politics, at least I try to anyways."

Marianne looked at the woman. She liked her.

"And, what the fuck, I'm a strong Canadian too, eh."

The cappuccinos arrived in large glass goblets, brown below, a perfect white, fluffy top—almost too perfect to stir. As Fred kidded Lynn and Mary Ellen, Marianne took out her notebook.

"You work for Western Energy. What do you do?" Janet asked. Marianne thought it was a little lawyer-like. But Mary Ellen again became serious and attentive.

"I'm the receptionist, extra secretary, gopher. I get coffee for some of the meetings and sometimes they ask me to take notes because I'm nice to the old farts and besides, I type real fast."

"Have you noticed anything unusual, Mary Ellen?" asked Janet.

"There's this American guy, his initials are JC and he acts like it. He's been coming to meetings at the law offices. Face looks familiar. Arrives by exec jet. It's kind of secret. No taxis. Always has to have a special ride to the airport. Comes from California, I think. He's also a real chauvinist pig. Even more so than the greasy Canadian senator on the board. Lots of guys. Think they're so important. They send a lot of faxes and do a lot of conference calls."

"To where?"

"To Quebec."

"Where in Quebec?" interrupted Marianne.

"To Quebec City and to a place called Jonquiere. And to a place in Alberta, 780 area code, named Cold Lake."

There was a pause and a curious silence at the table. The crack of a cue ball hitting a rack of eight balls broke it.

"Why did you say 'and I'm a strong Canadian, too,' Mary Ellen?"

Mary Ellen looked directly at Marianne. "I look at you, you're tall and you're good-looking. You're French Canadian. I'm not sure that I know you."

Marianne raised her head, moved slightly in her seat, put down her pen and was about to speak.

"It's OK. Janet tells me you're sort of working for, helping Clay. I worked for him the last election, making phone calls, because he sat right here and spoke to me and Lynn about politics and about Canada. He made time and actually listened to us. Told us our country is for everyone, even for people like me and Lynn. If you're on his side, that's good enough for me."

Marianne smiled.

Mary Ellen continued. "Some of these guys who came to those meetings I know from Canadian politics. They want to kill people like Lynn and me. They used to be called CRAPPers, not that guy Manning, but some of his followers. They really want Canada to be part of the US, I think. At least that's the part that I heard. They talked about 'after,' after it happens, there'll be one country, one English-speaking country, as the American said."

Janet and Marianne looked directly at each other. Janet spoke. "Can you tell us anything else?"

But Mary Ellen's serious look evaporated as quickly as it had come and she was smiling again and laughing at something Lynn said.

Marianne felt tired. The cappuccino had jolted her awake at first, but now its rush was wearing off. She thanked both women for taking her into their confidence, then told Janet that she would excuse herself and take a cab home. A very gentle rain was falling, but it felt warm. She hailed a cab.

"Take me to Kits beach just at Cornwall and Yew," she directed the cabby. She needed a moment to straighten out the thoughts rolling through her head. She got out of the cab at the beach where she could look up the hill to Fourth and her sister's apartment.

She sat on one of the neatly arranged rows of logs on the beach, and gazed across the dark, wet sand. The tide was in and she could hear the waves. She began to think about Clayton Greene.

He's young, she thought, got a full head of hair, fit, unlike most of the MPs she interviewed, lots of confidence. He seemed concerned about the environment, but maybe he just knew that was a good way to get his picture in the paper and on TV. He *seemed* to be different from the others—who were focused on themselves and not much beyond that—but how could she know for sure. Still, she couldn't trust the apparent chemistry, the bond she'd felt ever since they talked on the plane and he'd been so open about his past. Even that openness could be calculated, and she'd seen too many journalists get caught by it, reluctant to report stories that needed to be told because they had become friends with their subject. And she couldn't put out of her mind what the CBC reporter had told her about the rumours of Greene's past, the drinking and the womanizing.

Still, she wished Clay were closer so they could discuss the puzzle as they had done at Tony's. That was a good evening, but he couldn't resist trying to get her into bed at the end of the night. She remembered being half disgusted and half flattered and really wishing she could connect to this man at some deeper level. Instead it was back to being her comfortable workaholic self. Oh well, he was in Ottawa and she was in Vancouver and there was nothing to be done about it.

She looked out into the mist towards where she knew Grouse Mountain loomed. On the other side of it was the rest of Canada. She remembered Mary Ellen's words. I'm a Canadian too, she thought. She had made the choice even though she got angry sometimes about the past history, angry about the attitudes of some of those people, the redneck views she heard on the radio talk show the other day, the apparent inability to understand her people's struggle to have a culture and a language survive in an ocean of anglophones. If Quebec separated, the rest of Canada would surely be drawn into the American orbit in spite of what some of these people thought. If Canada sought to join the US by some means or other, Quebec wouldn't go away. Quebec would go it alone. It was an odd thought, sort of reversed, she thought. Looking up and getting a splash of rain on her face, she put the thought aside for the moment.

A gust of wind brought her back to the sound of the waves, their ripples coming up the beach. Anyway, she liked the people who were here; they were very open. She liked this place. When a bigger gust of wind caught and turned her umbrella inside out, Marianne got up and breathed the damp warm air, smiled to herself, and said to no one but the wind, "Get on with it, girl, you've got some work to do."

CHAPTER **1 3**

THE SCRUTINY OF REGULATIONS COMMITTEE, THE OLD "Stats and Regs," as the veteran hands around the Hill called it, started meeting at 9:30 AM in room 208 of the West Block on Parliament Hill.

Greene knew that the House committees could be useful tools for a backbench MP, especially in a minority Parliament. This particular committee had the power to examine regulations passed under various acts of Parliament to determine whether they were within the bounds of the statute and therefore legal. The water exports had been approved by cabinet regulation under the Environment Act, and now Clay was using the Regs Committee to probe deeper into the murk of water exports generally, and Western Energy Inc. in particular.

Clay Greene had another, bigger goal. He felt committees of the Canadian Parliament didn't have the resources, independence, and clout to make a difference in the way government worked. He was fighting to increase their influence. He argued that MPs should act more independently and use the committees to question government decisions or procedures, rather than bowing to the restrictions of cabinet government and party discipline that kept them from challenging their leaders.

The Regs meeting was to be televised, a recent innovation and one that Clay Greene recognized as a benefit to him. He knew if even a small portion of the Canadian public saw what was going on, it could make a difference, giving him more support for his inquiry. That's why most politicians and civil servants were reluctant to be grilled before a committee, afraid of looking foolish, or worse, in front of their constituents or their bosses.

Senator George Murphy wasn't a reluctant witness, however. He was brimming with confidence and eager to testify. Perhaps it was because Senator Samuels, as Chair of the committee, had requested that he appear.

Greene entered Room 208, passing a number of rows of seats reserved for spectators and media and a small booth for the translators, and moved to the middle of the room where some long tables were set up in a square. The Chair and committee clerk were sitting at the front, with members on either side of the square and the witnesses opposite the Chair, with their backs to the audience. There were microphones on the green-topped tables, with earphone plugs located below. There also were earphones in the audience chairs. At the front of the room, slightly elevated, sat a technician who controlled the microphones.

Greene was getting used to the company of a RCMP or CSIS officer—he wasn't sure which. Since the meeting at L'Agaric even though he had not requested it, the guy had followed him everywhere. He didn't tell anyone about it, but he did discreetly smile at the officer every so often and got a nice, not-too-discreet smile in return. It was unusual for an ordinary MP to have security, but the other members apparently didn't notice.

Senator Samuels called the meeting to order. In the absence of the other co-Chair, a Tory MP from Prince Edward Island, Senator Samuels would chair the entire meeting on his own. He explained that Senator Murphy could read a prepared statement if he wished, and questions would follow. A

A THIRST TO DIE FOR – 143 –

member of the official opposition, a Liberal MP, would ask the first question; a member of the government, either a Conservative or one of their Alliance partners, the second; followed by a member representing the New Democratic Party—meaning Clay's turn. A Bloc member would ask a final question. In the first round of questioning they would be allowed ten minutes each, followed by five-minute subsequent rounds so all committee members could put questions.

Greene thought to himself how ridiculously short a period of time this was; any good criminal lawyer in the law courts needed ten minutes just to get started on real cross-examination. But this had been the procedure of committees for a number of years, and it took many years to change custom around Parliament. He would have to live with it.

The clerk of the committee distributed a copy of the particular Orders-in-Council in question, together with a short paper on the legal background for such orders.

Senator Samuels hesitated and then spoke rather softly. "Before we hear our first witness, the Honourable Senator, let me remind the members of the committee what criteria we apply to government regulations like these Orders-in-Council. We all know that the statutes, the laws passed by Parliament, don't cover everything about the area legislated on, so it is necessary to give the government power to make orders from time to time that have the force of law. For example, a fisheries statute might allow the minister to regulate fisheries openings. An order-in-council closing the whole fishery might not be in conformity with the main statute. We're here to make sure the government doesn't abuse its power."

With that, Samuels looked to Senator Murphy, the witness. Murphy distributed a short text of his remarks and began to read from it, word for word. Greene's eye quickly skimmed ahead of the senator's reading. It was essentially the same statement Murphy gave to the Senate previously, with a little pitch for the water export business and a last paragraph that called for the member from Vancouver Centre to publicly apologize to this committee for his previous slanderous remarks. Greene was sure the press would fasten onto that last statement.

"The member from Toronto Downsview, first round of questions." The Chair looked to Bruno Pantalone, a small, intense man whom Greene knew to be deeply concerned with environment matters. The member questioned the need for any sort of water exports. Senator Samuels pointed out that the Canada-US Free Trade Agreement had further opened up the border for Canadian resource exports and that the deal had not chosen to exclude water exports.

"But wasn't it previous government policy—indeed, isn't it the policy of this government—to prohibit water exports?" Pantalone then quoted the words of a former Conservative Environment Minister. "'The water of Canada is not for sale. The federal water policy excludes inter-basin diversions for large-scale water export purposes.' Nothing could be clearer. If we wrote it in a million laws, the policy would not be clearer than that."

"Well, let me remind the member that Western Energy only proposes to ship water by tanker and not divert large-scale basins of water."

"Not yet," said the questioner under his breath, but loud enough for it to be picked up by the microphone.

"Besides, the water is wasted now. It's just falling into the sea," replied Senator Murphy.

"Your time is up on the first round of questions. I'll

come back to you later. I've been asked to give some questions to Mr. Johnson, of the Alliance Party."

Rob Faulkner was seated just behind Greene, and he leaned over to whisper, "Johnson's normally on the Justice Committee. He seems to be a close pal of the Deputy PM. As a matter of fact, the executive assistant of the Deputy PM is sitting just behind him. We'll get to see what their line is."

That wasn't too difficult. The questions were easy set-ups to establish that Senator Murphy didn't directly manage Western Energy and that the ministerial officials of the Department of Energy and the Department of Fisheries and Oceans had approved the permits, which, of course, put the Honourable Senator at arm's length. The other questions allowed Senator Murphy to expound on his theme of how his critics were simply anti-business. Very shortly it was Greene's turn.

Greene believed that the best way to get a witness talking was to shake him up, and since he had only ten minutes here, he had to do it quickly and theatrically. He had once examined a new Energy Minister, a woman who was presenting the estimates or budgeted expenses of her department to the Committee. She had thoroughly digested those estimates and had coolly dealt with questions from other MPs, some of whom she dismissed with a cold glare. Greene had simply looked at all her senior officials, who were lined up on the side of the committee room, and asked the Minister why none of them were female. It was not a question the minister expected and she lost some of her composure and answered a bit too candidly his subsequent questions.

Greene removed his jacket and rolled up his shirtsleeves, then looked directly at Senator Murphy. "So, you want to sell out Canada's water to the thirsty Americans, is that it?" Greene could see Murphy's temper rising.

At this point, Johnson, the Alliance MP, interrupted on a point of order. "Questions should be restricted to these particular Orders-in-Council."

"This was raised by the steering committee," said the Chair, "so I have had some time to consider it. I've decided that the questions can be fairly broad, but they must be more precise than that first question. If members object to that ruling, they can challenge the Chair."

Johnson looked around and realized that, because this was a minority Parliament, he just didn't have the votes.

Greene could see that he had succeeded in getting Murphy fired up, and he quickly continued. "Who in the US is the buyer?"

"I resent the implication of the first question, indeed the whole attitude towards . . ."

"Will the witness please answer the member's question?"

"The contracts are with Southern California Transmission."

Rob passed Greene a slip of paper, a cue for the next question. "That is the corporation, is it not, of which the Vice President of the United States is the former chairman?"

"That may be so."

"Have you or any of your company officials discussed this contract with the Vice President since he came to office?"

"Point of order!" shouted Johnson.

"Please answer the question, senator." Samuels ignored Johnson.

"I'm not part of the Canadian government, in case the member hasn't noticed."

"That was not my question."

"We may have had discussions—the Vice President and I are old personal friends, but, I repeat, ministry officials approved the permits, not I."

Senator Murphy didn't look pleased.

Greene asked a few more questions about the timing of the permits and reasons for secrecy. Murphy responded by calling Greene anti-business.

At eleven o'clock, the Chair apologized and said the clerk had informed him that another committee had booked the room. Their committee would continue at 3:30 PM in room 371 of the East Block.

Two TV news cameras were waiting outside for Senator Murphy. Greene could imagine the story: "Secret Water Exports Discussed with US Vice President." He turned to Rob Faulkner in the hall. "Where did you get that information, Rob?"

"I have this woman in Vancouver, very smart, very well connected, very keen on helping you."

"Do I know her?"

"Marianne Tremblay."

Greene laughed, put on his jacket, and winked at his security tail, who smiled back. He also laughed to himself. If anyone really noticed this guy, they could easily identify him as a cop because all cops wore the same little pin in their buttonholes.

On the way to their office, Greene asked Rob if he noticed anything peculiar about the witness. Faulkner couldn't think of anything except that he looked like he wanted to punch Greene in the face.

"He did point out rather strongly that he is not part of

the Canadian government. Why isn't he? After all, he's a former campaign manager."

"I told you Clay, too right wing for Sandy MacKenzie. The PM used him only reluctantly and then cut him loose. Murphy belongs to the Deputy PM's and Defence Minister's side of the party. They see MacKenzie as a liberal, if you can believe it."

"I'd believe anything about these guys—well, almost anything. The question is, how ruthless are they and what are the real stakes here?"

—◆—

Greene walked to the Centre Block and rode the elevator, which was packed with large, hungry MPs, to the sixth floor and the Parliamentary dining room. He was greeted by the maitre d' and taken to a table for two in one of the alcoves. The table had a magnificent view of the Ottawa River and the Chaudiere Falls to the west.

"Thank you for joining me, Paul."

Sitting across from him was Paul Havel, one of the veteran journalists on the Hill. He had covered stories all over the world and was a former bureau chief for the CBC in Washington. His full head of grey hair, his slight European accent, and his gentle eyes made him recognizable anywhere in Canada.

After they had gossiped about people and political parties for awhile and were into the main course, Greene finally asked, "So tell me, Paul, about the business background of the American VP."

"Oh, I saw the story from committee on the wire just before I came up here. You got lucky with that question.

That guy was up to his neck in the California defence industries and some energy transmission companies. He's a multi-millionaire and proud of it. Made most of his money building and selling weapons, of course, and in his spare time was a prominent spokesperson for the Christian right. Sort of "praise the Lord and pass the ammunition." Was put on to balance the ticket, the right wing side of the ticket that is, to get the votes of those folks. And it worked."

"Paul, you've got a great memory—think back."

"Now I remember, Clay," said the journalist. "Yes. At the time of the Mulroney/Reagan trade deal, the future VP was quoted as talking about the marriage of the two nations. More precisely, he spoke of merging a resource-rich country like Canada and a capital-rich country like America. 'I think it is something we are looking at down the pike.' I believe those are the exact words he told us on camera."

"Let me buy lunch this time. You're just a poor journalist." They both laughed.

Greene skipped Question Period and returned to his office. Just in time, because Marianne was on the line from Vancouver.

"Marianne, your stuff on the VP helped a lot. I confirmed it with Paul Havel and he has an old story quoting the as-yet-to-be VP on water exports."

"That's good, Clay. Washington is full of research institutes and they now have everything, and I mean everything, on computers. I'll call CBC in Toronto and get them to send you a tape of that old interview. Meanwhile, if you get another crack at Murphy, try to get some more details of the deals."

That afternoon the Committee reassembled at 3:30 after Question Period. This time the Tory and Alliance members of the committee were prepared. On a number of points of order, they argued that the Regs Committee must look narrowly at the legality of the Orders-in-Council and not at the general policy area of water exports. They argued that it was a question for another committee, perhaps environment or energy or trade and finance. Greene advanced a spirited counter-argument, but Senator Samuels finally ruled that the mandate of the Committee was indeed a narrow one.

"I thought he was on our side," whispered a disappointed Rob Faulkner.

"He is, or was. Actually, he's probably right. We'll just have to find another way to skin this cat."

"Are there any other questions before we move on to other matters?" asked Senator Samuels.

Greene put up his hand, leaned forward, and pressed the small button to activate his microphone in front of him. "I have just a couple of final questions for the Senator, Mr. Chairman. When did Western Energy first apply to cabinet for an order-in-council to export water?"

Senator Murphy checked his papers and replied, "Last June, I believe."

"That was just after the last federal election?"

"Yes, but the election had no relevance."

"Did the company discuss its application with any environmental groups?"

"I believe I have indicated that the environment is in no way put at risk. The water is surplus."

At that, the member from Toronto Downsview sighed loudly.

"Did the company discuss its application or its intention with any Native groups?"

"No," replied the witness.

"Did the company discuss the exports with ministers or officials of the provincial government of British Columbia?"

"Order, order. The Member heard my previous ruling. I think I have been more than generous in allowing his questions. On behalf of the Committee, I would like to thank the witness. And now we will move on to other business, after a short break." With that, the Chairman gently brought down his gavel.

"Come on, Rob, let's get back to the office. We have a lot of work to do."

At the office, Greene looked at his phone messages—a pension problem, an Employment Insurance question, a tax problem, more immigration cases, grants for environment and cultural groups, a leading Vancouver company in financial trouble, complaints about Customs.

"If I want to be re-elected, I'd better get on to these constituency matters. Besides, we may be almost at a dead end."

"What do you mean, boss, by 'almost?'" smiled Faulkner.

"Well, the good—make that not-so-good—senator argued that the bigger policy issue of water exports was a matter for another committee. At least, his minions argued that."

"Like the Finance Committee, Clay?"

"You got it, Rob. Ann, can you get me Don Harris on the phone?"

"Will do, but first do you want any more of your phone messages? Your favourite woman caller from Saltspring Island—the one who always calls the Rafe Mair show—and your friend, that sincere and good-looking producer for the CTV News, and a lot of other press have called."

"Not at the moment, thanks."

"And I have a caller holding. Says he's Grand Chief Joseph George."

"Put him through."

Greene knew most of the Aboriginal leadership from the old days of the constitutional fights, but things had been quiet there lately and he hadn't spoken to Chief George for months.

"Clay," said a slow steady voice on the line, "I watched you on TV. Your committee was televised."

"I usually watch you, Chief, so this is quite a reversal."

The speaker laughed and continued deliberately. "Your big important senator was lying. The company did talk to us. But it wasn't a long discussion. We told them the water belonged to us. They sent a fellow up from the States and he talked about a lot of money and deals they had made with the Navajos. I told him there are some things money can't buy. Besides, we're not Navajos." The Grand Chief chuckled to himself, "Just thought you might like to know."

"Thanks, Chief, I appreciate that."

Greene paused for a moment and then quickly dialed a BC number. He heard the lilting accent of an Indo-Canadian secretary.

"Of course, Mr. Greene, I'll put you right through to the Premier."

Within seconds the Premier of British Columbia was on the phone. Greene knew that she had the reputation for being more liberal than her predecessor who, like a lot of other BC premiers, was recently forced out of office. She was also a bit of an environmentalist.

"Clay, how can I help you?" she asked briskly.

"Joan, I need to ask you a couple of questions."

"Go ahead."

"What is the provincial government's latest policy on water exports?"

"Our latest policy is our earliest. We're against them and we have said so repeatedly. BC has even passed legislation. No change."

"Has anyone asked for a change of policy?"

"Well, let me see. One old guy who used to work for Wacky Bennett called me, and a couple of lobbyists have raised the matter indirectly with me. You know how this place is crawling with lobbyists. And that columnist for the *Vancouver Sun* suggested that we could cash in on the resource and pay down the debt. Luckily, nobody pays attention to him anymore. I guess that's about it Clay."

"What if the government of Canada called you?"

"Are you kidding? We'd tell them to take a hike. It's our jurisdiction. We'd probably threaten to take them to court. You know BC politics, Clay."

"Thanks, Joan."

"Okay, if you need more information, just call me. And if you can't get me, try my assistants, David or Ron. They're always here and ready and share the western view of Ottawa."

Greene laughed to himself and hung up the phone.

"I can't get Don Harris on the phone," Ann told him when he came out of his office.

"Well, what now?" asked Rob Faulkner.

"Rob, I'm having trouble putting it all together. These guys want to export our water in a big way. They're going to have a lot of trouble getting the go-ahead from the BC government. Even if they did, they would then run into the Natives. I haven't even mentioned Greenpeace and the other environment groups. Then, there's Maude Barlow and the Council of Canadians. She'd throw a hundred thousand emails at them to begin with. They got a trial run out of the PM, but he seems rather cool to their project. They'd have to go around or get rid of the lot to succeed. They'd be taking on the whole country, so to speak."

"Poor Captain Kim, why did they get rid of him?" Rob asked with a frown.

"I suppose he may have known too much. Perhaps he was honest and was going to spill the beans."

"Jeez, I need a drink just thinking about it."

"Good idea, Rob. I think it's time to visit the Press Club Bar."

CHAPTER 14

THE PRESS CLUB, OR MORE CORRECTLY THE NINE-STORY building that houses most of the media on the Hill, is at 150 Wellington Street, right across from the West Block. The bar is on the second floor, above the main studio for press conferences. Some people say you can learn more at the bar than at most of the press conferences. The bar starts to fill up in the late afternoon. There are a series of tables facing a big TV set in the corner, and in the back is a room with two pool tables. But the main feature is a long bar. A number of media types, various lobbyists and flacks, and some MPs with drinks in hand spend most of their day appearing to prop it up.

Sure enough, Greene saw the Honourable Member from Saskatoon Centre in his element with journalists on both sides hanging onto his words. He saw Greene enter. "Well, young man, can I buy you a drink or will it be just water today?" Don Harris gave a great belly laugh.

"Yes, and you can add a touch of Scotch, please."

As the bartender put the water glass on the bar, Greene held it up to the light. "Buy a surplus oil tanker, Don— there are plenty around these days. Scrub its tanks, line them with epoxy—not too expensive a job. Moor it to a fjord 100 kilometres north of Vancouver, put a pipe into a stream, let gravity fill the 250,000 tonne ship with the equivalent of 7,500 tanker truck loads, and you have about 75 million gallons of water. Ship it to California. Collect 800,000 bucks. That's US dollars too. Now that our forests are disappearing, what do we have left? Cool, clear water."

The Tory MP laughed again. "You're getting to sound more like a Texan, young man. Want to be an entrepreneur, now?"

Greene poured some of the water into his Scotch and continued. "California has 30 million people now and they're still coming. Combine them with six years of drought and you have a big thirst. What's more, Don, you know who are the big users? Of course, you do. 85 per cent of California's water is used by farmers. Cheap water to produce cheap vegetables. Now, if Canada's water is diverted to the US, it may not be available to Canadian farmers. There's been a little bit of a drought recently on the Canadian prairies, hasn't there, Don? So ex-Albertan and ex-Texan oilmen, now water entrepreneurs, get rich again, and of course their banker friends, at the expense of the Canadian farmer. Sound familiar, Don?"

"You want committee hearings bad, don't you? Well, I'll tell you something. I'm interested in your argument. It's clever, but it's not enough. This afternoon, the Deputy PM and some of his Alliance Party friends approached me, told me not to have hearings on this water business. So, I got news for you . . . and them. Your hearings start next week. They should know better than to threaten me."

At this, Greene noticed a couple of reporters slink away from the bar, suddenly remembering an appointment at their newsrooms. Greene smiled back at the burly Saskatoon MP, who was proposing a toast.

"To entrepreneurs!"

"To the truth," replied Greene, "and to our hearings."

Greene offered his RCMP bodyguard a drink, but the officer stuck to soda water and politely suggested that

Greene should take a cab home, which he did. He had rarely felt lonely in his small apartment since coming to Parliament, but now, for some odd reason, he did. Perhaps it was the tension of the last week, the need for a bodyguard, making him feel less comfortable in the city. He wanted to go back to Vancouver.

When he picked up his telephone messages, he heard Marianne's voice and wondered whether he should call her. Instead, he called Janet's cell, but only her voicemail answered. He opened his small fridge and took out some cold chicken and munched on it. He was still fidgeting when he finally called Marianne. She answered quickly and sounded glad to hear from him. She told him about her experience on the Drive. "They were outrageous, Clay, but I loved them. And they sure are loyal to you."

"That's the problem here in Ottawa, Marianne. Sometimes I feel so far away from my friends and supporters, not to mention my constituents."

"How do you think I feel about Quebec and my family?"

"You know, maybe someday I could meet your family. I bet they're interesting people if they're anything like you."

There was a pause on the other end of the line and Greene had to ask her if she was still there. After a moment he told her about his visit to Quebec City, leaving out the more dramatic parts about the freighter voyage.

After an other awkward pause she commented, "You did very well in the Regs Committee, Clay."

"That was thanks to you and Paul Havel. You especially would have enjoyed being at that lunch with him. He's an unbelievable guy."

"Then why are you still so down, Clay?"

"I was thinking about what Senator Murphy said in his testimony, something about water being wasted falling into the ocean."

"Why does that bother you?"

"Because it's a fundamental misunderstanding of our environment, of our whole planet, Marianne. Water is not a renewable resource. Water can't reproduce itself like trees or even humans. Water is recycled by means of the hydrological cycle: evaporation plus transportation by plants, to cloud formation, to rain and snow, back to plants, rivers and ground water, to the oceans and cycling around again by means of evaporation, transpiration and precipitation."

"Why is that so important, Clay?"

Marianne could hear him suck in his breath. "Because the hydrological cycle is a life support system for all living things, including us. You screw around with it and you fundamentally change the world." He paused for a moment and then laughed: "I don't mean you personally."

"We *are* getting a bit serious, aren't we?"

Greene looked at his watch and realized they had been on the phone for over an hour. "I apologize for the lecture, but I feel strongly and I get so damn frustrated that this debate always becomes an economic one. You know, under international trade rules once one company is allowed to export water in bulk, a precedent is set allowing other companies, be they American or Mexican or whatever, to do likewise. But the real issue is bigger."

"Clay, enough. You need some sleep. And you're three hours ahead of me."

"You're right, and I've hardly let you get a word in about your research. Look, I have to come out to Vancouver to deal with some constituency matters—you reminded me of that when you mentioned Lynn and Mary Ellen. And I need some rest before the Finance Committee hearings next week. How about a couple of days skiing at Whistler?"

Again there was a pause which lasted even longer and prompted him to say, "Oh, come on Marianne, I promise to be a good boy. And I do need to talk to you without my staff."

"Clay, I've heard these words before from guys. I'll tell you the truth. I really do want to ski Whistler, but I'm going to keep you to your promise. So, you're on, Mr. Greene, with conditions."

When he hung up the phone, Clay got undressed, slipped into his bed and was about to turn out his bed lamp when a book of poetry on the shelf beside the bed caught his eye. He reached over and pulled out the blue-covered volume, thumbing through it till he found the spot he was looking for in Coleridge's "Rime of the Ancient Mariner:"

Water, water, everywhere,
And all the boards did shrink;
Water, water, everywhere,
Nor any drop to drink.

It made him think. Was this going to be the future? No water unless you could pay for it? Canadian farmers staring out over parched fields while the country's resource went south to help American farmers? Like the Ancient Mariner, Clay felt he was caught in the middle of something he didn't fully understand. Who was involved? Where were the mysterious payments of money coming from and going to? And why were people willing to murder for the water and the money? His mind worked over these questions for a long time before he went to sleep, and he also wondered if inviting Marianne on a ski trip was a wise idea. When he finally fell asleep, he dreamed of running waterfalls and falling snow.

CHAPTER **15**

MARIANNE TREMBLAY LOOKED INTO THE BACK OF
Greene's old blue Volvo. She wondered what kind of
guy would carry around scuba gear and all that other athletic
junk. She also wondered why she was taking a chance in
going away with him. Shaking her head, but at the same time
smiling to herself, she helped him load his skis.

"Clay, ever clean your car out?"

"You know how busy I am."

"When is the last time you went scuba diving?"

"Actually, quite recently. I love diving. It's now my main
hobby, next to skiing, of course."

Marianne looked at him and laughed. Then they were
off on the road to Whistler, 150 kilometres north of
Vancouver.

On the road Greene told her that when he had first
started skiing on what was now a booming city for the international jet-set, and a possible future Olympic site—with
bilingual signs in English and Japanese—it had been the
garbage dump. "It only took a decade or so to make the place
is almost unrecognizable. But this road to Whistler hasn't
changed much. It's been widened and straightened a bit, but
it still winds along this beautiful ocean fjord, and it's still
dangerous. There are rock falls and car accidents every year,
and sometimes major washouts when it rains hard in the
winter."

Marianne saw a sign identifying it as the "Sea to Sky
Highway," and after they passed through the logging town of
Squamish at the head of the inlet, the rain gave way to the

snow of Whistler-Blackcomb, the best skiing area in the world.

Two hours after they left Vancouver, they parked outside the condo, one in a line of snowed-over units just above Whistler Village.

"Is this yours, Clay? I didn't know that MPs made so much dough."

"You don't need to be rich. You only have to have rich friends." Greene fumbled with the key that finally opened the door.

Marianne peered into a cozy living room with a couple of white couches and a pine kitchen table. She saw a small balcony with a covered over jacuzzi. "I guess it belongs to one of your poor NDP lawyer friends, n'est-ce-pas?"

"Well, as a matter of fact . . . but he works so hard he hardly uses it. So much the better for us."

"Well, I like it. Beats St. Jovite hands down," Marianne smiled.

Greene was looking out the window. "You know, if we hustle we could get in a half day of skiing."

"On one of those cheap half-day passes. You are part Scottish, right? By the way, what's the other part?"

"Gwitch'in."

"What?"

"I'll tell you on the chairs."

Within half an hour they were skiing in Whistler's back bowl underneath huge snow crevasses, still his favourite part of the resort after all these years and all the new trails. As she passed him on one of the long straight stretches, he noticed how her blonde hair flowed out from under her ski toque and caught in the wind. He noticed, too, how snugly the one-piece blue ski suit fit around her hips. He had to work to catch up to her.

They came to a long downhill stretch of moguls, small mounds cut into the side of the hill by the turns of many skiers. Marianne didn't hesitate and in no time had cut a path right through them. They took the Red Express chair up to the Whistler Round House rest stop, not talking, but savouring the exhilaration of looking toward the Whistler bowl. From the top, Greene led her down under the Big Red chair run to Whistler's midstation.

As they got on the old slower orange chair that climbed back up the mountain, Greene finally spoke. "I've always liked this chair, even though it's slow. You get some time to talk to your partner on this chair since it's just the two of you."

"So talk," Marianne said as she carefully brought the safety bar down on them, then took off her toque and shook out her hair. When she looked up she thought she saw Greene staring at her.

"Well, where's the talk?" she said. Her tone sounded a little too harsh, a little like an interviewing journalist, even to her own ears.

"About water exports or about me?"

She relented a bit and softened her tone. "First you, and then the water exports."

Leaning against her on the orange chair, he told her what he knew about his childhood in Old Crow, about the death of a beautiful mother he never knew, about his Gwitch'in family still there, and even a little, a very little, about his dad.

"That explains the eyes."

"Pardon?"

"Nothing, I'm sorry."

"Can I talk about the present, Marianne?"

"Of course."

"Even when I was skiing the back bowl, I kept thinking about the PM, the money, and the water exports."

"Think of snow, not water, Clay."

"It's the same thing. Besides, I keep asking myself, could the PM actually be that corrupt, and why is the bank ratting on him?"

"You know, some people have a dignified exterior and a somewhat shabby interior. Besides, perhaps the bank didn't leak the story to the *Toronto Star*."

"Then who did?"

"Maybe his friends. Anyway, let's ski and think snow. I'll tell you my theory about water tonight."

With that, Marianne put her toque back on, raised the safety bar, and sped ahead of Greene as they got off the lift. They raced down the old green chair run and past its new Emerald Express lift to the Olympic run, then followed that run down for almost seven kilometres in what seemed to Greene his fastest time ever. They finally arrived, Marianne one ski length ahead, at what used to be the old dump site—now Whistler Village. As they were taking off their skis, they could see the crowd that spilled out of the Longhorn Saloon, a western-style bar with a large outdoor patio. The après-ski beer drinkers were engulfed in a cloud of country music and talk. Marianne and Clayton stopped for an Okanagan Pale Ale and a plate of cheesy nachos, but it became hard to hear themselves talk.

"Let's get out of here and go back to the condo, Clay."

Greene was actually enjoying all the people and all the

noise. He also felt a little hesitant about what might happen next. He still wondered about the wisdom of bringing Marianne to this place. She had already been invaluable to him and he had already admitted to himself that he was attracted to her. She sure could ski, too. Was he getting in over his head? Could he keep his hands off her?

"OK, let's go," he heard himself say.

After dinner, they set aside the dishes and moved with their wine glasses to sit in front of the fire.

"Now, if the Honourable Member is relaxed enough, I'm prepared to talk about water."

"Okay," smiled Greene, "but why don't we talk in the Jacuzzi."

"All right, I suppose it's a Whistler ritual, but I brought my bathing suit. Put it down to being an Easterner."

Dressed in bathing suits, they moved outside to the porch and into the large cedar tub and its pulsating waters.

"This is really decadent."

"No, it's only British Columbia. And if you're comfortable, tell me your water theory?"

Marianne Tremblay began to recite what she had learned in the last few days from her contacts in Washington, Los Angeles, Houston, and Calgary.

"Since the 1980s, water's become a major political issue, and an emotional one in Canada. There have been protests, sometimes verging on violence, over the Rafferty-Alameda Dam in Saskatchewan, the Oldman River in Alberta, the Kemano project in BC."

"And James Bay in northern Quebec," Greene interjected.

He moved over closer to her, picked up a coarse brush from the edge of the tub and began gently to scrub the top of her back. She was about to object, then seemed to lose herself in her story.

"Of course. They're all examples of political struggles between developers, governments, Aboriginal people, environmentalists, and fishers. But water exports will make these other political issues seem like playground squabbles. For years, the export of Canadian water was just a fantasy in the heads of some business executives. One group led by Francis Dale, a US Ambassador, once proposed a grand scheme in which 'surplus' water from northern Canada would be exported to thirsty customers in the US and Mexico."

"The world's biggest waterslide, so to speak," laughed Greene.

She was surprised to hear herself say: "Keep scrubbing my back, Clay, it feels good." But she didn't pause long.

"You'll recall that I told you about a group of businessmen, supported by the ex-premier of Quebec, Robert Bourassa. It's all in his 1985 book *Power From the North*. That group wanted to construct dike enclosures to change James Bay and divert the water to the US."

"I remember you telling me at dinner in Vancouver that that project would cost some $100 billion. Is it really worth it?"

"You bet it is. The 1988 drought in California cost seventeen billion dollars. Cities like Santa Barbara discovered that water desalination costs a fortune. California has a runoff of 71 million acre feet a year. They're already short a million acre feet, and the shortages are just beginning. The immediate future of their cotton and alfalfa crops are at stake. The vegetables come later. You can see why the potential profits from water sales are enormous. They'll dwarf hydro, oil and gas, and telecommunications."

"What's it mean to BC?"

"A lot. Large rivers like the Fraser flow out of British Columbia. That means the province has an estimated annual runoff of 665 million acre feet of water, which is 2 per cent of the world's total water. Canada has 9 per cent in all. You can only imagine how much we have."

Greene turned his head, wiped some bubbles from his eyes and looked outside. At the bottom of the mountain, a gentle rain was falling. "Who controls water anyway, Marianne, other than God, of course?"

"That's murky. Transport and the use of bulk water is a provincial matter. The federal government controls exports, a trade matter. The feds have promised a water policy since way back in 1993 and have never completely delivered. The World Bank has said the wars of this century will be about water."

"How do Senator Murphy and his friends fit into this?"

"I found out that Coronation Transit, a subsidiary of Western Energy Inc., has placed orders for a number of old oil tankers. And there have been meetings in Calgary in which a plan was presented to dam BC's North Thompson River and to divert it at a point 75 miles west of Jasper National Park to flow downstream to the Oregon border. A pipeline company based in Houston is already doing the technical drawings for a water pipeline across Oregon to California's Pit River. That river feeds into the Lake Shasta Reservoir near, you guessed it, Redding, California. Canadian water would thus sustain California."

Greene, who had been looking intently at her as she told

him the story of the water plans, closed his eyes for a moment and then raised himself up, sitting on the edge of the tub.

"Where did you get that last piece of information?"

"I never reveal my sources."

Greene smiled. "So tell me Murphy's problem."

"Clay, to get these schemes going, you'd need a mountain of permits—the last one I mentioned would need permits from three states, a province, and two countries. Not to mention Native land claims and environmental injunctions."

"Well, they won the last court case and it appears, for some reason, that the Government of Canada is changing its policy. BC and Ontario might be difficult, I suppose, but could the promoters use the North America Free Trade Agreement to get around provincial moratoriums on water exports?"

"You're clever, Clay. I checked with my sources in Washington. It could be argued under the trade deal that Americans farmers have to be on a level playing field with Canadian farmers, and to achieve this they could demand Canadian water at Canadian consumer prices or claim that we are obliged to give them equal rights to water even in the event of a shortage in Canada. Take your pick. And of course we also have to factor in Mexico as part of the trade deal. But it's iffy, this whole thing. Besides, if MacKenzie loses his working majority in Parliament, another government might finally abrogate the deal. What the Americans need, as one of Murphy's American business partners once said, is control over the source of the water."

Greene's eyes narrowed and he frowned, "'Control over the source of the water.' What does that really mean?"

"Well, some people think if we start exporting water, the Free Trade Agreement will make it impossible to stop, so Murphy may just be pushing to turn the taps on a little bit in hopes that it will be impossible to turn them off. If a government got in on the act and wanted to cancel the Agreement, it might be harder to do that. But there's still that possibility."

"So if they wanted to be sure," Clay mused, "they'd have to make sure no government changed the Agreement. We could be talking about rigging elections, payoffs . . . murder . . ." He hesitated. "Marianne, I've got to tell you. This could be dangerous for you."

She looked up at him and saw the worried look on his face. She was going to speak but decided to let the silence hang above them; perhaps it was the journalist in her. As ever larger flakes of snow fell on them, Greene began to relax and open up. He told her about the personal attacks on him in Toronto and on the St. Lawrence. She listened intently; he was confiding in her. As she got out of the tub, she handed him a towel and put on her white dressing gown. She was surprised, surprised at how open he had been with her.

Greene himself got out of the jacuzzi and turned it off. As the bubbling jets stopped, they gazed out of the window together at the gentle snow.

They were standing close to each other. Marianne spoke first. "We both could be in danger, Clay."

The music on the tape came to an end. Water dripping on the skylight above them was the only sound to break the silence. For an instant their bodies touched. Then, at the same moment, they stepped apart.

CHAPTER 16

MARIANNE AWOKE TO THE AROMA OF FRESH COFFEE, slowly opening her eyes. It was hard to believe. Last night she expected to say an awkward no. She had been dreading the moment all day. Eventually they all made a pass at her; they all wanted the same thing, and once they got it, their interest in her dropped off very quickly, sometimes right off the map. But this guy, despite what she had heard about him, didn't come on to her. He even led her to a separate bedroom, and gave her a gentle good night kiss. She began to dream again sleepily. She didn't trust men. She had long ago determined that she didn't need a man to fulfill her life. She had her career. She knew when to cut them off. Besides, none of them could live up to her dad. At this thought she woke up again. As she gently rubbed her eyes and smelled the sweet cedar smell, she saw Greene standing by her bed, offering her a mug. "Just cream, right?"

"How long have you been up?" She saw his briefing notes spread out on a table in the kitchen nook. She also saw a gentle snow falling outside the window and smiled.

"Oh, for about half an hour. I'm not exactly a morning person, but I try to do a few breathing exercises when I get up and I find I can think, especially before the phone starts ringing. Besides, I slept particularly well last night."

"It must have been the skiing," said Marianne. "Clay, do we have to go back?" She was surprised how quickly the words came out of her mouth.

"You know we do."

"We're crazy, Clay. Here we are in one of the most

beautiful spots in the world. There's a whole range of mountains at our doorstep and you're going back to work in Ottawa. How do you do it?"

"Don't ask me. Someday I'll stay here and enjoy it. If all the world were to play, then to play t'would be as tedious as to work."

"No Shakespeare, please. Certainly not this early in the morning." She got out of bed and slipped into her dressing gown.

"I have a little surprise for you. Come out to the kitchen"

The table was set, with a plate of fresh croissants as a centrepiece.

Marianne smiled, then became suddenly serious. "We're breaking the rules, Clay. Journalists are not supposed to socialize with the people they interview, not CP journalists, anyway, but I did enjoy yesterday."

"We have the same rules. Made to be broken on special occasions."

They both sat down and ate the croissants.

"You know," said Greene, "I feel different and I was trying to figure out why. I haven't touched the phone this morning. That's a miracle. And I didn't give the number to my office, so they haven't called."

"That's the real miracle," said Marianne. "Clay, you haven't put Senator Murphy out of your mind, have you?"

"I haven't. And I've been thinking over what you said last night. 'Control over the source of water.' That means control over Canada. Some people say the US already has that, with the Free Trade deal and globalization and the business agenda. But we could be looking at more."

The phone rang. Almost instinctively, Clay picked it up.

"Yes, she's here." He glowered at Marianne.

"Sorry, Clay. I am a journalist, and I was waiting on a call, so I gave the number out last night as a last resort." She smiled awkwardly.

He handed her the phone.

"Yes? Where should I come?" She reached for a pencil and paper near the phone and wrote down "Cold Lake," some directions, and the name "Major Renée Bouchard."

She hung up the phone.

"Well, what was all that about?" Clay asked a bit grumpily.

"I'll tell you on the way to Vancouver. I may have a detour to make before coming back to Ottawa. I'm sorry about giving out the phone number. I know you didn't want anyone to know that we were here, but I'd been waiting for that call." It sounded a bit lame, even if it was important.

"Oh, well. It's your job." But Greene was wondering, again, if he could trust this woman. I'm letting my feelings dictate, he thought. I like her—she's different. Sometimes, like last night, the attraction seems mutual, but then she puts up this huge guard.

He was glad he didn't try to make her last night. He was surprised at having been able to resist. After putting her to bed, he had quietly phoned Jerry in Vancouver and told him his feelings. Jerry had said that maybe for once, there was more to this attraction. Anyway, he probably could have laid her if he really wanted to. But last night he had been able to put the thought out of his mind and had fallen asleep surprisingly quickly.

"Do you ever get away from journalism and the news, Marianne?"

"Well, I like it. I—I've always liked my job." Marianne Tremblay looked down at the pine floor, hesitated, and continued. "I worked really hard to get where I am, Clay. It's still hard for a woman journalist to get sent to Parliament Hill. That's usually considered a job for the big guys. I'm proud of where I got to."

Greene softened, noting the red blushes on her cheeks. "I bet you'd do anything for a story, right?" She thought to herself: well, wasn't that why I came to Whistler, to pursue a story?

"I'd do a lot, but not 'anything' as you put it. I think I'm good at what I do."

"Well, I can vouch for that judging by the research you've been feeding me on the water issue."

Greene poured himself another cup of coffee and refilled Marianne's cup. She nodded, but remained silent. As he was taking the plates away he heard a cracking sound outside. "Oh, I forgot to tell you we a have family of raccoons here. The owner of this condo calls the mother raccoon, 'Big Susy.' His wife claims she's jealous. That noise. It must be Susy."

Marianne nodded. She looked out the window at Whistler Mountain, at the white ski runs cutting the tree lines, and thought how there was still some tension between them, even in this beautiful spot.

Silence, that awesome silence of the wilderness, had returned to the mountains. The light snow muffled noise, and the only sound now was the gentle bump-bump as the chair of one of the distant ski lifts crossed over the lift tower. She was enjoying this silence and feeling less apprehensive about Greene. After all, he hadn't make a move on her.

Had Clay and Marianne looked out the side window, they would have seen a man standing by the Volvo, putting tools into a bag. He had just closed the hood of the old car. In spite of his careful efforts, there had been a sound—the cracking noise that Clay and Marianne had heard. The man slipped silently out of the carport, lit a cigarette, and slunk away to a waiting car.

It was about noon when Clay and Marianne finished their skiing, packed the equipment back in the car, and started for Vancouver. The road was mostly downhill to tidewater at Squamish, where the snow would turn once again to rain.

"So, why Cold Lake?" asked Clay. "That's in Alberta, right?"

Marianne replied, "I've been thinking about your conversation with the Governor General and her remarks about the armed forces. It was very strange. After all it's a known fact that the GG *is* the head of Canada's armed forces. Why should she tell you that? So I made contacts with some of my sources there, specifically a woman friend who has risen rapidly through the ranks. She referred me to a captain stationed at CFB Cold Lake who refused to talk to me over the telephone but invited me to Cold Lake, which in itself is very unusual. I agreed to go, even though I'll miss the beginning of the Finance Committee hearings on the water exports."

Greene fished the last brown croissant out of the paper bag. Between bites and with one hand on the wheel, he stared ahead with what seemed to Marianne an odd look.

She turned to him. "Clay, you look afraid. It's the first time I've ever seen you like this."

He looked straight and gripped the wheel. "I haven't often been frightened in my life, but this thing is starting to frighten me. It's just so strange. I'm not afraid for myself, but I'm concerned about where it may lead. Of course, on the other hand, I should be grateful that it led me to get to know you."

Marianne smiled. "God, you lawyers are all the same— on the one hand, on the other hand. What did Herbert Hoover say—'Give me a one-handed lawyer?'"

Clay lightened his grip. "Thanks for that," he said and smiled at her. As his eyes flicked back to the road, he glanced in the rearview mirror. A large car with two men in it was awfully close behind him. He saw an Alberta licence plate and was about to joke about prairie drivers when he realized there was something menacing about the car. It was bearing down on them. He pulled as far over on the narrow, winding road as he could, but the driver didn't seem to want to pass.

"Clay, that car is trying to force us off the road!" He heard panic in Marianne's voice.

The speed of the two cars was increasing. As they came to a corner, the bigger car moved up beside the Volvo and tried to force them off the road, but Greene spurted ahead. He had travelled the road for years as a skier, so he was able to continue negotiating the turns ahead of the Alberta car. He knew that if they could reach the long straight stretch down to Porteau Cove, he might get some help there.

As they swayed through the final series of turns before the straightaway, he told Marianne, "We're going to make it. Hold on!"

As the Volvo started downhill, Greene put his foot ever

so gently on the brakes to maintain control. His foot went to the floor; the brakes were gone.

"Marianne, we're not going to make the last corner. Don't panic, just tuck your head in your hands."

He noticed that Marianne's eyes opened wide and her mouth closed tightly, but he was concentrating on manoeuvering the car around the corner.

"This is Porteau Cove," he said, almost conversationally. "It's a special underwater park for scuba divers. I was here last year. I've lost the brakes, so we're going for a rough ride. Just stay tucked and keep breathing."

As the Volvo reached the bottom of the long hill, Greene turned hard right into the entrance of a gravel car park for recreational vehicles that extended for a long distance, jutting out into the water. At high speed, the Volvo virtually flew across a railway line, then returned to earth with a thud, spinning out of control across the parking lot. Marianne could feel an incredible sensation in her stomach, as if it had been left in the air above the railway crossing.

The car came to the edge of the gravel and flew over a small mound of grass, down a sandy beach, and into the ocean.

It sank fast in about twenty feet of water.

Greene tried to picture how close to shore the steeper ledge was. All he could remember was that this was the only scuba diving spot along this part of the coast because the fall-off was so gentle. Howe Sound itself was very deep, up to four hundred feet. The car was now on the shallow sandy bottom very close, too close, to the drop-off.

The Volvo began to fill up with water, but relatively slowly as the windows were not broken.

There was a look of panic on Marianne's face.

"Take off your seatbelt and don't panic." Greene tried to speak slowly and calmly. "I've been here before."

The last sentence seemed so strange to Marianne that she did tackle the seatbelt, and then she just looked at him.

Greene turned his head to the back of the old station wagon. The back seat was folded down so that they could more easily store the skis. There was a lot of other stuff in the back.

He reached under a tarpaulin, past his skiis, and pulled out his battered scuba tank. An air hose was still connected to the tank. He had been meaning to clean it out of the car, but thank God, he hadn't. He put the air hose to his face, turned on the tank, and hoped. After a few seconds he knew that there was still some air in it. He took a deep inhalation and passed it to Marianne.

"Inhale," he said, "and breathe out slowly. Do *not* hold your breath under any circumstances. You must breathe out slowly on the way up to the surface. That's crucial. Trust me. Now, in and out. In and out."

Marianne closed her eyes and did as he said. The water was not yet over their heads.

After he took a couple of breaths, the cold water filled the inside of the car. This would be the big test. He grabbed Marianne's hand, squeezed it hard, and held it. With his other hand, he passed the breathing apparatus.

She took it and breathed, in and out, in and out. They continued to breathe like this together for about five minutes until Marianne was relatively calm. Then Greene, with great effort, rolled down the driver's window. He signalled to Marianne—two more breaths and they would ascend. She looked terrified, but she was still taking the breaths and she had not panicked. First Greene and then Marianne squeezed through the open window and floated to the surface. As their heads came out of the water, Marianne gasped for air. Greene held onto her. They heard cries from the beach, and the next thing they knew some young people in a boat were grabbing for them.

"Man, that was wild," said one of the young men, who was wearing a wet suit.

When they got to the rocky beach and were out of the boat, the diver explained that he and his friends had been packing up to leave when the Volvo went into the water. "Man, it just flew! Wow!"

Another diver said that a car with Alberta plates had stopped and waited for about five minutes. "The two guys just stood there and looked at their watches and then at the water, she said. "They didn't try to get us to come out after you or anything. Then they just left. Maybe they went for the cops."

And a RCMP cruiser did arrive on the scene shortly after. The officer had brought blankets, and Clay and Marianne were huddled up in these when coffee mysteriously appeared.

Clay looked at Marianne. She seemed speechless and almost in shock, but finally she looked up at him. "Those skis were borrowed," she said.

He laughed and said, "You're amazing."

"You too, but get me out of here."

CHAPTER 17

THE SKY ABOVE THE PARLIAMENT BUILDINGS WAS A brilliant clear blue, and the Ottawa morning was crisp and cold. A young tour guide stood amidst some crimson maple leaves, slightly behind a group of thirty Japanese tourists. Her right arm moved in a slow sweep from left to right. As she described the scene, the sound of clicking cameras broke the morning silence.

The guide pointed out the statue of former Prime Minister Lester B. Pearson, frozen in bronze and sitting on a small grassy hill just to the west of the Centre Block. Pearson, who won the Nobel Peace prize for inventing the idea of a UN peacekeeping force, perpetually regards the Peace Tower some five-hundred metres away.

Below him, even closer to the Peace Tower, rests a statue of his arch rival, Prime Minister John George Diefenbaker, although people will tell you that "Dief the Chief" never rested for a minute in his long parliamentary lifetime.

"The architectural style of the Parliament Buildings is Victorian Gothic, a design derived from the medieval architecture of England and Europe, popular in England when the plans for these buildings were drafted in 1859," explained the guide. "The Gothic style reflects the origin of Parliament in the Middle Ages. The towers are German in origin, the mansard roofs French, the pointed windows Italian, and the library is modelled on an English chapter house."

She could have added that, according to writer Heather Robertson, the organic style, with shapes and motifs derived from nature, captured the spirit of the Canadian wilderness and the aspirations of a young nation. Nor did she mention the other side to the Gothic style, the notion of barbarity—uncivilized, mysterious, with even a touch of horror.

If a bird had flown in a straight line from the end of the guide's finger as it swung to the far east side of the great Gothic building, it would have landed on the open third-floor windowsill of the office of Senator Murphy. Inside that office, six men were sitting in dark red leather chairs scattered around a light, oak-panelled office. Murphy himself sat behind a big walnut desk with a red leather top that matched the blood red carpet. He was dressed in an expensive blue silk suit with thin grey stripes and a blue striped dress shirt with a starched collar. A gold tie clasp at the neck of the shirt. He held the desk telephone to his ear. Behind him hung a huge painting depicting young soldiers fighting on a World War I battlefield. Several silver-framed photographs rested on a credenza near the desk—Brian Mulroney, Ronald Reagan, George Bush Sr., and the present Speaker of the Senate.

"Good. Excellent. They should come back right away. They have? Good."

Senator Murphy put down the phone, lit a cigarette, smiled, and glanced at the other men seated around his desk.

The man in the biggest chair, just to the Senator's right, immediately filled the brief silence with a southern American drawl. "I don't understand why there's always delay here. Delay, delay. Can't you Canadians ever get things done without all the red tape?"

James Roberts, the Deputy PM, straightened his thin body and coughed slightly before he spoke. "We are making progress, Jeff. We got our first tanker shipment after a bit of trouble, which we easily solved. We had to, well, change captains after the first one was going to reveal our little experiment. And we defeated those greens in court."

"You mean the tree huggers," Murphy exclaimed. "Christ, between them and the Indians, nothing is going to get moving. We sent some people to talk to the Indians. They think they own the whole damn store."

"We're working on that." This voice, too, was unmistakably American. "The Embassy, or should I say, our people, my bosses, are looking into that."

Jeff Conway, the American Vice President, was glad the CIA man at the US embassy was with them. There had been a change in the administration in the US, but nothing had changed with the CIA. They were still there when you needed them. Besides, he had made sure to guarantee this guy a future job in Southern California Transmission and to cut him in on a piece of the action.

"We're also looking at your Prime Minister. We're not sure if he is with us or not."

Senator Murphy immediately looked up. "Let us handle that, Jeff."

But Conway still didn't seem pleased. He stood up and began to pace around the large office. He was a tall man. After a moment, he spoke. "The worst is that young bastard, the MP from the coast. He's a prima donna all right, but his information is awfully accurate. He's really the only one we can't handle at the moment."

Senator Murphy leaned back in his chair: "Don't worry about him, Jeff. Seems that he's just had an unfortunate car accident on a very dangerous provincial highway. Drove his car right into the ocean and drowned, poor fellow. Too bad, it'll be a tight by-election in Vancouver Centre, usually is." Murphy laughed and lit another cigarette. The room was quiet for a moment.

Conway nodded his chin up and down a few times and then broke the silence. "What about the main part of the plan, the water diversion from the North Thompson to California?"

"We're working on that," replied the Deputy PM. "The first step is the official change in policy which we expect to get through cabinet." On the outside he appeared to be the most cautious guy in the room.

"Shit, you know how difficult it was to get those Orders-in-Council for the tanker export," Conway blustered. "Old MacKenzie was pretty reluctant, wasn't he? Now you've got to get the whole shitbag."

Senator Murphy frowned. "Well, we have in process the means to pressure the PM. Don't worry about that. It just takes time."

Conway stopped his pacing, sat down in the large red leather chair, leaned back and, looking like a portrait of the young LBJ, looked directly at Senator Murphy. He saw a middle-aged man in apparently good physical shape, not large and with rather a small mouth, but with a confident air, at least for a Canadian. Yet there was something he didn't quite understand and it made him uncomfortable. In the States when you met Senators, damn them, you could feel how comfortable they were in the corridors of power. They all felt they owned the place. And you could tell in an instant their alliances. They were either your friends, the good guys, or your enemies, the bad guys. Here, for all his connections and for all his domination of these other nobodies around him, he still talked like an outsider. Wasn't he the god-damned campaign manager—shouldn't his word be the law? Canada, he had to remind himself, was a different place. Well, perhaps not for long. He smiled to himself and spoke up: "There is, of course, Plan B, which I think is the real solution, the inevitable solution. Are you guys ready?"

At that, the Defence Minister, who had remained very quiet so far, shuffled in his seat. He was a big man, with an enormous belly hanging over a thick black belt with a silver horseshoe belt buckle. He didn't have a Texan accent, but he spoke slowly and deliberately like the Calgary oilman he had been. "I can tell you, Jeff, that we are ready. I just got back from Cold Lake and the peacekeepers are ready to move."

They looked at each other, paused, and all began talking at once.

Murphy took Conway aside and in muted tones said, "Look, I can see you're worried, but we should have clear sailing. We can pressure the PM. We've got rid of Greene.

"What about the Frenchies?" said the big American. "Have you got any of those Bloc guys on board?"

"We don't need them. They don't matter much now anyway. We've got their real boss onside. Why do you think we spent all that time in Quebec City. They won't stand in our way. If Canada goes, they're on their own, which is what he wants anyway. Why are you smiling?"

"I always thought American politics were crazy, but you folks beat it all. The Separatists and the Alliance Party. Same damn goal really."

Murphy moved away from the Vice President and picked up the large crystal glass decanter on his credenza.

"Here, let's have another scotch and relax a bit. It's coming together in our Canadian way, Jeff. We will see the Prime Minister tomorrow and then go through the formality of those damned Finance Committee hearings. And then we'll put the pressure on."

He filled up their glasses with scotch. "I propose a toast."

"To the five richest men in the world!"

The Vice President raised his glass. He was beginning to feel more comfortable.

CHAPTER **18**

THE SOFT FIRST LIGHT OF DAWN GRADUALLY OPENED up the huge Northern Alberta sky. The dawn was like a dark curtain rising to reveal a stage set of green fir and pine trees that seemed to go on forever. The lawyer and poet F. R. Scott had once described Canada as "cold, silent, vast—awaiting the struggle."

But it was not silent here. The engine roar of three F16 fighter jets filled the chilled air and broke the northern silence. The air itself smelled of jet fuel. The jets screamed off the long runway over the pine forests at one of Canada's largest air bases, CFB Cold Lake, Alberta.

It had taken a shivering Marianne Tremblay three and a half hours to drive up from Edmonton. Now she stood at the main gate of the base as a young guard intently examined her press identification.

"I'm sorry, but the base has been closed. No one can visit."

"But there must be some mistake. I'm expected."

"Sorry, I have my orders and they are firm orders."

"What about my orders, son?"

Major Renée Bouchard was tall and erect with close-cropped black hair, imposing in her green braided uniform, someone you didn't talk back to.

The young guard was temporarily taken aback. Then he saluted and said, "These orders are very specific, Major."

"I'm making a very specific order, too. This woman is my guest and she will come in to see me. The visit won't be long. I'll sign her in and she will be out of here in an hour."

The guard was reluctant, but he finally agreed on the basis that Major Bouchard would take full responsibility. Marianne entered the base with Renée. Together, they walked behind the married quarters to a small brick residential building where they entered a neat apartment, painted light green, with a bedroom and a small sitting room. Two cups of hot tea were already on the round pine table. Marianne helped herself.

"I remember where I first met you. I did a story on you when you became the first female aide-de-camp to a Governor General."

"Correct. I loved that job and I loved the GG. She was great to work with. And, to tell you the truth, I liked your story a lot. I think it helped get me my promotion here."

"Well, I recalled your connections with the GG and your senior rank in our armed forces. I'm looking for some information."

Major Bouchard frowned slightly and took a sip of her tea. "Marianne, you've come to the right place. Something strange is going on here. I've been almost completely shut out of the decision-making process and the information loop, so to speak, and I'm a senior officer. At first I thought it was the old boys thing or something like that, but now I don't think so."

Major Bouchard explained that the base had gone on a series of alerts a few months ago as part of a special mobilization exercise. She was told that this was practice for dealing with a national emergency.

"When some of the plans seemed rather odd—for example, the control of the CBC national news and items like that—I began to raise questions. At that point, they explained it as a form of peacekeeping, even "peacemaking" in the new world order, if you can believe it."

Marianne knew from her previous article that Major Bouchard had always had a precise and logical mind. She had topped her class in engineering at the College Militaire de Saint Jean. She wasn't someone who could be fooled.

"Why is the control of the news odd, Renée?"

"Because peacekeepers don't need to control a country's media. That's what *invaders* do."

Renée told Marianne that one night she had telephoned a friend who worked for the new Governor General to wish her a happy birthday and she had mentioned the nature of the exercises. She was shocked when the friend called her back a few days later to say that the Governor General, who normally was kept informed of affairs of state, knew nothing of the exercises. After that call, she had the sense that her phone was being tapped, that she was being followed. She certainly was completely excluded from the base planning.

"About a week ago the preparations began again. There is no major new UN initiative at this time, and unless these guys are clairvoyant, we don't have any more Okas happening at the moment."

"What is it then?"

"I haven't quite figured it out, but I know the Defence Minister was here recently, and the Deputy Prime Minister was with him, along with American liaison officers. Oddly, our Chief of Defence Staff was not in the group. A couple of really weird mid-level officers accompanied them. These were the same guys that, the rumour has it, have been involved in some extreme right wing political movements. They come from the old paratroops gang. The base commander was there. He's somewhere right of Attila the Hun. I found out that they had been referring to the operation or some future operation as Operation D'Arcy McGee."

"What are they capable of doing with it, Renée?"

The tall officer looked down at Marianne, pursed her lips, and lowered her voice. "They are capable of sending out of here, to anywhere in the world, on a few hours notice, a tactical assault force—in short, a small army that could invade and operate a small country. I just can't figure out which country the UN wants them to go to."

Marianne began to cough, a sort of choking cough, which forced her to put her cup down.

"Are you all right, Marianne?"

"Yes. I think I know what country it is." Both women looked at each other. Neither spoke.

Their silence was broken by a knock. Then a group of armed soldiers opened the door. "Major Bouchard, you have disobeyed the order of the base commander. You are under arrest, as is your guest," barked one of the soldiers.

Bouchard was still protesting as she and Marianne Tremblay were led away.

—

They were in a room about twenty feet by thirty feet. The soldiers had hustled them along a narrow corridor, down two flights of stairs, and along another corridor to a room marked "Utilities." The leader of the group opened the door and the women were pushed into the small room, which was painted stark white and lit by a simple yellow light. It contained a small chair and a couch. Big metal pipes ran across the top of the room.

It took the women a moment to catch their breath. Marianne looked scared and was about to open her mouth. Major Bouchard, on the other hand, looked angry—angry and determined. When Marianne saw that look she closed her mouth and took a deep breath. Bouchard put a finger to her lips and whispered to Marianne, "This is not a normal detention room. There are no cameras and there don't seem to be any hiding places for microphones. That means they are likely to come to get us sooner rather than later."

"What do we do, then?"

"Get out of here and get out of here fast."

"The door's locked and it's pretty thick."

"You, and they, forget that I'm an engineer by trade and that I directed the recent renovations of the base. I really got into blueprint reading for the first time in my life. Let me think a bit and try to visualize where we are."

Major Bouchard sat on the chair and closed her eyes. Marianne sat on the couch. It seemed like a long time, but in reality it was only a minute until Bouchard spoke again, this time in French. "It's the pipes. We opted for buying sectional attachments locally to save money."

"Sectional attachments?" Marianne didn't understand.

Major Bouchard took a small Swiss army knife out of her jacket pocket, opened it up, and gave it to Marianne.

"I'll boost you up Marianne. Move along the pipe until you find the end of a section, then pry the fittings apart with the knife."

Just as predicted, Marianne found the divide and, surprisingly easily, cut a hole in the tin pipe.

"Keep cutting as round as possible."

When Marianne had cut around the full circumference

of the pipe, one end fell down a foot or so. The other part didn't move, except there now was a large round hole.

"What do I do now?" asked Marianne as Major Bouchard lowered her down.

"Well, ma chérie, we pile the chair on top of the chesterfield and I help you to scamper into the pipe."

"Good, but where will that take me?"

"Not far. A few feet. Into the next room. But you will be surprised at the room. Just find another attachment, cut a hole, break part of the pipe down, and lower yourself through the hole into the room."

"But I won't have you there. It's a long way down!"

"I think you'll find something there you can stand on." For the first time, Major Bouchard's face broke into a smile. "Once down, get into the main corridor, approach the first enlisted man you see, and ask for a key."

Marianne looked horrified, but she obeyed the firm order. Up she went, and crawled a few feet. Where two pipes met, she cut through easily, then pushed down one segment of the pipe and lowered herself to a white porcelain object just below her. It was the top of a urinal, a men's washroom. She smiled. Renée really did know her blueprints. Luckily, no men were there.

Marianne left the washroom and turned right, running into a sitting soldier who was guarding the detention room. He was half asleep at this hour in the morning, but not so drowsy as to miss her. He grabbed her right arm and spun her around, muttering, "Your friend. Where is she?"

"Still inside," stammered Marianne.

At this, the young soldier produced a key with his other hand and opened the door. He saw an empty room, with the chair perched on the couch and a hole in the ceiling duct. Leaving the key in the door lock, he took out his revolver with his free hand and dragged Marianne into the room with the other.

The door closed.

The last thing the guard saw was the tall figure of Major Renée Bouchard standing behind the door. Her right arm shot out and hit him in the solar plexus. He doubled up and fell to the floor without a sound.

"I'm sure those cute little abs will be a bit bruised when our boy wakes up, but he'll be OK. I bet he won't tell the boys that a woman hit him in the stomach."

Marianne was in awe.

"Come on. Don't just stand there. Follow me."

Marianne followed her back down the corridor, past the stairs they had come down, to another flight of stairs at the far end of the building. They went up two flights and emerged through a door that opened to the outside. Marianne was about to push at it.

"Wait, Marianne. No sense telling them where we went out of this complex. Let's keep them guessing."

Major Bouchard went down the hall about thirty feet, poked at something in the wall, and eventually opened a box. Then she hit a fuse switch and the lights went off. "You can open the door now. The alarm's not working for a few minutes."

The two of them stepped out onto a narrow piece of grass next to a long cement runway. A lone F16 fighter jet from the Canadian Air Force slowly taxied by them, and they ducked under its wing, holding their hands to their ears to block the scream of the jet engine as much as possible.

The aircraft wasn't large, but it was enough to shield them from the view of the tower and the main section of the building opposite.

Slowly, painstakingly, gagging from the smell of the jet fuel and almost deaf from the roar of the engine, the two women stayed in the airplane's shadow to the corner of a metal fence, where the jet turned to the main runway. They slid into a ditch, still holding their ears as the engine revved up and the plane whined down the runway and took off. Marianne would never forget looking at the round engine glow like a small sun as it faded away.

"My God," she panted, "what's next?"

"We climb the fence, my dear. It's back to boot camp."

It wasn't as hard as it first looked. Marianne felt her body shaking. She bit her tongue slightly, pursed her lips, took a deep breath, and got up and over the metal fence.

"Let's get your car, gas it up, and get the hell out of here to Edmonton," shouted Major Bouchard. Suddenly they were laughing, and they slapped their right hands together, palms up.

CHAPTER 19

THERE IS NO WHITE HOUSE IN CANADA. THE PRIME minister lives in a rambling mansion at 24 Sussex Drive on the banks of the Ottawa River, about a kilometre from Parliament Hill. Here he entertains and sees special visitors. Like any other MP, he keeps an office at the House of Commons where he does his daily work.

Prime Minister MacKenzie was an early riser. These days he was having trouble sleeping because of bouts of prolonged coughing. The more he tried to hide the cough in public, the more it seemed to break out in private.

Sitting in a small sunlit room overlooking the river, he took the coffee cup with its foaming milk from his private secretary, Adrian Horgan. "Sir, you didn't want me to bring in the morning papers?"

"No, Adrian. You were right when you told me to avoid reading the daily press. I can only imagine what they're saying today. I'll read the press scan on the way to the Hill later."

A few minutes later Adrian came back into the room. "Your guests have arrived, Prime Minister."

"Sit them down in the dining room, give them coffee and orange juice, and let them wait a bit."

This sunlit room was MacKenzie's favourite spot, apart from his house on the Atlantic Ocean in Cape Breton. Here, alone, he could look across to the church spires of the little villages on the Quebec side of the river that divided English and French Canada. He was looking in a northerly direction and he could imagine kilometre upon kilometre of trees and rock stretching all the way to the arctic. The vastness, the north, the solitudes—it was part of every Canadian's heritage, he thought.

The Prime Minister pondered his fate. He hadn't been prime minister long and he knew he wouldn't last much longer. He didn't have time to create any big projects or solve any of Canada's interminable problems—Quebec, Aboriginal relations, north-south issues with the US, the correct balance between the public and private sector. He was unlikely to have any big international successes, although he would have liked, and indeed had some plans, to move in the area of greenhouse gases and other international environmental issues. He knew that Canada had entered the millennium on an environmental high. No, he thought, he would be satisfied if he, as the British philosopher Michael Oakshott had said, could keep the ship of state just floating, never mind bringing it to port. He had sailed small boats in Atlantic storms and done just that. But could he continue? Well, he had gotten through the parliamentary storms of the last two years and was still floating. Though barely.

One last glance at the early morning view and the outline of the Gatineau Hills on the horizon, with, to the east, the faint signs of the Laurentian Mountains, and he finished his cigarette, now the only one of the day as he had promised his doctor. He was ready to meet Senator Murphy and his group.

Senator Murphy, the Deputy Prime Minister, the Defence Minister, two backbench Alliance MPs, and an Alliance Party official were seated at a large, formally decorated table. They rose when the Prime Minister entered.

"Please, gentlemen, be seated. The staff will come

around and you can tell them how you like your eggs. And please help yourselves to some good old Canadian bacon."

The PM was smiling as he made himself comfortable in his chair and unfurled his white linen napkin. His guests were serious, to a man.

James Roberts, the Deputy PM, spoke first. "We will be straightforward with you, Sandy. We'd like the cabinet to move forward to next Tuesday on the change to the water policy, in the national interest. It's been delayed too long."

MacKenzie kept smiling and slowly buttered a piece of brown toast. Even more slowly, he reached for the marmalade. He seemed to take even longer to put it on his buttered toast. Then he took a slow bite out of the piece of toast and chewed it for awhile. His guests in the silence of the room could hear clearly the crunch of the chews. The PM could feel another spasm of coughing coming on. It was all he could do to hold it back. He reached down and took a drink of water from the crystal glass goblet near his coffee cup. "You know I reluctantly agreed to the trial run. Well, we got sued. The BC premier is hysterical. Some sensitive negotiations with First Nations have been broken off, and the environment groups are up in arms. Now you are asking me to escalate the first decision into a major policy change with God knows what policy implications. Gentlemen, I'm afraid it's not on."

Technically, in the Parliamentary system the Prime Minister is the first among equals, the other equals being the thirty or so other ministers in cabinet. Yet everyone, including all the people at the breakfast table, knew that if the PM wouldn't support a submission to cabinet, that submission wouldn't go through.

The Minister of Defence moved his chair back, making

a screeching sound on the wooden floor, coughed, and turned directly to face the Prime Minister. "The way I see it, Sandy"—he drew out the name—"you don't have no choice. You'll lose the support of us Alliance guys and that means the government goes down. Down like a dead duck."

There was a pause while the waiter filled the PM's cup with more coffee. He thanked him with a smile and then turned and moved his chair slightly so as to more directly face the Defence Minister.

"You know, I used to be a red Tory. You fellows don't even like the sound of that word. I could be again. The Liberals don't want an election now and the NDP will support me on this issue. No, the government wouldn't fall. It just might be made up a bit differently."

The Prime Minister paused, turned to whisper something to his private secretary and then turned to face his guests again.

"My car is ready to take me to the House so I will be saying good . . . "

Senator Murphy stood up and cut him off in mid sentence. "Sandy, we were afraid you might say that. But we think you should look at the alternatives. I don't know if you've read the morning newspapers, but we have. They contain some pretty terrible allegations. You could fall in one of the worst personal scandals in Canadian history. Not a very nice legacy. They've never been able to pin such things on past Canadian prime ministers, but they seem to have you, Sandy, as my western friends would say, in their gunsights. We'll give you today to think over our reasonable request. We may even be able to help you with your personal problems. Let us know by six PM."

Murphy pronounced the word "personal" very slowly and deliberately.

The rest of the table smiled and turned their heads towards the Prime Minister. John Alexander MacKenzie rose and looked directly down to Senator Murphy at the other end of the long table. He coughed slightly, but his look was firm and confident.

"Senator, I enjoy reading Canadian history. Perhaps you do too. A group of Prime Minister Diefenbaker's ministers came to him right at this very table and asked him to resign over his refusal to put nuclear weapons, armed Bomarcs, on Canadian soil to keep a commitment they thought we had to the Americans. They even had the audacity to offer him the position of Chief Justice of Canada. Dief told them to get lost. I'm sure when Sir John A. was drunk he must have had ministers wanting him to go. Laurier survived the resignation of Henri Bourassa and later his Quebec lieutenant. When John Turner resigned as Minister of Finance, Prime Minister Pierre Trudeau just shrugged. I will not be as direct as Prime Minister Diefenbaker or as nonchalant as Prime Minister Trudeau, but I can tell you this, Senator. In Canada nobody bullies or threatens a Prime Minister."

MacKenzie accepted his briefcase from Adrian Horgan and moved quickly towards the door. Just before leaving he stopped for a moment. "Good morning, gentlemen. See you later in the House."

And with that, the Prime Minister of Canada was gone.

CHAPTER **20**

DON HARRIS, THE PORTLY CHAIR OF THE HOUSE Finance Committee, looked around the packed committee room and, with his big Cheshire cat grin, raised his right hand, which contained his favourite gavel. He brought the gavel down on the green table with a loud thud.

Today, because of the sudden scheduling of this hearing and the fact that other committees were also sitting, the Finance Committee was holding its meeting in Room 250 of the East Block, one of the original buildings on Parliament Hill, the site of the office of John A. MacDonald, Canada's first prime minister. Guards claim the spirit of old Sir John still haunts the building.

"Order, order, this Finance Committee will come to order. We have already heard this morning from officials of the Privy Council office, as well as the Departments of Energy and the Environment, about Canada's water policy. I must admit I was surprised to learn that our water policy is in the process of changing."

The Chairman looked to his right, to the government side of the room.

"We will hear from the officials of the Finance and Agriculture Departments this afternoon. However, do I have the consent of the Committee to sit late this morning and into the early afternoon to hear from Senator George Murphy and employees of Western Energy, whom I understand want to appear now?"

As the debate continued in the committee, Senator Murphy and two of his staff waited in a small annex room.

The Senator had initially been surprised that the Finance Committee would actually hold a hearing on water, but he had determined to go on the offensive. He needed to keep control of events at this critical moment. He didn't want his allies to get cold feet. He thought to himself that MacKenzie would eventually collapse. In the end all politicians want to remain in office; they really don't want to rock the boat. He was surprised that MacKenzie had held out so long. And he still couldn't understand why MacKenzie had passed him over for cabinet. Why wasn't he Government Leader in the Senate? Hadn't he got the prick elected leader? If he were running the Government things would be very different. Canada needed a right wing revolution on the national level. The Alliance screwed it up because they got into abortion and all those crazy social issues. No, Canada had to be in the new global world economy or it would be left behind. Why didn't they listen to him? He lit another cigarette.

Back in the Finance Committee there was some murmuring among members. A Liberal member pressed a small button on the microphone in front of him and a small red light went on. "Mr. Chairman, this is a bit of an extraordinary procedure because we could end up sitting right into Question Period in the House."

"I'm sure they can get along without us for one day," the big chairman chuckled. The gavel came down again. "Hearing no dissent, we will begin. Call in the Senator."

Senator Murphy put out his cigarette and said to himself—Go on the offensive. When he sat down and spoke into the microphone, he did just that.

"It is in Canada's economic interests to open up water exports to the US. It is a logical extension of the Free Trade

Deal. Indeed, if committee members take the time to reread that deal, you will see in the energy provisions that Canada would benefit, would make a lot of money in energy exports—including water. We made a good business deal and we should exploit it. As a matter of fact, we should have a closer business association with the US, maybe even join the currencies. This is the twenty-first century and Canada has to be part of the new global economy."

The Senator's assistant touched his arm and he stopped talking abruptly.

"Perhaps I could take some questions, Mr. Chairman."

The questioning started with the Liberals, whose members pursued, to the delight of the Chair, questions about the impact on Western Canadian farmers. Then the Alliance member lobbed some softball questions at the Senator on free trade. The Chair announced it was the turn of the NDP member. A tall, thin, soft-spoken MP from Saskatchewan, Vic Sutherland, asked one question on agriculture, which was deceptively simple but clearly pinpointed the future danger to Canadian farmers if Canadian water was equally allocated or sold out to the Americans. Just as he was about to ask his second question, Clayton Greene entered the committee room and sat down at the table next to his colleague.

Senator Murphy's jaw fell. His face reddened. He jerked his head up and back to the right. His brown eyes opened wide and in a second narrowed down to almost a squint. He glared at Greene.

Sutherland continued, "I would like to have Mr. Greene complete our round of questioning."

"I will allow that but we will take a short break as the Chair has a short rendezvous. Adjourned for five minutes."

Don Harris banged the gavel, turned to his clerk, and asked directions to the washroom. At the same moment a page approached Clayton Greene. "Mr. Greene, there's a telephone call for you." Greene saw Murphy pass a note to another page as Greene went to a small table in the corner of the committee room where a telephone had been plugged in for the meeting. He picked up the receiver.

"Clay, it's me."

"Marianne, are you okay?" He could detect the tension in her voice.

"Clay, I can't tell you the whole story now. I'm at a gas station almost halfway between Cold Lake and Edmonton. Renée is unbelievable. They actually locked us up, but she managed to get us out of the room and she knew an underground way out of the base. We're on our way to Edmonton and we've got to move it. This is big stuff. They have an operation—Murphy, the Deputy PM, the Defence Minister, and some Yanks. Code name is Operation D'Arcy McGee. They have a military force back-up. I've got to go, Renée is urging me. Be careful, Clay."

"Marianne, call me from Edmonton. And get back here as soon as you can. I *will* be careful."

The Chair was just about to lower the gavel again. Greene's head was swimming. D'Arcy McGee? That name was so familiar. Something to do with journalism? He couldn't put his finger on it. He returned to the table and the Chair recognized him for the remaining time in the NDP round of questioning. Senator Murphy glowered at Greene

"Senator, we have been through questions about exports of Canadian water by tanker and we agreed to disagree. Now I want to ask you about 'overland' exports. Do you see a need to export Canadian water overland? By that, I mean by diverting Canadian waters."

Senator Murphy, who had now regained his own composure, looked up at Greene and tried to answer calmly. "As a matter of fact, if the demand were there, I see no reason to exclude what you call overland exports or export by water diversion."

"Senator, wouldn't that violate the policies of at least three provincial governments and the national government of this country? Wouldn't that clash with Aboriginal land claims and wouldn't that run smack into the opposition of every environmental group in the country?"

The Senator didn't take the bait and simply smiled. "If it were in Canada's national interest, I'm sure that opposition could be overcome. It happened after the great debate on free trade."

Greene decided he had nothing to lose by being blatantly confrontational. "Senator, isn't it a fact that the company you control has resorted to violence to pursue its goals? You've been exporting water by tanker, skirting provincial laws and manipulating national laws, and you want to divert rivers to make more money. In fact, aren't you and your friends simply traitors to Canada?"

The Senator began to turn red again, but before he lost his temper, he appeared to steady himself. He paused and gave Greene an icy stare. "This is a peaceful country, Mr. Greene. Violence is never used to bring political change against the will of other businessmen, other political interests, or against other MPs."

Some committee members seemed to find the last part of the answer rather odd, and Greene's colleague on his immediate right, the Saskatchewan MP, interjected. "Not exactly never—the Fenians did assassinate Thomas D'Arcy McGee."

It was meant as a light interjection, and some committee members laughed.

"Mr. Greene, you have a few more minutes," said the Chairman.

But Clayton Greene was trying to still his mind and think. Of course. McGee had been a father of Canadian Confederation, and he had indeed been shot by an Irish American, just off Parliament Hill on what was now the Sparks Street Mall. He had been shot because . . . because he was against the Fenians, the Irish Amercans who were planning to invade Canada. Wasn't this use of violence similar to what Murphy and his guys were doing to get their way?

"Mr. Greene, you can continue."

Greene ignored the Chair for an instant and glanced towards his security guard at the end of the room. A second man was standing beside him, quietly talking, and suddenly the guard nodded and left the room. Greene recognized the new face—a face he had last seen, briefly, behind the wheel of a car on the Squamish Highway.

D'Arcy McGee. Suddenly Clay knew what was going to happen.

He looked up at the clock. The Committee was going to sit right into Question Period, which would begin in ten minutes. Now he knew. There was a killer loose in the East Block and he could be after the Prime Minister.

"I have no further questions, Mr. Chairman."

Senator Murphy looked a bit dumbfounded, as did the Chair.

Greene quickly turned to his colleague and whispered, "Vic, put another question on agriculture and water. I've got to get out of here. I have to get back to the House."

With that he got up and slowly moved to the one exit door behind the Chair. Once outside the committee room he turned right, then left past a row of pictures of old senators, and right again to the top of a stairway. He quickly descended two flights of carpeted stairs past a Senate guard and down another stairway to the basement of the East Block, then hurried down a corridor. He could hear his own heart pounding. At the end of the corridor he opened a steel door and found himself at the entrance to a narrow tunnel that led off at a diagonal to the door.

This utility tunnel, with a series of small pipes running along the left side of the ceiling, connects the East Block to the Centre Block of the Parliament Buildings. The walls and floor of the tunnel are painted grey, and the white pipes are marked at intervals with red ribbons so people who use the tunnel don't hit their heads. A person of average height has to duck slightly to get through. The tunnel goes gently uphill, swinging left after the first fifteen feet or so, then continues for a distance before swinging right and again left.

Clay saw a yellow sign that read "Wet Floor/Plancher Mouille," illuminated by low lights on his left that barely lit up the grey stone floor.

As Greene was about to turn the first corner in the tunnel, he heard someone else opening the door from the East Block basement. Greene paused and looked back, recognizing the man who had taken the place of his security guard. The man had a nine-millimetre Browning automatic pistol in his hand, and he fired it just as Clay darted around the corner. The shot ricocheted off the wall.

Greene began to run. He zigzagged like a fullback going through another team's defence. This was the crucial time and Greene knew it. If he could just get to the next bend in the tunnel . . .

Pierre should have had a clear shot in the long straight-away, but he hit his head on the roof of the tunnel. Clay's side-to-side movement also threw him off. He took aim and fired again, but missed, barely. He aimed again and took one step forward to steady the shot, but slipped on the wet floor and the shot went high. It tore into what looked like white asbestos padding on the pipe near Greene's right ear.

Greene rounded the last corner and bounded another fifteen feet to another door that opened onto a short stair-way up into the bowels of the Centre Block. Its basement pipes were large and green. A small set of grey steel stairs led him up to the ground floor of the Senate of Canada.

There were a number of large red-leather chesterfields, above which hung a huge portrait of King Edward VII, who seemed to be looking down right at him. Greene had never been so glad to see a monarch. He took a deep breath. Just ahead were some Senate guards. They looked startled at his haste, but he composed himself, smiled, and proceeded down the main corridor west towards the lobby of the House of Commons, fast.

CHAPTER **21**

CLAY SAW ROB FAULKNER WAITING FOR HIM IN THE foyer at the entrance to the lobby of the House.

"Is the Prime Minister in the House?"

"Geez, Clay, you look like you just came from the gym and skipped the shower!"

"Is the Prime Minister in the House?"

"Nope, he ducked QP today."

Greene looked puzzled, a little disoriented, Rob thought. He motioned for Rob to come into the Opposition Lobby with him. Rob flashed his pass at the guard on the door and kept on talking. "The House is going wild. The Deputy PM is refusing to answer questions on the scandal. He says wait for the PM. The Speaker seems to be going along with the government line. The opposition is furious. I expect all after-noon will be taken up with points of privilege. You know the shtick. There's a scheduled vote on the order paper just after six PM. Jesus, the government could go down."

"What's happening outside, Rob?"

"The town's going a bit ape, what with a sitting PM caught in a scandal. Hasn't happened since John A. got kick-backs on the building of the transcontinental railway and those moneys went to the party. They tried to pin Mulroney after he left office, but that went nowhere."

"Nor should it have," interrupted Clay.

He still thinks like a lawyer, thought Rob. He was tempted to comment, but continued. "Now all the papers are on the story and the TV vultures are waiting. The 'scorps,' the scorpions in the media are ready to pounce. You know how you often say that it takes time for a story to percolate from here out to the country at large. Well, this one's getting out there quickly."

"What about the vote?"

"The opposition has an amendment of non-confidence on the government's budget. The Bloc has tacked on a sub-amendment. Since it covers a major financial bill, the budget, it is deemed a vote of confidence. If the motion, the sub-amendment, carries the MacKenzie government is finished."

Bill Allen, a Manitoba member sitting in the Opposition Lobby, a large man with a rather scraggly beard finally turning white, couldn't resist interrupting. "Greene, I was here, right here, in 1979 when a young NDP MP named Bob Rae proposed a similar motion to a Liberal non-confidence motion on the John Crosbie budget. Damn, the thing passed, to the surprise of some of us. Prime Minister Joe Clark dissolved the House the next day and called an election, which he lost. Looking back, we blew it. We had the Liberal Party in opposition and leaderless, on their deathbed. All we had to do was keep their head under the water an extra minute and they would have been gone—and we the clear party of the left and eventually government. We won't make that mistake again."

Greene was still having trouble focusing. "Is it really going to pass, Rob?"

"I don't know. I do know that you have a caucus at five PM. You look like you need a coffee now."

Faulkner was right. The time after Question Period was taken up by numerous motions, Speaker's rulings, and endless procedural debate that went on all afternoon, right up to six PM.

Greene returned to his office. After instructing Ann to put through only calls from Marianne, he closed his door. Never, ever, in his life had he felt unsafe, insecure, anywhere in Canada, but this afternoon, in the capital of the country, in the office of a member of Parliament, he felt that anything could happen, anyone could come through that door and take him away. Could he trust the guards? The Hill guards, yes. He felt they were safe. The police? Maybe not. Could he now trust the army? No. What a thought. He was actually shaking.

I should get out of here, flee, and get as far away as possible from this place. But I can't. What would Uncle Jim do?

He slowly closed the curtains on his windows, flicked on the desk lamp, put out the overhead light, and tried to take a few quiet minutes to meditate, to get inside himself and to still his mind. Jim had taught him as a boy that when he got overexcited he had to pause and renew his body's energy. He could still see Jim standing over the little boy on the grassy tundra at the muskrating camp in the Old Crow flats. He remembered Jim's gentle lecture.

As he tried to focus, his mind, however, kept jumping around. Why am I pushing this? I'm going to get myself killed. God, they've tried three times already, and now I can't even trust my guards. Why don't I just back off? Forces beyond my control are at work. I just want to be out skiing, out in the mountains. Where is Marianne? I have a feeling we're in too deep to get out of it now . . .

He thought about how he had first learned to still his mind. As a teenager he had worked on an archeological dig near Old Crow, and a shaman there had taught him a song. He concentrated on the words of that song and began to hum it. Gradually his mind stilled and he felt more in control. The meditation didn't last long—about twenty minutes—but it replenished his energy and helped to unite his mind, his heart, and his spirit. His fear wasn't gone, but he had at least stopped shaking.

As he stretched out his arms and then his legs, a strange thought crossed his mind. Who did I expect to come through the door? At that moment he thought of King Charles I bursting into the English House of Commons, and some of the members fleeing by the back door. He shook his head slightly as the bell on the Peace Tower struck five times.

On the other side of Parliament Hill, in Senator Murphy's plush office, a group of men were watching the Parliamentary feed on a large TV. All they saw was interminable procedural debate arising out of the PM's absence from the Question Period. On a smaller TV set behind the senator's massive desk, Newsworld was preparing to carry the vote live, and a panel of experts was talking about a "Parliamentary crisis."

In a large caucus room in the West Block, the NDP caucus was meeting to decide how they would vote. Jack Hepburn had not spoken. He looked even paler than usual. The House Leader chaired the meeting, and the feeling of the meeting seemed to be to vote for the sub-amendment on the budget, the Bloc motion, and thus against the government.

Clay was about to be recognized to speak when his cell phone rang in his pocket. A few members looked at him with annoyance; he could feel the cold stare of the Whip, and he quickly excused himself from the caucus room.

"Marianne, thank God."

"Clay, you remember those pull-out phones on the back of the aircraft seats. Well, this old Air Canada jet still has them. We're on our way to Ottawa. We're on Air Canada flight 711 and we arrive in Ottawa at 8:45 tonight."

"I'll be there to get you," Clay began, but Marianne broke in.

"You won't believe this, but a group of Native elders are on the plane and I have made friends with a sweet old man who wants to talk to you."

"Clayton."

Greene immediately recognized the voice and his spirits were lifted. It was his Uncle Jim.

"They are going to give us, give Old Crow, a medal to mark the sixtieth anniversary of our war effort while some of the old ones are still alive. We're going to meet the Governor General."

Clay smiled. This was part of the GG's efforts to reach out of Ottawa to Canadians in even the remotest parts of the country. And it was about time the country recognized Old Crow's tremendous efforts during World War II, when the small population contributed soldiers, meat, and knitted goods for the war effort.

"I thought you couldn't move around Uncle, couldn't hunt?"

"Just because I can't hunt them caribou doesn't mean I can't travel anyways."

Greene laughed and felt good inside, felt good that Jim was still there for him and would be near him, especially now. "I'll pick you up at the airport."

"The Governor General is going to do that, Clay, but I'll

talk to you soon." A big belly laugh came through the phone. "Here's Marianne."

"Clay, another surprise. I'll be dressed in black and white."

Did he hear a giggle? The phone went dead.

Greene hurried back into caucus and the House Leader called on him to speak. He rose slowly and, thinking of Jim and his common sense about everything, he looked around so that he had made eye contact with most members of the caucus. "You heard from Bill Allen about the past and our part in the defeat of a previous minority government. Like all Manitobans, Bill's got good political judgment. That's why he's been here so long." Some of the caucus members smiled and the tension was relieved a bit.

Clay continued, "Let me put his point another way. We don't have to do what's always been done—vote automatically for a non-confidence motion against the government because we are 'the Opposition.' Let's look at politics in a new way. For God's sake, let's put aside the argument that I heard here this afternoon, that we shouldn't support a Bloc motion because, well, they're the Bloc. We are bigger than that. Instead let's consider whether the motion, if passed, will serve the cause of Canada."

There were a few audible coughs now in an otherwise very silent room. They were listening. Greene could feel it. The picture of Prime Minister MacKenzie sitting in that little café in Chelsea flashed in his mind. He continued speaking: "Look, the PM, MacKenzie, in spite of the recent water Orders-in-Council, has shown a great deal of openness to environmental causes, and they're the really big issues we have to face as a country, as a world. We can't predict the outcome of an election. The Alliance stalled in the last election campaign, but they could come back as a majority and move the country far to the right."

He took a sip of water from the glass in front of him and hoped they didn't notice how unsteady he held it. He sucked in his breath and continued.

"If you watch a bear fishing, you'll see that there are different ways to catch the salmon. There is a time to wait and a time to pounce. Now is the time to wait. We need to see how this scandal plays out, and that will happen tomorrow or Monday."

There was a lot more Greene could have said, but it would take too long and probably sound too far-fetched for the caucus members. He chose not to for the moment.

There was one more speaker on the list, the caucus's most radical member, openly gay, outspoken, who had even spent time in jail for one of his causes. He despised the present government, so Greene was stunned when he said, "I want to agree with Clay Greene." The MP went on to repeat in a succinct way the points Greene and others had made and added that he felt "in his gut" that there were bigger issues being played out that would soon emerge. They therefore should wait until things became clearer before bringing down the government. Greene was grateful for the support and for the remarkable insight.

The straw vote was close, but the caucus voted not to support the sub-amendment.

The occupants of Senator Murphy's office did not, of course, know what was going on in the NDP or Liberal caucus meetings. They had another agenda.

"Well, he has ten minutes left to call," growled the senator.

"MacKenzie will fold. He's got no choice." It was the voice of the Defence Minister. "The heifer is roped."

They all helped themselves to a drink of scotch and filled the room with small talk.

At one minute to six, the senator's phone rang.

Murphy put his hand on the receiver, but didn't pick it up. He let it ring a second time. There wasn't another sound in the office. On the third ring he slowly picked up the white receiver. "Murphy here." There was a slight pause and then simply "I see, I see."

With that the Senator put the phone down gently, rubbed his chin with his right hand, and faced the people in his office. "That was the PM's chief of staff. The message is no thanks and MacKenzie is going into the House to vote."

The clock in the Peace Tower tolled six times.

The Senator clicked up the volume on his TV set. Members were taking their seats in the House of Commons. The senior clerk took a sheet of paper to the seated Speaker, who put on his glasses, then stood up and, after waiting a few seconds for silence, read the sub-amendment.

"All those in favour, please stand up."

As members stood row by row, the three clerks scrambled to check off their names as the Speaker recognized each by name. Once their names were recorded, the members sat down. All the Bloc members stood for the Ayes. Some Liberals stood, but every other Liberal seat was empty. The few Independents in the House also stood in favour of the motion. The New Democrats stayed seated and then rose for the Nays. There were a surprisingly large number of absent members, including many from the government benches and a handful of Alliance MPs, including the Deputy Premier and the Defence Minister. Prime Minister Sandy MacKenzie was in the House. He stood and voted Nay.

The senior clerk passed the tally up to the Speaker who stood and announced: "For the Ayes 94. For the Nays 125."

The government was still standing.

The government House Leader rose to formally move to adjourn the House, normally a routine motion. But unexpectedly, both the Liberal and NDP House Leaders rose to call for a continuation of the procedural debate. The government House Leader called this "absurd," and the Liberal House Leader, an old veteran of Parliament, called for a "division." The bells of the House rang again, and members filed back in, only this time many Liberal members who had been absent for the vote joined them.

On this vote the Bloc, the Liberals, the NDP, and the Independents all voted against the government. Eighty-four voted for adjournment, while 140 voted to continue.

The Speaker then called the next member on his list on the procedural debate. Above the din and the cries of "order," it became clear the government couldn't even adjourn the House. The opposition, like a cat, would play with the government mouse for a few hours and then allow it the adjournment. The kill would come tomorrow or the next day.

Senator Murphy and his friends watched the proceedings with looks of disgust and disdain. Finally the Deputy PM spoke up. "Well, Senator, what do we do now?"

Murphy took a long drag on his cigarette, put it out slowly in the round black ashtray on the left of his desk, and looked up to face his colleagues. "It's Plan B, I'm afraid."

Looking at the door to his office, the Senator noticed that two tall men had silently entered while the others were watching the House on TV. Addressing the man who had pursued Clay Greene through the tunnel, Murphy added, "And it will be the full Plan B, Pierre." The emphasis was on the word "full."

CHAPTER **22**

A GREEN FORD VAN APPROACHED THE SERVICE entrance of the West Block and parked between two House of Commons vans that were unloading paper products. Rob Faulkner flicked open the automatic lock on the sliding passenger door.

Clayton Greene emerged from the side door of the West Block, slid open the van door, jumped in, and pulled the door closed. He lay on the floor behind the seats. The van left Parliament Hill by the exit near the Confederation Building and turned left across Wellington Street to Bank Street. As Greene looked up he could see the tower offices of the Bank of Canada. About ten blocks down Bank Street, and after a few red lights and one brief period of parking at a meter, Rob finally motioned to Greene to get into the front seat.

"After what you told me, Clay, I borrowed my brother's van. My God, you look pretty laid-back for the guy at the centre of a storm. A hurricane I'd call it."

"Let's say I'm trying to stay focused, Rob. Besides, I'm looking forward to picking up Marianne and seeing my uncle again."

It took them twenty minutes to reach the airport in the light evening traffic. As the van rounded the curve past the departures section and pulled up to arrivals, they saw a large black limousine with red Crown licence plates idling by the exit door. A number of policemen were standing near the car, and two motorcycle cops were just in front of it.

"Jeez. This only happens when the Queen arrives," exclaimed Rob.

They could see the Governor General herself out among the people. Two reporters were interviewing her on the run. She was making herself very visible.

"I'm here tonight to welcome the First Nations elders from the north and west. Tomorrow I will honour them on behalf of all Canadians at a special ceremony at Rideau Hall. You know it was one of my predecessors who persuaded the government of the day to make a formal apology for past actions against Native people, like the residential school system and other abuses. With the success of the Nisga'a treaty in BC, I believe we are finally seeing the beginning of a new relationship." She smiled her warm smile.

Rob Faulkner proceeded in the traffic line slowly past the GG's car. One of the motorcycle cops put up his hand. The other came quickly to Greene's side of the van.

"Mr. Greene?"

"Yes."

The policeman opened the van door, put a hand on Greene's shoulder, and firmly but quietly said, "Come with me, please."

Greene hesitated but then slid out of the van's front seat. The policeman took him by the right arm, led him across a lane of traffic, opened the back door of the limo, put his other hand on top of Greene's head, and gently pushed him down and in. It was like a TV news scene, where the arresting cops put the crook into the cruiser, but there were no cameras here because all eyes were on the Governor General, near the airport door away from the limo.

Inside, sitting in the jump seat was a man in a braid uniform. "Don't worry, you'll be safe here." Greene recognized the GG's aide-de-camp.

Greene wondered, but he held his tongue. The back windows of the big stretch limo were blacked out, so he couldn't see what was going on inside the airport, but he expected that the Edmonton plane had landed. A few minutes later he heard some noise and cheering, and looking out the front window ahead and slightly to the side, he saw camera flashes illuminating a group of Native people, some in the ceremonial headdress of the plains Indians. In the middle of the group was the diminutive Governor General.

The back door suddenly opened, catching him by surprise, and the same policeman gently pushed two nuns into the back seat with him. Greene gasped.

"Ever kiss a nun?"

It was Marianne. She hugged him tightly and then pulled away. "Clay, this is Major Renée Bouchard. Renée, Clayton Greene, MP."

Greene quickly regained his composure and smiled. "Black and white, eh? Welcome to Ottawa, sister. Or, should I say, sisters?"

They laughed, but then Marianne became serious. "You can't imagine what we've both been through. Renée's wonderful. She saved my life. And this, this dress up, was her idea. Her sister is in a convent at St. Albert near Edmonton. We borrowed the habits. We figured they would be looking for Renée. We came in with the Native people. A soldier at the Edmonton airport even tipped his beret to us as I guess he thought it was natural for us to be with the Natives. No one has bothered us since. The police put us in this limo in a flash."

The back door of the limo opened and the Governor General got in. They were silent as the big car moved off behind the motorcycle escort. Clayton Greene looked directly at the Governor General. She smiled at him ever so gently and he looked down.

"We must all summon up all the courage we can. The Chinese letters for danger also show opportunity. So, let's remember that. We're first going to stop at the Chateau Laurier Hotel. That's where the elders are staying. I'll get out there. After three minutes, Mr. Greene, you and Marianne will get out of the car and go into the hotel through the front door; you will walk to the far hall through the lobby, turn right, and proceed to the elevator. Go down one floor and then out the side door onto Nicholas Street. Renée, my dear, you stay put. We have much to talk about and work to do later."

The Chateau Laurier, one of Canada's great railway hotels, sits like a castle just past the Parliament Buildings on the bank of the Rideau Canal. As the limousine pulled into the narrow entrance of the Chateau, a bus containing the Native elders pulled in behind it. The two vehicles filled the narrow driveway.

The Governor General slipped out of her car to be greeted by the hotel manager. Her driver closed the door quickly. Her aide left by the other door. A Mountie in full red serge accompanied the official party into the hotel. Inside the limo, Marianne and Renée slipped their black habits over their heads. Both women were casually dressed.

Marianne gave Renée a worried look and opened her mouth to speak, but before a word came out, Renée said, "I'm in good hands now, as you can see. I'll be alright. When the GG returns I'll go with her. We've some catching up to do. You and Clayton must go somewhere safe tonight."

"Can you imagine feeling like this here in Ottawa?" Marianne wanted to cry. Instead she reached over and hugged Renée.

Both women looked up when the driver opened his door, got out, lit a cigarette, looked around, and quickly opened the rear door. Clayton and Marianne scurried into the lobby of the Chateau, moved through it in a few seconds past tourists, turned right to the small bank of elevators, and got in the first open one.

It seemed to take forever for the door to shut, and when it did they saw themselves reflected in the ornate mirrors on the elevator walls. Two unfamiliar, haggard people looked back. In a few seconds they reached the basement and headed for the side door of the hotel. Rob Faulkner's green van was parked in front of the exit.

As they reached the glass doors, a small figure came out of the shadows. Clay pushed Marianne to the other side and tensed.

"It's only me, Clay. She told me to catch you before you go and tell you not to worry." Jim Sichinly was smiling.

"Uncle!" Greene threw his arms around the old man and hugged him. As he drew his arms away he remembered Marianne standing next to him. "Did you meet Marianne, Uncle?"

The old man's smile got even bigger.

"We met on the airplane," Marianne told him. "Your uncle is charming. After I talked about our friendship, he invited us to visit his fishing camp. Isn't that wonderful?"

"You still have a fish camp on the Porcupine River, Uncle?" The words escaped Greene's mouth a little too quickly.

The old man smiled and winked at Greene. Marianne didn't see the wink.

Rob Faulkner came in the exit door, holding the keys to the van. Marianne moved towards the door, towards Rob. Greene held back so only he could hear Jim's soft voice.

"Clayton, I used to go with my Inuit cousins to hunt the big bear, that polar one. They used to tell me they had one big rule: 'Be a hunter, never be the hunted.' Second rule was to keep your eyes open."

Greene looked at him intently, lovingly, and tears came to his eyes. He held back. "You enjoy Ottawa, Uncle. Rob here will take you back to the reception, and I'll try to attend the ceremony tomorrow if I can."

Jim looked at him. "I have only one question."

"What's that, Uncle?"

"Does this joint serve caribou?"

CHAPTER **23**

AS THE GREEN FORD VAN CROSSED THE INTERPROVINcial Bridge into Quebec, Marianne looked over at Clayton Greene. This was not the confident man she had seen at Whistler. His face was flushed, his stare directly ahead on the road, both his hands tightly gripping the wheel. She finally broke the silence. "We're quite the pair, aren't we? Like two bank robbers on the lam."

Greene wiped a bit of sweat off his forehead and turned slightly to look at her. "You're right. Here we are, sneaking away. Not exactly Whistler, is it?"

"I was thinking the same thing," she said in a low voice. "Where are we going anyway, Clay?"

"My friends, Darcy and Nancy Rosslands have a cottage, a log house actually, in the Gatineau. It's right on the Gatineau River. And it's relatively remote. No one knows we're going there."

Greene then asked her if she had her luggage from the plane.

"Rob was good enough to put it in this car's trunk, along with a bag that arrived from your Vancouver office."

Greene gave her an odd look, but kept driving. Twenty minutes later they left the freeway at the same exit Clay had taken to meet the Prime Minister at L'Agaric restaurant, but this time he turned east instead, then north up the river road for two kilometres. The Ford rolled slowly over railway tracks and past a series of dirt driveways to the little cottages now closed up for the winter. Marianne could see the outline of a large log house. Behind the house and down through a rock garden shimmered the Gatineau River, in the moonlight looking more like a small lake than a river.

Greene reached above the door, took down a small key, turned it in the lock, opened the door, and switched on the light.

Marianne saw a large living room framed by walls of raw shining logs. A few rugs were scattered here and there on the floor. A kitchen opened up to the left, and directly across the room was the fireplace that heated the house.

"How about a scotch, Marianne?"

Greene rummaged through the kitchen cupboards and found a decanter and two crystal glasses. Marianne began to raise her glass in a toast and then lowered it awkwardly. This wasn't the time for toasting. Instead she continued her exploration of the house. In an alcove opposite the fireplace was a piano, and as Greene moved to put wood into the fireplace and light the kindling, Marianne sat down at the piano and began to play a showtune, "If We Only Had Love."

A slight smile came to Greene's face. "Jacques Brel, one of my favourites. I can still remember hearing Anne Mortifee and Leon Bibb singing that song at the Arts Club in Vancouver years ago." He stretched out on a white couch near the fireplace. "You play well, where did you learn?"

"My mother insisted."

"I know so little about you, Marianne. Do you . . . are you in a relationship?"

She stopped playing and looked up. "I was married, Clay."

Greene took a long sip of his scotch.

"And he was a lawyer too. Political as well. A committed sovereignist."

"That was a problem?"

"Not really. In Quebec you learn to live with, how should I put it, differences, even in the family. No, he was my first real love. I was quiet. I was learning my trade as a journalist. He was the life of the party. And what a party it was, at least for him."

"And then?"

"And then, one night I came home a day early from an out-of-town assignment. There was a small table in the living room, a glass on it with a razor blade and straw beside it and the residue of white powder on the plate. Then I went into the bedroom. He was in bed with Madeleine, my best girlfriend. When I left him, I vowed I would be on my own for awhile."

"You liked being on your own?"

"At first no. I tried to date again, but I felt awkward. I was, am, too intellectual, too quiet, and I felt somehow I couldn't trust the guy, any guy. I gradually began to like being on my own."

She saw Greene looking at her in a puzzled sort of way. He hesitated and then spoke softly: "Marianne, I must tell you, I was suspicious of you at first."

This time it was Marianne's turn to look puzzled.

"After my Quebec trip. I wondered . . . it seemed possible that you might have tipped the bad guys off. I told you where I was going, remember? Same was true of Toronto."

"Clay, you've got to be kidding."

"It seemed far-fetched, but everything was so unreal that anything seemed possible. But I have to tell you, when I was numb with cold in that St Lawrence water and when I felt myself slipping away, I thought about you."

Her smile came back. "At Cold Lake I thought about you too."

"And at Whistler . . ." The words came out of their mouths at the same time. They both laughed.

"So you were feeling some of the same emotions I felt," he asked as the logs in the fire crackled.

"Yes."

Marianne moved over to sit on the couch and faced him.

As they looked at each other, Greene's eyes lost their tiredness. "Speaking of Whistler, are you up for an outing? Something I love doing?"

She looked surprised, but nodded.

Greene walked over to an antique Quebec blanket box, opened it and took out two Cowichan wool sweaters. "Here, put this on and come with me."

He led her outside onto a wooden porch, and then down a path half covered by dead maple leaves through a wilted hillside garden towards the river. At the edge of the water a small boathouse appeared out of the river mist. A red wooden canoe lay on a dock beside it.

Greene turned the canoe right side up and slid it into the water.

"Have you gone crazy, Clay?"

"No, you'll see. Come on. Can you paddle a canoe?"

"I may be a 'habitante,' Clay, but yes, I can paddle a canoe."

He tossed her a paddle and then slowly got into the canoe. As the canoe slid out into the current, Marianne could see an outline of the rocky opposite shore reflected in the moonlight.

"It's beautiful, Clay. You'd think this was a lake. We could be anywhere in Northern Canada."

"My friends who own the log house are on an external

affairs posting in the Caribbean and I keep an eye on their place for them. The river and the rocks of the Canadian Shield remind me of the Canadian North. When I'm really stressed out I come up here to canoe. I've always wanted to share the feeling with someone." Greene paused in mid-stroke and looked at her. "Am I being crazy?"

"Not at all. Clay, I understand what you're going through."

"Marianne, at first I was scared. I'm still afraid, but I'm also angry—angry that I can't trust people in my own country, angry at the violence and at the corruption."

"But can they succeed, Clay?"

"I don't think so. The Canadian people are not stupid. And mostly we're a progressive people. We're northerners, not American. We're still defining ourselves, but I think we know where we want to go."

"Where's that?"

"We want our kids, I think, to be citizens of the world, right up there with our American friends, but a little kinder, a little gentler, more compassionate. Our weakness, I suppose, is that we don't realize we've developed a distinct culture both in English and in French. We need to have more confidence."

As she watched Greene put his paddle back in the water and begin to stroke, she wished her father could have heard that and have understood her wish to be part of a bigger world.

"Sorry, Marianne I can be a bit of a dreamer sometimes. Let's paddle around this little island. It'll take us past the Gatineau Yacht Club and back to the house."

"Clay." Now it was Marianne who stopped paddling.

"Yes?"

"I never thought I'd want to, well, open up to someone again. Half of me is really scared."

"And the other half?"

"Loves it."

They both laughed and began to paddle hard. In a few minutes they glided into the boathouse dock.

"Clay, the journalist in me, the analyst part, is coming back."

"What do you mean by that?"

"I mean, we have to consider where we go now. How do we deal with these guys and what's going to happen to us? Remember, we are really in hiding."

Greene turned the canoe over on the dock and returned the paddles to the boathouse without answering. They retraced their steps up the hill to the main house, and when they were finally settled on the couch again, he spoke. "Normally my mother's people, my people, when they were in trouble, consulted their elders. Uncle Jim, I suspect, is probably pleasantly asleep now."

Marianne looked across at him. "Clay, what about your father? Is he still alive?"

Greene frowned. "I haven't talked to him in years, but yes, he's still alive, living with his new wife in Cape Breton."

"Why haven't you talked to him?"

"He's a cop, sort of old school. Got into spying and all that stuff."

"So he disowned you for your radical, well, almost radical, politics?"

Greene's frown lightened somewhat. "No, he had abandoned me before that. After my Mum died he drank a lot and wasn't really there when I needed him. Later, when he had sorted out his own life, he did give me some good advice when I got arrested in Vancouver at the anti-clearcutting demo. I didn't like his work with the RCMP, spying on people like the Cubans and the Chinese. I thought it was a waste of time."

"But that was his job, wasn't it?"

"I suppose so."

Marianne saw Greene's expression soften, as if his mind were somewhere else. She persisted. "Why don't you call him?"

"I . . . it's late and I . . . I could call Jerry on the West Coast.

Marianne frowned: "Try your dad, Clay."

He looked her directly in the eyes, got up, and went over to a small oak table in the corner. He picked up a green phone and punched in a number. His back was to her but after a few moments she heard him speak.

"Dad, it's Clay. Yes, I'm OK. Dad, I . . . I need your help."

Marianne left the big living room and found a small mirrored bathroom down a narrow hall. She splashed cold water on her face. It seemed to give her new energy, but didn't ease her worry that she had touched a nerve in Clay that she shouldn't have. When she returned to the living room he hung up the phone and turned towards her looking serious.

"I guess I shouldn't have suggested that, eh, Clay?"

"No, Marianne, you were right. He says we're in real danger, more than we know, because they'll know where we are. Twenty-five years ago the RCMP had homing devices and all sorts of electronic monitors. He says now these guys will have the same things and we could be wearing them. We're to search our clothes and bags. And CSIS will be looking for us too."

"Whose side are they on, Clay?"

"Dad says probably ours, but we may have to assume that they have been neutralized by the CIA. Anyway, he says we should get the hell out of this building."

As Greene was talking, Tremblay began to run her hand through the bags she had brought in from the car. Greene reluctantly did the same. It was Marianne who handed him the small black leather bag from his BC office, the one Rob had put in their car. The larger pockets contained a note from Janet Wong. Greene had quickly pulled the papers out of it and was about to throw the bag into a corner when Marianne took it from him. She patted down the bag with her right hand, turned it inside out and then opened up a small pocket in the inside of the bag. She pulled out a rolled up UBC T-shirt, which she removed and shook out. A small blue platted object, looking a bit like a little transistor radio, fell out with a clang on the wooden floor. They could see a minute red light flash from the object ever so faintly. They both looked at each other.

Greene recovered first: "We are getting the hell out of here now. Put on one of Nancy's tracksuits hanging in the bathroom. I'll change too. Then go to the van and take it a few driveways over to the neighbour's place. Here—." Clay pulled out a notepad from the phone table, "I'll draw you a sketch. See the end of the point? Just keep turning right on the gravel road until you can't drive anymore and then I'll pick you up."

"With what, Clay?"

"With the canoe, what else? We're Canadians, eh!"

After she arrived at the point, Marianne turned the lights off in the green van and locked the doors. As she walked down to the river past a darkened, abandoned small cottage, she almost didn't see the canoe.

"Jump in. My dad said we don't have much time."

In a few minutes they had paddled around the point, past the yacht club, and back down to the boathouse on the Rosslands' property.

Marianne finally said, "What do we do now, Clay? I'm afraid."

"Come into the boathouse, Marianne. And you're not the only one who's afraid, believe me."

The first small room inside boathouse was cluttered with a couple of mattresses, some old sailing gear, a broken canoe paddle and a number of dry Hudson Bay blankets. Greene led Marianne through a thick wooden door into another, even smaller, darkened room. When he switched on the light, she laughed. "Don't tell me we're going to have a sauna."

Greene smiled. "Marianne, you asked me to call my father and I'm taking what he told me seriously. Now, open up that bench, the sauna seat to your left. Can you fit into the space under there?"

At the same time, he was opening up the opposite bench, and she saw there was room—barely—for one person to lie down inside each bench.

"I think I can," she said, "though I don't know for how long."

"We don't need to get in right away. We may not have

to at all, but we've got to be ready. Until then we can just sit in here."

He sat down in the cold sauna facing her and flicked off the light switch. Through a small window the moonlight streaked in from the river. It took a minute for her eyes to adjust. She saw his face half in shadow as she inhaled the sweet smell of cedar.

"We've got some time. Can you tell me more about what happened at Cold Lake?"

Marianne described the events, from the sentry who would have refused her entry to their escape from the base. She told of their shock when she and Renée realized that the country in need of "peacekeeping" might be Canada.

"Did anyone at any time implicate MacKenzie?"

"Never."

"So, Marianne, what stands in their way of changing government policy and really taking control of the source?"

"I suppose only two people, first MacKenzie and then you—us."

Just then they heard the sound of a car engine on the road above, and the crunch of tires over the dried leaves. Had they been outside the boathouse they would have seen the headlights swing into the circular driveway of the log house. As two car doors slammed shut, Marianne and Clay froze.

It took only a few minutes for the two men to go through the house.

"The logs in the fire are still smoldering, Pierre. The van's gone."

The two men left the log house, got back into the car, and drove down the road.

"Is it OK now, Clay?"

"I'm not sure, but let's not take any chances. My dad says they never leave a stone unturned, that they're pros."

"I'm scared, Clay. I've never been so scared in my life."

"So am I, but we have each other here."

He moved over to her bench and put his arm around her. She didn't resist.

"You survived Squamish, Marianne."

"But that happened so quickly, I didn't have time to . . ."

Greene put his fingers to his lips and Marianne stopped talking. Both heard the river water gently lapping at the side of the dock and saw some stars out of the small sauna window to their left. But nothing else broke the eerie silence.

Marianne was about to speak again when Greene cupped his hand over her mouth. She didn't hear the new sound at first, but gradually she could make out a dull thud, then more clearly the sound of oars slapping river water. She also heard the engine of a car returning above and then the rowboat gently hitting the dock and the sound of footsteps on that dock. At the same time, she could hear someone running down the path from the log house above.

"I'll open the door. Pierre, you go in."

The door to the boathouse slammed open and the two men kicked over the mattresses and rustled through the sailing gear and blankets. Then the sauna door creaked and the lights went on.

The sauna was empty. The two men entered the small space and sat down on the benches facing each other. Each one had a gun in his hand.

"I thought for sure they were still here, Pierre."

"Fuck it, we've got other things to do. After tomorrow

afternoon those two will become irrelevant anyways. Let's get out of here."

Their footsteps receded up the hill, then the car doors slammed and the engine started. The sound grew fainter as the car pulled out of the driveway and headed up the road.

The lids of the sauna benches came up simultaneously.

"Now I'm really angry, Clay. I don't like being irrelevant."

Greene saw her forced smile and quickly reached over to take her hand, helping her out of the sauna bench and leading her into the outer room. He cleared a space for the larger of the two mattresses, spread it on the floor, and put the Hudson's Bay blankets over it.

"Ready for bed, Marianne?"

This time her smile was genuine.

"You bet."

They made love as the Gatineau rippled past below them. This time they were oblivious to all sounds except their own.

CHAPTER **24**

AS THE SUN ROSE OVER THE GATINEAU HILLS, CLAYTON Greene opened his eyes and stretched his legs full out. Rarely, he thought, had he slept so soundly. Next to him, Marianne Tremblay was curled up on her side. He was tempted to wake her. Instead, he bent over and gave her a gentle kiss on the cheek. She stirred, but didn't wake up.

He got up quietly, left the boathouse, and climbed the hill in the cool morning air, all the while taking slow deep breaths. He especially noticed the chirping of the small birds. After he entered the main house he brewed some coffee. As he was pouring into two mugs, the slight squeak of the main door caused him to turn abruptly, almost spilling the coffee.

"It's only me, Clay."

He handed Marianne one of the mugs.

"You remembered cream and no sugar, but where are those croissants you got for me at Whistler?"

Greene laughed and toasted her with his mug, then swept her up and hugged her.

"You sure gave me good advice about calling my dad. So, Madame l'analyste, what do we do now?" Before she could respond, he continued, "I'd love to just hang out here with you."

A frown came to Marianne's face. "But remember they've written us off as irrelevant. The one guy said, 'After tomorrow afternoon they'll become irrelevant.' Well, it's tomorrow now, Clay."

Greene leaned back in the chair and stretched out his

arms and legs. Marianne could see that he was thinking.

"A penny for your thoughts."

"Trust, I was thinking what you have been saying about trust, you know, trusting men, how they let you down. I'm thinking that I never trusted myself, maybe that's why I spent so much time chasing women, trying to seduce them and then moving on, just leaving them wondering God knows what. You've helped me feel different Marianne."

Marianne smiled ever so slightly at him. "You know, Clay, we all have some demons in our lives. 'Seduced intellectually,' you used that expression when we first talked on the plane flight. Strange. Women don't usually do that to men. They do other things. Or, at least men don't speak that way about women. Was it the Professor, Jerome?"

Greene stiffened up in his chair withdrawing his stretched out arms and legs back into his body. His expression looked saddened. She had never seen him this way, vulnerable, almost childish.

"It's all right, Clay, you can trust me. It's OK to love in different ways, as long as it's real."

"Like you and your father?"

Marianne just smiled. "Yes, I'm now beginning to understand about that love too. It wasn't sexual abuse or anything like that. When he cut me out of his life because of my supposed disloyalty to the 'cause,' it hurt deeply and I think I was lost for awhile."

"Jerry helped me out when I put a girl in the ditch in Richmond after a frat party. Uncle Jim was too far away and wouldn't have understood. My Dad was drinking. He never really got over my Mum's death. He used to look at me as if he saw my Mum in me. Jerry was always there for me. I could always call or hang out at his place. I still call him almost every night."

Marianne noticed Greene's head lift up and his mouth open slightly.

"What's the matter, Clay?"

"Jesus . . . I . . . I called him every night. You remember that Janet and I wondered if you were on our side, especially Janet. Well, Janet told Jerry about English Bay before we went to the freighter. Jerry also knew that I was going to Toronto, that I was going to Quebec City, that we were going to Whistler. And he has been a little strange. He wanted more of the relationship. I said I'd moved on a bit. And . . ."

Greene got up and picked up the bag on the corner, the one in which Marianne had found the electronic device.

"Tell me again where you got this, Marianne."

"Rob gave it to me at the Chateau. He said it was from the riding office, some papers from Janet and . . . and from Professor Jerome Howie."

Greene picked up the UBC T-shirt and slowly returned to his chair. This time he drew his legs into his stomach and lowered his head. She noticed tears coming to his eyes.

"I don't understand why he would help them," he sobbed.

"Clay, maybe there are some things we'll never understand."

She stopped and let the silence fill the air between them, and then she reached over and stroked the leg of his jeans very gently. He put his arm up around her. All they could hear was the chirp of a small starling sitting on the outside windowsill.

After a few minutes, Greene released his grip on Marianne and slowly uncurled himself. As he stood up he wiped his eyes with his shirtsleeve and took a deep breath. Marianne had never seen a look like this on his face. He looked determined.

"Marianne, Janet's with him on the coast. Senator Murphy is still scheming. We can't hang out here, as much as I want to. Remember what my Uncle Jim told me? 'Be the hunter, don't be the hunted.' And you said last night that nobody at Cold Lake implicated MacKenzie, that only MacKenzie and we stood in their way."

"What are you going to do, Clay?"

Greene looked up to the ceiling and then back down and into her eyes. "First MacKenzie, he's in danger. We're going back to Ottawa, to the House of Commons. Then we need to make sure Janet Wong isn't in danger. When I last spoke to her she told me she had a special meeting."

"Who with?"

"With Jerry Howie."

CHAPTER **25**

WHEN GREENE ARRIVED IN THE OPPOSITION LOBBY of the House, he saw a small group of his colleagues, including his leader, the House Leader, the House whip, the director of caucus research, and a few MPs in what looked like a football huddle. On one of the television sets he could see Don Newman, the CBC Newsworld commentator, reporting on what he called "a widening scandal in Parliament."

Clay joined the group of NDPers. The director of research had a plain brown envelope in her hands and was saying, "The media are reporting that the PM is involved in some foreign bank account which held kickback monies. But now we have received, anonymously, these documents which seem to show the leader of the opposition is also involved."

The House Leader immediately interrupted, "We can kill the Liberals in Question Period with this. They won't know what hit them. We can get both of those bastards."

Jack Hepburn was not quite so sure. He hesitated, wiped his cheek with his right hand, and coughed slightly. It was plain he had no stomach for scandal politics. Question Period was literally seconds away, and Greene's adrenaline was flowing. Without hesitation, he grabbed the envelope, motioned the group to follow him, and led them onto the floor of the House.

———

Janet Wong had planned to watch Question Period in the Vancouver constituency office and to fly to Ottawa later that afternoon. She hadn't heard from her boss in two days. This was unlike him. In Ottawa, Ann didn't know where he was either. Both women were worried. Professor Jerry Howie had called and invited Janet for a "special urgent meeting" for coffee in the small boardroom of a big Vancouver law firm. They could watch Question Period there, Howie said. It was strange but he was, after all, a good friend of Clay's.

She was led into a small corporate boardroom on the twenty-ninth floor with a magnificent view of the Vancouver harbour. Jerry Howie was seated in one of the leather chairs. He looked distraught.

"Janet, you might have guessed that my relationship with Clay was pretty close."

She just nodded and he continued: "A group led by Senator Murphy and some Americans approached me. They offered me a very senior position with a corporation in California and a part time position at Stanford Law School. I had invested poorly recently and I was very tempted. When I hesitated, I was told that they had evidence that my computer had been connected to some bad sites. They mentioned child pornography. I found that my computer had been connected, but not by me. But I couldn't prove that. I began to realize that these guys played hardball. At the same time, I was angry with Clay. It was irrational, but he had drifted away from me.

Janet looked hard at him. "So they got you to spill the beans on what he was doing."

Just as she spoke the boardroom door opened and two large men entered. Behind them was Senator Murphy who closed the door firmly. Janet began to get up. One of the men put his hands on her shoulder and pushed her back down. She could see that the other man had a revolver in his hand.

"We're going to watch Question Period together and you'll see history in the making," Murphy laughed.

Both Janet Wong and Jerome Howie looked up helplessly as one of the men opened up a TV cabinet and turned on the House of Commons channel.

The Speaker rose and recognized the leader of the opposition. René Jourdain got up from his seat and fidgeted nervously with his hands. "My question is to the Prime Minister of Canada. I have in my hands a cheque for $500,000, drawn from the Bank of Hong Kong for deposit to a secret Bahamian account in the name of John Alexander MacKenzie. How does the Prime Minister explain this, and can he tell the House whether there are more cheques like this one?"

The Prime Minister rose in his place. He looked tired and his face was ashen. "Mr. Speaker, I can honestly tell the House that I have no knowledge of that cheque or that account." With that he sat down.

"Supplementary question, the leader of the opposition."

René Jourdain rose again, looked at the Prime Minister, and then at the Speaker. He spoke in French. "Again to the Prime Minister. I have in my hand another cheque for $500,000, this time drawn from a branch of the Caisse Populaire, again in the name of the Prime Minister, to a Bahamian account. My question is, can the Prime Minister explain this cheque?"

"I have no knowledge of this cheque, Mr. Speaker."

"Final supplemental question, the leader of the opposition."

"Can the Prime Minister explain what favour or favours were granted for these obvious kickback monies?"

There were some cries from the government backbenches, but they were rather muted. The Prime Minister arose again, this time with a bit more spirit, but he again coughed. "Mr. Speaker, I can assure you, the House, and the Honourable Member that there were no favours."

There was none of the usual applause on the government side as the PM's two lieutenants, the Deputy PM and the Minister of Defence sat in silence.

Senator Murphy had pulled the blinds on the windows and put out the boardroom lights. As they all intently watched the TV and Question Period another door to the darkened room opened gradually and silently.

"The Chair recognizes the leader of the New Democratic Party, the Honourable Member from Ontario." Jack Hepburn started to get up, but then he paused, looked over his shoulder, and motioned to Clay Greene to stand and lead off the questions.

The Speaker also hesitated and then said, "The Chair recognizes the Honourable Member from Vancouver Centre."

Clay Greene quickly rose, steadied himself, leaned slightly forward, and looked directly across the aisle. "Mr. Speaker, my question is also to the Prime Minister. The

Prime Minister and the House may recall my continual questioning on the matter of water exports."

As a few audible sighs and groans came from various parts of the House, Greene took a few seconds to look up and scan the public galleries of the House. "Is it not true that the government recently changed its policy on water exports, allowing them but only by tanker and only on a limited basis?"

The Prime Minister smiled slightly, stood up, and said, "Yes."

"Supplementary question, the same Member."

Greene took his time getting to his feet. He was very cool and very measured. His eyes focused on the Prime Minister across the aisle. "Again to the Prime Minister." Greene began to hold up the brown envelope and rotated it in his fingers. The Deputy Prime Minister and the Defence Minister leaned back in their seats. "While the Prime Minister can't reveal cabinet discussions, I can tell the House that the Deputy Prime Minister wanted to go further, much further, but was blocked by the Prime Minister."

The Speaker began to rise but hesitated as Greene plunged on.

"Will the Prime Minister confirm to the House that there have been extraordinary troop exercises at Cold Lake, Alberta, at our Canadian Forces Base—exercises that were not authorized and indeed were a surprise to the Prime Minister and to the commander-in-chief of the Armed Forces?"

Now both the Deputy Prime Minister and the Defence Minister leaned forward in their seats. As they did, Greene turned his head and looked up at the Members' Gallery above his head. He recognized the face of his pursuer.

The Prime Minister rose quickly, looked at the Speaker, and answered. "Yes, Mr. Speaker."

The House was silent.

———

As Janet Wong, Jerry Howie, Senator Murphy, and his two henchman stared intently at the TV set, two burly men and a much smaller Asian man entered the boardroom without a sound. One of the big men raised a longshoreman's pick at the neck of the man with the gun. The other burly man snatched the revolver out of his hand. Senator Murphy and the other two hardly noticed as their eyes were still on the TV.

———

Greene again looked up quickly at the Members' Gallery opposite him, above the government benches. His eyes again picked out an athletic figure that was making a slight motion with his hand.

"Final supplementary question. The Member from Vancouver Centre."

"Isn't it a fact, Prime Minister, that your two lieutenants there seek to discredit not only you, but also the leader of the opposition, the parliamentary system, and the government of this country? Isn't it a fact, Prime Minister, that they are traitors to Canada?"

Both the Deputy PM and the Defence Minister spontaneously began to rise to their feet and the House erupted in cries. But Greene ignored the gathering pandemonium. With a quick glance over his shoulder at the Members' Gallery, his eyes caught a flash of silver.

The Prime Minister had hesitated after Greene's question and the outcries from his colleagues, especially the two on either side of him. He began to stand up again, almost by rote, for Greene's final question.

Clayton Greene didn't hesitate. He took two steps down from his seat to the floor of the Commons, one step across the floor, and then he leapt full length and caught the rising Prime Minister at the shoulder blades.

As MacKenzie fell backwards and downward with Greene on top of him, two bullets tore into the top of the Prime Minister's padded green chair.

CHAPTER **26**

I T WAS AN INDIAN SUMMER DAY ON TOP OF THE PEACE tower. The slightest cool breeze blew in from the Gatineau Hills. In all his years in Parliament, Clayton Greene had never been here, although it was one of the favourite tourist spots on Parliament Hill. On one side, Greene looked out over the lawns of Parliament, where he could see the statues of MacDonald, Laurier, and, to the side, Pearson and Diefenbaker, all former Prime Ministers. On the other side was the beautiful Ottawa River. But for Greene the best view of all was his view of Marianne Tremblay, who was standing beside him. Her blonde hair floated in the wind.

"Marianne, it was your idea to meet here. What have you got in mind?" he smiled.

"Well, Clay, I thought this is the one place we might actually get a little privacy. The tourists are so busy looking at the view, and the media never come here. You know you're practically a national hero and the press are looking for you."

The Governor General had ordered the arrest of the Deputy Prime Minister, and the Defense Minister. Tommy Gow and Janet delivered-up Senator Murphy. Good for them and good for the GG, thought Greene. Journalist Michael Valpy was right after all—there is a use for the monarchy!

"You know, I'm glad it's over. I love this place and I guess I don't want it to change. With all our problems, we're still blessed, Marianne, whether it's water or those nice tulips in bloom down there."

"What about me, Clay?"

"You too are a national asset."

"Well, thank you, but . . . where do we go now?"

"We're going to get married, I hope. I suppose a new government will be formed and we'll have elections soon, in which case I'll never see you. It'll just be the same old political life, but it will be quieter and sweeter. I will be a normal struggling backbencher once again."

There was the sound of a phone ringing, and Marianne looked embarrassed.

"Is that a cellular phone? If it is, I'm going to divorce you before we get married."

"Clay, Rob and Janet told me I had to bring it. Besides, remember you promised your Uncle Jim you'd attend at least one of his events." Greene smiled as Marianne answered the phone, then scowled as she said, "It's for you, Clay."

The expression on his face changed immediately. "Yes, Madame, I will be there."

"Marianne, it was the Governor General. She wants me to come to Rideau Hall right away, says it's very important. She told me to bring you." Greene smiled at Marianne and faked annoyance." I had other ideas about what we might do today."

⎯⎯•⎯⎯

As Greene and Tremblay got out of the taxi in front of Rideau Hall, they were confronted by a large crowd of reporters in a roped-off area surrounding the large portico near the front door. When the reporters saw Greene, they went into a frenzy. Several TV cameras rose above the crowd and began filming, while the clicking of a dozen still cameras made it difficult to make out the questions the writers were shouting. Greene spied a Vancouver reporter and focused on him. He thought the reporter asked him why he was here, so he yelled that he was joining the Native elders. A few of the journalists in front of the pack looked incredulous.

The large wooden door of Rideau Hall opened and an aide to the Governor General stretched out her hand to welcome them. As they crossed the threshold, they were greeted by applause. The entire staff of the Hall had gathered in the entrance room, not in an organized receiving line but in little groups or singly. Some people had tears in their eyes even as they smiled, and others broke out in cheers. Marianne moved closer to Greene.

The aide ushered them immediately into the Governor General's office, a large room, full of bookshelves and books, with a fireplace and many comfortable looking sofa-chairs. Greene was surprised to see René Jourdain and Jack Hepburn in these chairs. The Governor General was seated at a huge desk in front of a window overlooking the grounds. Captain Renée Bouchard was at the Governor General's side. Beside her sat a beaming Jim Sichinly.

Greene was about to go over to Jim when a small man in an expensive, tight-fitting blue suit and shiny black patent leather shoes rose to speak. He recognized the Prime Minister's private secretary, Adrian Horgan. Instead of speaking, however, Horgan walked over to a closed door on the far side of the room. He opened the door and John Alexander MacKenzie, white sling holding up his right arm, entered the room. Greene was speechless. He was not expecting to see the Prime Minister there. Renée Bouchard got up immediately and offered the PM her chair. He smiled and declined. Instead he leaned slightly on the back of René Jourdain's chair and spoke in a quiet but firm voice.

"Your Excellency and friends, I wanted to come and explain to you personally what has happened and why. Given the crisis Canada is in and our narrow escape—thanks to Clay here and your Excellency—from an even greater one, no hospital bed was going to keep me away."

MacKenzie coughed slightly and looked around the room, seeing a lot of worried looks. After a slight pause he continued: "My reputation has been viciously smeared and this has caused me great anguish, as you may well have imagined. The truth is that the revelation of an account in an offshore bank in my name was a surprise to me. I entered politics as a moderately poor man and I expect to leave politics the same way. Although I'm a Scot by family background, money has not been my motive for a political career. The thrill of politics is the thrill of stimulating people, moving them, and accomplishing change. For me, politics was always challenging work, but always enjoyable. That is, until recently.

The Prime Minister paused a second, took a white handkerchief from his pocket, blew his nose, replaced the handkerchief and looked at the Governor General.

"After the last election produced a minority Parliament and after I won the leadership of my party, you were gracious enough to ask me to form a government. That government was kept in power by the support of the Alliance Party members in Parliament. People were surprised by that development because I have always been a Progressive Conservative. I made a point of dealing straight up with those members, yielding to their views when I could while keeping my own political integrity. Most members responded accordingly. But about six months ago, I began to suspect the loyalty of some of my own colleagues in very high places in my government. I feel, given the circumstances, I can reveal to you that Cabinet debated the extraordinary proposition of a further economic and political treaty with our American neighbours that in my view would eventually lead to union of the two countries.

This I could not accept under any circumstances. I did compromise on the issue of water and gas exports to the US and reluctantly agreed to change our present policies in part, especially as they related to water, on a limited trial basis. The Member from Vancouver Centre shrewdly picked up on this change. I thought this would end the matter, but it didn't. There seemed to be a movement to discredit me. Now I realize not only were moderate Tories like me to be discredited, but the Liberal leader was to be set up as well. Parliament was to be dissolved after I was out of the way, and an act of union with the US was being prepared. I had no idea until last night exactly how far the plotters were prepared to go, engineering what amounted to a coup following my demise."

The handkerchief came out of his pocket again.

"I will be eternally grateful for the tenacity of the Member from Vancouver Centre and, of course, for his good sense and duty. As I think back on the last few months I'm amazed at how Mr. Greene here tracked those plotters so accurately."

Marianne leaned over to Jim Sichinly and whispered in the old man's ear. "Someone must have taught him those tracking skills."

Jim smiled broadly as the PM continued, his voice now

much stronger and firmer: "Last night as I lay awake in the hospital I asked myself where is this wonderful country to go? The people, up until now a peaceful people, are shocked. Parliament is in turmoil. I thought of handing in my resignation."

He paused, and the politicians in the room looked at each other.

"But I have decided, with Your Excellency's concurrence, to try to keep my Government afloat."

There was a slight shuffling of feet in the room.

"I have been thinking of what motivated Senator Murphy and his gang. I'm only beginning to comprehend their greed. But I do now realize how important Canada's fresh water resource is, not to mention the thirst of others for it. Indeed, it is a thirst that they were prepared to kill for."

MacKenzie paused, turned and gazed towards the fireplace. After a moment he turned back and faced his listeners.

"I ask myself what motivates this new generation. That's why I asked my friend Clayton Greene to come here this afternoon. What is your vision of Canada Mr. Greene?"

Greene looked up rather sharply. He began to speak, slowly at first and then he became more animated.

"Well, Prime Minister, I know my generation is supposed to be motivated by personal greed too, but at heart I don't think they are moved by the fight against the deficit and debt as much as the business press believes. I come from the Canadian city where the worldwide Greenpeace movement was founded. It's making a difference. I think my generation's vision is a clean, livable country and world. Canada could make a difference. We could lead the world in environment issues, if we wanted to. Why should we be afraid of the Kyoto agreement on global warming? We should embrace it and set our goals of living up to it. And why shouldn't we control our own water and finally pass a strong bill to exclude large-scale exports? While we are at it, we should make money available to our Provinces so our own drinking water is clean in every city, town or hamlet in Canada."

Greene realized that all the people in the room were looking up at him. Slightly embarrassed, he turned towards Marianne. There was silence in the room. It was the Prime Minister who spoke first.

"I have decided to try to continue to govern with a new coalition and a new direction, at least as long as I am able." Again he coughed slightly. "I will ask selected members of the NDP and the Liberals to join this Government. Some may turn me down. Others, I hope will join with me. René and Jack, this is my invitation to you. If Your Excellency lets me, I will again face the House of Commons."

The Governor General nodded her head.

"There is one member of the opposition who I particularly want on my side in what I hope will be the lead portfolio in this new Government. So, I'm asking Your Excellency to swear in this afternoon Clayton Greene MP, as Canada's new Environment Minister."

This time Greene looked stunned.

The Prime Minister finally took the chair that René had offered him.

Now it was the Governor General who stood up.

"It's my responsibility as head of state in Canada, as the late Senator Forsey correctly insisted, to make sure a government is in office. I'm satisfied that this new coalition proposed by Prime Minister MacKenzie should be given a chance to meet the House of Commons as a Government."

The other two party leaders present nodded. The GG looked directly at Greene.

"And I would be delighted to accept your advice on its composition. First, Mr. Greene. I'm now prepared to swear you in as Environment Minister for Canada."

When Clay turned to Marianne he noticed that his Ottawa staff—Ann, Rob and even Janet, back overnight from Vancouver—had been invited into the room. He looked up. Jim Sichinly smiled at him.

"Can we do it, gang?"

They nodded in unison.

Clayton Greene looked at the Governor General and spoke clearly and firmly. "Yes, I accept."

The Governor General smiled. "Come forward, Minister."

Ian Waddell was the Minister of Culture in the government of British Columbia. He previously spent fourteen years as an MP in the House of Commons in Ottawa. Born in Scotland, educated at the University of Toronto and the London School of Economics, he moved to Vancouver to become Assistant City Prosecutor, a storefront lawyer, counsel to the Berger Commission on the Mackenzie Valley Pipeline, and Chair of the Fraser Basin Board. He is currently lives in Vancouver where he is practices law and is a film producer.

Another Great Political Mystery from NeWest Press

Guilty Addictions
A Political Mystery
Garrett Wilson

An investigation into the death of a local MLA and the ensuing disappearance of 15 million dollars reveals political corruption—including murder. Oxford LaCoste, a lawyer called upon to recover the money, must ultimately decide whether revealing the truth is more important than the race to stay alive.

"This is not just an entertaining and well-plotted read but an insider's guide to an elite of corrupt politicians, greedy business people and baffled police in an extraordinary story."
—Stevie Cameron